Also by Janine A. Morris

Diva Diaries

She's No Angel

Playthang

drama 99 FM

JANINE A. MORRIS

KENSINGTON PUBLISHING CORP.
http://www.kensingtonbooks.com

DAFINA BOOKS are published by

Kensington Publishing Corp.
119 West 40th Street
New York, NY 10018

All Kensington titles, imprints, and distributed lines are available at special quantity discounts for bulk purchases for sales promotion, premiums, fund-raising, educational, or institutional use. Special book excerpts or customized printings can also be created to fit specific needs. For details, write or phone the office of the Kensington Special Sales Manager: Kensington Publishing Corp., 119 West 40th Street, New York, NY 10018. Attn. Special Sales Department. Phone: 1-800-221-2647.

Dafina and the Dafina logo Reg. U.S. Pat. & TM Off.

ISBN-13: 978-0-7582-7144-0
ISBN-10: 0-7582-7144-1

First Kensington Trade Paperback Printing: November 2009
First Mass Market printing: October 2012

10 9 8 7 6 5 4 3 2 1

Printed in the United States of America

This book is dedicated to my parents,
Carolyn and Julius Morris,
for helping me become the woman I want to be.
And also to my uncle Joe, who passed while I was
writing this book.
One of the last Mohicans—RIP.

The Life . . . it's not for everybody

Acknowledgments

This is my fourth book and in my previous books I have acknowledged pretty much everyone in my life who has influenced me, inspired me, helped me, befriended me, and loved me. Therefore I am going to keep this one short.

All four of my books, including this one, were written while I was in law school and I am FI-NALLY done. I graduated May 17, 2009, from Hofstra Law School and I am happier than ever. I thank God for giving me the ability to write these four stories all while completing law school. He has been so good to me, and this is just one of the many things I have to thank Him for.

Professor Folami, my one law professor who inspired me to continue on the exact path that I am on and inspired me to never change because I see that you are genuinely you—thank you!!

My parents—Carolyn and Julius. As always, thank you and I love you for EVERYTHING! I am strong, Mommy, because you are strong and you showed me how.

My siblings, Tasha and JR, are my shapers and molders. I love you both. My twin brother, who is not here in flesh but FOREVER with me in spirit, we did it, Jason.

Hammy, Tylah, Leila, and the new princess

Jewel—love you all. You are my interim children and every one of you brings me joy.

My baby, best friend, and the love of my life, Ahmad—each book I write, you are still there to toast with me when I turn in the manuscript. Thanks for staying by my side. Thanks for being my air. Regardless of what happens between us, I treasure every day that we have ever spent together because they are magical 99 percent of the time. (OK, maybe 98 percent) ☺. Love ya, babes.

Mommy and Daddy Meggett—I can't tell you enough how much I love and appreciate you both. If ever your son drives me crazy, I remember that I couldn't live without you guys ☺ and so I stay. Rashida, Les, Rashard, and the boys—love you guys.

Kim Ginyard, Alicia McFarlane, Wendy Lattibedeure, Tiffany Ballard, and the rest of my law grad buddies, we did it, sisters!

Lauren, Gordon, Brandi, Brian, Troi, Candice, Tanika, Darryl, Anthony, Malik, Janice, Nay, Monique, Nikki Bigelow, Chrissy, and all my other cousins and fam—love you all.

In this music industry, as A Tribe Called Quest said, record company people are shady. Then there are those who are just true blue! DJ Envy, my brother, I love you always. Tracy Cloherty, I am thankful to have had the opportunity to work with you, learn from you, and have you as my friend. Fatman Scoop, I love to see you still doing your thing. Love ya, Isaac. Funkmaster Flex, I appreciate all that you have done for me throughout my entire career; your words of advice until this day and your help in making moves. You don't have to, but you do, and I appreciate you. Cocoa, you are always my girl. Crazy behind Clue, Absolut, Camilo, and Whookid—I love all of you guys repping for my Qboro ☺. My fellow author and scorpio Miss Jones, Ang, Koren Vaughn—my girl forever, Enuff—my big Spanish, Jazzy, Rod-Ness, Bobby Trends, Donyshia Benjamin, Travia Charmont—nothing but love. Ebro, thanks for all the many lessons. Nikki Smith, my girl forever. Alex Cameron, congrats! Of course, I have to acknowledge my Bugsy for always being exactly who you are. Kyser, Hollywood, next book is all about you, lol. James Brown, Pecas, Yvette, Helen Demoz, Jay Brown, Nels, Karen Rait, Blue Williams, Pia, Buttah Man, Dave House, Marilyn Lecointre—you guys make TCQ wrong and prove not all record company people are shady. Love you all.

Chapter 1

This wasn't something Madison ever would have expected. As she cruised down Hughes Avenue, she saw DJ KD being put in the back of the police car. There were some onlookers watching, but it wasn't clear if any were fans of his or if they were all just people coincidentally passing by. Madison knew she should have pulled over instantly and approached the police and KD to see what had happened, even if just simply to show concern for her employee, but quite honestly, she just didn't feel like it. *I'm getting too old for this nonsense,* she thought as she turned the corner, pretending as if she hadn't seen what she'd just seen.

She knew the drama and constant goings-on in the entertainment industry were what made her job exciting. But after twelve years in the industry, she had to admit that sometimes enough was enough. Why couldn't these damn adults just get their stuff together? She knew firsthand that once certain kinds of people were blessed with money and fame, those same blessings could have terrible effects on a person. Most of these celebrity figures, even if they were known only on a local level, had huge egos—so much so that they formed more enemies and brought on more legal issues than any one person needed. The reality was most of these issues occurred because these people seemed to forget that they, too, were mere normal humans at the end of the day. Fame and money could evaporate just as easy as they came, but these folks hadn't gotten the Staying Humble 101 handbook—at least not most of them.

Madison finally found parking in the busy uptown area of Manhattan and began to walk over toward the radio station. She was hoping the scene she'd passed in front of the building would be gone by the time she got there. Just to up her chances, she stopped in a store along the way to get coffee, though she usually just welcomed herself to the free coffee in the cafeteria at work. She sipped her warm coffee as she walked down the two long city blocks between the store and the station. She arrived on Hughes Avenue and noticed there was no sign of the cop car or DJ KD, and she said a silent "thank you" to herself. There were still a few onlookers standing around, probably just gossiping about what they had seen and putting pieces of their own accounts of it together. Madison walked past them all and directly into the building.

Once she got into the lobby, the drama began. The security guard in the lobby looked eager to be the bearer of bad news as he saw Madison walking up.

"They just arrested KD," the security guard said.

Madison wanted to roll her eyes at him. Not just because he couldn't even let her get in the damn building all the way before he bombarded her with information, but he wasn't minding his business. He was the security for the building, not the radio station, so at the end of the day he was just gossiping.

"Yeah, I heard," Madison said as she walked by him in a hurried manner. She was hoping her short response and her body language made it evident she didn't wish to have that conversation with him. It must have worked because he didn't say anything more about it, at least not to her.

Madison made her way to the elevator without seeing anyone else, and she was relieved as she enjoyed her lonesome elevator ride to the twelfth floor. As she exited into the lobby of the radio station, she noticed a tall Asian man dressed in a police uniform. By the time she'd registered that he was standing there, she heard the receptionist's voice.

"There she is. That's the program director right there," Felicia said.

Madison could've just pulled out a gun and shot Felicia right then and there. Well, in her imagination she could have. The officer seemed surprised to see that such a little woman was the boss of such a large man, but Madison's expression made it clear big things came in small packages. Madison was only five feet five inches, with a milk chocolate complexion and a shoulder-length bob. Her bangs were growing back, so she had them slightly swooped to the side, just enough for folks to get a good look into her eyes.

"Hi, Madison Cassell. Can I speak with you for a moment?" the officer inquired.

"Sure, but as you see, I just walked in. I will need a few moments," she replied as she cut her eyes at Felicia, hoping she got her gist.

Felicia was new on the job, so she needed a hint to let her know Madison wanted Felicia to keep the officer occupied. Madison had been questioned by the police many times before, and she was not about to get the story from a police officer as he tried to gain information from her. Madison didn't give the officer the chance to object—not that he could; she knew she wasn't under arrest, and he couldn't hold her there in her lobby. She swiped her security card and walked through the door to the other side where the officer was not welcome. She walked toward her office, and she could see the eyes of some of her colleagues watching her as she made her way toward her department. As soon as she made the left turn down the corridor leading to her office, she saw her assistant standing a few feet away.

"What happened?" Madison asked.

Now, her assistant, Alexis, was the person she wanted to hear the story from. She knew Alexis would tell her what she needed to know, and she knew she would likely be well informed because everyone went to Alexis with the news and business. She was the type of girl everyone trusted and got along with. As Madison expected, she knew exactly what had happened.

"KD was leaving the station this morning after doing his morning mix, and that new artist Tryme was upset that KD didn't spin any of his records because he'd been a guest on the morning show. When KD stepped out of the DJ booth, Tryme approached him and said some things. One thing led to another, and they started fighting. Somewhere along the line KD grabbed a phone off the console and hit Tryme in the head with it. Someone called the cops—I'm not sure who—but by the time KD was leaving the building to get his car, the cops approached him and arrested him."

That was the part Madison had seen, but she wasn't interested in commenting on it just yet. She stood there for a second taking it in, trying to see exactly what she would have to face when she got back to the lobby with the officer. She already knew he was going to ask if there was a video camera and if he could get the tape, etc. This was the prime reason Madison had gotten mad when they'd installed a security camera back by the studio—too many industry secrets would be contained on those tapes, always subject to being subpoenaed or found and looked at.

"How is Tryme? Is he OK?"

"He didn't leave in an ambulance or anything, but he was bleeding a little bit," Alexis said.

"From the phone?"

"No, I don't know why KD even threw the phone. I think he was just caught in the moment."

"It was a phone, not a fire extinguisher. How much damage could it have done?" Madison asked, clearly frustrated that this nonsense was starting off her day.

"It didn't do any damage, really. I was back there by the time he threw the phone, and he was already bleeding a bit. Truth is, KD was kind of beating him up, and he threw the phone as like an insult, because by that time Tryme wasn't really fighting anymore."

"This is bullshit." Madison knew Alexis could run on forever if she let her. Her long-winded story wasn't what was getting under her skin, it was knowing she had two meetings today and that this was going to consume most of her valuable work time. It didn't help that she wanted to get home at a decent hour to finally cook dinner for Jamahl, her fiancé.

Madison headed back toward the lobby. When she got there, the officer spun around as though he had been counting every second she'd been gone.

"Hi, what's your name?" Madison said as she extended her hand. She blurted this out before the officer could say anything. Madison knew this was her way of dominating the conversation—by starting it and showing her confidence and lack of fear.

"Officer Lewis," he replied.

"Hi, Officer Lewis. As it seems you have been notified—" she gestured toward the receptionist area where Felicia had been sitting not that long ago—"I am the program director for Drama 99. How may I help you?"

"There was an incident on these premises between a DJ from Drama 99 and an artist by the name of . . ." The officer looked down at his pad. "Tryme."

"I am aware of the incident and that my DJ was arrested. What would you like to speak with me about?"

"I have some questions, and I also want to retrieve the video from the security camera by the studio."

"Honestly, Officer Lewis, I would love to be of help. However, I wasn't here, and it is my policy that I answer no questions regarding legal matters. As for the video, I am unable to give that to you at this time. The camera is not always recording, and there is a process for checking tapes and retrieving footage. I will look into it for you, but it's going to take some time."

The officer looked like he wasn't impressed by her evasion, but he also knew there was nothing more he could do. He didn't have a warrant, nor was there a subpoena. Instead of pushing further, he reached into his pocket and handed her a business card.

"Here's my information. Please call me," he said.

"Sure, no problem," Madison replied.

Without hesitation, Madison walked off. The officer stood there, a bit shocked for a second at her unfriendliness, but then he, too, turned and walked away.

Madison had been in the business way too long and had seen way too much to let one little police investigation get her bent out of shape. She knew she had to handle it, and that was all she was concerned about. She had to minimize the press and make sure to give the right quotes for the news papers and news stations, and she knew she would. Everything else was secondary, despite what Officer Lewis might think. She understood he had a job to do, but so did she, and hers was to maintain the image and entertainment value of her radio station, Drama 99 FM.

Chapter 2

It didn't take much for Reyna to realize there wasn't going to be a chance for her to get what she wanted out of the situation. Michael had already made it clear he wasn't ready for much more in their relationship, and Reyna knew deep down that she was beyond fed up with fighting for her relationship all by herself. She had never understood how she could have a boyfriend, yet feel so alone. She was finally realizing it was because even though he was a decent boyfriend, he wasn't willing to give her anything more than that—but she wanted so much more.

Reyna and Sereeta were friends, and they'd known each other half their lives. Sereeta told Reyna, every time the conversation called for it, that she needed to leave Michael alone. Sereeta felt strong about a man's role, and as far as she was concerned, Michael's $55,000 income wasn't enough to fulfill his obligations. So she didn't know why Reyna was sweating him to begin with.

Reyna respected Sereeta's point of view, but she

couldn't keep herself from feeling those same strong feelings she'd felt for Michael since their junior year of high school. It was going to take more than words to convince Reyna that she and Michael weren't meant to be together forever, even if those words were coming from Michael himself. The way Reyna saw it, they hadn't come this far just to go their separate ways after all these years. Although she didn't have any desire to wait for the day, she told herself Michael would eventually come to his senses. In the meantime, though, she had been stuck feeling dumb and dumber. For some reason, hearing him say it this time really hit home for her.

"I'm just not ready. Why can't you just accept that?" he said.

The look on his face was disgust mixed with frustration. Reyna looked him dead in the eye and as it registered, it made her body freeze.

Why can't *you accept that?* she asked herself again. *You were able to accept your sister's death. You were able to accept that you had to do a whole extra year of medical school because of some administrative errors at the school. You were able to accept Michael's apology for asking you that one time to move out after living together for two years (she had won and stayed with him at home). And you were able to accept nothing less than a six-figure salary from your first employer out of medical school. But yet you can't accept that this man isn't ready?* After talking to herself for a few moments, even Reyna had to admit something was wrong with this picture.

How she could stand here and let Michael once again make her feel less than worthy of his love and commitment was beyond her understanding.

She was well aware that love was a powerful thing, but she didn't understand how it could numb all your senses at times. She was dressed in a multicolored tunic top with some dark blue leggings and black knee boots. Her hair was combed back under a baseball cap, and she had on no makeup or earrings. She had been at his condo for the weekend, and she had just planned to make a quick run to Wal-Mart and grab some things. The conversation had gotten so deep so suddenly. It had started just because Reyna had asked if he wanted her to buy a hamper with a separator in it. When he'd asked why, she'd told him so they could have their dirty clothes divided, and Michael had begun to express that that wasn't necessary because she could take her dirty clothes with her back to her place. Confused, Reyna had asked what was wrong, and it had led to an argument Reyna wasn't expecting. The beautiful, sunny Saturday morning had turned into a gloomy day when Michael began saying hurtful things.

This wasn't the first time he'd mentioned not being ready for something, but Reyna had always accepted it. Marriage and children and living together were one thing, but not ready for a dual hamper? Reyna just couldn't understand what this man's issue was. The embarrassment and anger had hit her just about instantly. Reyna looked him right in his eyes and turned to walk away—no response, just an exit. She couldn't afford to respond because she knew, just like he did, that her words meant nothing. She had allowed her words to lose all their value over the past few years because she had said a lot of stuff she didn't mean, and her actions had contradicted a lot of things she had said she would or wouldn't do. She knew at this point that only her actions could speak for her.

Reyna tried to ignore how silly and angry she felt about Michael's inability to compromise for her happiness. She was ashamed to admit to him or to herself that she still wasn't sure she could accept that he wasn't ready.

Once she got to her car and sat down, she picked up her cell phone to call her sister Nelcida, but as she was dialing the number, an incoming call from Sereeta came through. Filled with all the emotions from her discussion with Michael, Reyna really didn't want to speak with Sereeta at this moment. She wasn't in the mood for any smart comments that would only cause her to yell at Sereeta for having the nerve to tell somebody how to handle their relationship. Sereeta was the type of friend who never looked in the mirror before she spoke; she was quick to tell someone how they should be, but she never looked at her own reflection. Reyna knew if she told Sereeta what had happened, chances were Sereeta would tell her how she needed to leave him alone and that she was a dummy to be waiting around any longer for him to "get serious" or propose—yet Sereeta was single and had been for years. Though Reyna knew she was crossing the borderline to foolishness for her patience with Michael, she really didn't need Sereeta-funky-butt's words of wisdom right now. By the time Reyna finished thinking all that through, the phone had stopped ringing.

Reyna pressed the button to clear her missed-call message and began to dial her sister's number. As she pressed the sixth digit of Nelcida's number, Sereeta's number appeared on her screen again.

"What!?" Reyna said aloud in frustration. She answered on the third ring.

"Hello," Reyna answered with her obvious attitude hanging out.

"Dag, a sister gotta hunt you down," Sereeta said with a snicker.

"Knock it off," Reyna said. "My phone was in my purse."

"You are the worst with answering your phone, but anyway—"

"Yeah, anyway," Reyna interrupted. "What's up?"

"I got the job!" Sereeta shouted.

"Oh, wow. Congratulations!"

Despite the tears she was fighting back, distracting her thoughts, Reyna was genuinely happy for Sereeta.

"Thanks," Sereeta said. "My starting salary will be seventy-eight thousand with benefits, and you'll never guess who I'm assisting."

"Who?" Reyna said, trying to sound excited to cover up her impatience.

"The Flash."

"Who?" Reyna said.

"Corey Cox, the NBA player they call the Flash."

"Oh, I kind of know Corey Cox, but I didn't know about no Flash."

"That's what they call him—I guess because he's fast or something. He just started playing with the Knicks a month ago."

"Well, that's good. When do you start?"

"Next week, but I met the entire team last night at this ESPN party."

"How was that?"

"It was really cool. Corey is so fine, and so are a couple of his teammates. I felt like I was in heaven."

"Uh-oh. No mixing business with pleasure; you do know that much, I hope."

Sereeta just laughed. From the sound of her giggle, Reyna could tell that Sereeta already had some rule breaking in mind. If Reyna didn't have her own problems on her mind, she would've pulled it out of her friend, but Sereeta's drama was the least of her concerns right now.

Chapter 3

"*Naomi, you have been working here for some time now. I expected that you would get the hang of things by now.*" Naomi could hear her boss's comment over and over in her head. She was devastated that she was still not on point at her job after four months already. Even though it was a simple mishandling of a message, it didn't take much to irritate Naomi's boss, Tiffany. Tiffany had been working in the music business for over ten years, and she had a reputation for taking no nonsense. Every executive assistant who had the honor to work for her was well aware that there would be more pain than pleasure. However, the benefits and experience from working for someone like her were well worth the pain.

Although Naomi had a college education and had learned a lot in her life, it was apparent she wasn't that worldly. She was a naturally inquisitive but shy person, and the intimidation from this position had caused her to be humble and even more shy since her very first day. She hadn't made that many friends at the company yet. She seemed to be overlooked a lot by most of the staff. It seemed as if people in the office just stepped over her to get to her boss—like she was just a voice to be heard before connecting staff with Tiffany on a phone call. Naomi hadn't become comfortable enough yet to show Tiffany all her talents and smarts because she was too afraid to come out of her shell. She knew her boss didn't give two craps about any of her insecurities—she had to get it together.

There was only one coworker who knew the real Naomi, and that was Kevin. Kevin worked in business and legal affairs, and he was a nice guy. He was Spanish with a lot of spunk and personality, and he had introduced himself to Naomi on her first day and extended his help if she needed anything. Kevin was five-nine and medium built with black hair he usually wore slicked back in a Brad Pitt kind of style. If everyone didn't know he had a girlfriend, they would have assumed he was gay, and some people still thought that he was even after meeting his girlfriend. Naomi didn't know too many gay people back home, but she had instantly fallen in love with Kevin. He not only amused the hell out of her, he made her feel comfortable. She only wished he worked next to her to make the day that much easier. He had accompanied her to lunch on most days—initially it had been just to help make her a bit more comfortable as the new girl, but eventually they had formed a little friendship. Kevin had been working for the record label for four years. He swore to Naomi that any day could be his last because he was ready to find a new job, but it was obvious that he, like several of the other employees, was a label whore.

Naomi was still beating herself up over her fumble with Tiffany, but she stopped to call Kevin.

"I just got in trouble with Tiffany."

"What happened?" he asked with a chuckle.

"Hollywood called, and I told him she was in a meeting."

"Was she in a meeting?"

"Yes, but she said I should have told her he was on the phone because she was waiting on his call."

"Did she tell you she was waiting on his call before she went into the meeting?" he asked.

"No! So how was I supposed to know that?"

Kevin laughed. "You'll catch on. Certain people are too important to be too busy for."

"I see. Well, I wish I could figure out who is on that list and fast. This isn't the first time she was upset because I mishandled a VIP, not knowing they were a VIP."

"The list changes constantly. You just have to fine-tune your senses for it."

"OK," Naomi said with a hint of sarcasm.

"Let me go. I have to run this order sheet down to the art department."

"OK, talk to you later."

Naomi hung up and instantly opened a document on her computer. She began to type the letters VIP across the top. She then began to list all the names she remembered to be pretty damn important—those were the people she had found herself getting in trouble with over the past few months—and the list started with Hollywood. She continued to add the artists who Tiffany stopped everything for, and she also added the bosses at the record label and a couple attorneys and other executives. Naomi knew some of the names probably didn't belong on the list—and there were many names missing—but she figured she would use this list as a temporary point of reference. Whether it would help her a little or a lot, it was worth the try because Naomi wasn't trying to lose this job.

Naomi was wearing a pair of faded blue jeans—one of her favorite pairs—and a sweatshirt with FORDHAM printed on it. Naomi hadn't attended Fordham, but it was a promotional shirt she had received when she was in high school. Her hair was pulled back in a loose ponytail, and her glasses were sitting close to the end of her nose. She had four pictures hanging in her cubicle and no other decor aside from her office supplies. Her pictures were framed in oak—there was a photo of her with her boyfriend, Charles, from back home; a photo of her parents; one of her dog who had passed a few months before she had moved from Texas; and one of her college graduation. Her cubicle was a reflection of her personality and style: pretty simple and laid-back. Back home Naomi had never been the center of attention, and moving to New York alone was the most excitement she had experienced in her life so far.

It hadn't been easy to just uproot her whole life and move to this new city all alone. Despite the serious nature of the decision, it hadn't taken long for her to accept the offer. Naomi had been trying to get a job for months in whatever field she could, but she wanted more than anything to work in the music business. She took an extra year to finish her bachelor's degree in liberal arts—and a "no set goals" minor. When she'd finished school and those school loans were fast approaching, she had applied to every posted paid position she could find. Initially, she had wanted a job making big bucks; she'd thought that, with a degree, her sky was the limit. She had spent four years and thousands upon thousands of dollars on this degree, and she assumed she would have no problem getting a job upon graduating. That reality had begun to fade as the months went by and there were very few callbacks and only two interviews, neither of which had led to a job offer.

Almost seven months had passed since her last interview, and she had sent out dozens more résumés, when she'd finally gotten a call for an interview in New York. Moving to New York definitely had pros and cons, but she knew it was worth pursuing. After a long journey, she had finally ended up sitting at her very own desk at a company, and she felt like she had graduated all over again. All her friends and enemies back home were so envious she would be working at a record label in New York City. She had come too far to have to start all over again—so she was willing to try anything to show Tiffany she could handle her job, fit in at the company, and be a hit in New York.

Chapter 4

"**W**hy is it that you seem to think everything is always about you?" Madison asked.

"Whatever—I'm not in the mood for this right now," Jamahl replied.

"When are you ever in the mood to discuss anything serious? All you want to do is soar by all our issues."

"Whatever. I'm watching television. Can you please go back to whatever you were doing?"

Madison began to walk away and then turned back.

"No, you aren't just going to dismiss me like I'm some child. I'm talking to you, and I'd appreciate it if you would listen."

"And I would appreciate it if you didn't talk to me right now."

Madison could feel her stomach tying in knots from the frustration. She hated when Jamahl put up this wall; because he was so damn stubborn, it was hell trying to break it down.

"So you are just going to sit here and magnify the situation by ignoring me?"

"I'm not ignoring you, and you are the one magnifying the situation. All I said is I don't want to go to some stupid event with you, and you are turning this into me being a selfish partner and thinking everything is about me. This is you making a big deal out of nothing."

"There you go, saying it's nothing. It *is* selfish of you because it's a work event, and I would really like you to attend with me, and you are saying no without a reason."

"I do have a reason: I don't want to go, and I would really like it if you stopped pressuring me about it. So I think that makes you a selfish partner because you keep bothering me about it."

Madison couldn't take it anymore. When Jamahl got like this, there was no talking to him. He was determined to be difficult and not see things from her point of view, so she just figured she would save herself any more aggravation and go back to the bedroom where she'd been before she'd brought all this up again.

Jamahl didn't say anything when he saw that Madison had gotten fed up and walked out of the living room. He just readjusted himself in his seat and turned the volume up some. Madison didn't turn back this time; she continued into the bedroom.

She was cuddled up reading a book, with a recorded *Tyra* show on mute, when she began to want to go back into the living room and ask Jamahl yet again why he couldn't join her at the

MTV Video Music Awards preshow dinner the following week.

The only explanation he had given thus far was that he wasn't interested in dealing with a bunch of fake industry people all night—whereas most people would die for the chance to go to the award show or any of the star-studded events surrounding it. Still, since he had said no a few days ago, there had been a bit of tension between them. Instead of going into the living room, though, she pulled the covers back over her legs, realizing that her badgering didn't help at all—technically, she just made it worse.

Jamahl chuckled loudly at something on television. Just hearing his contentment while she was feeling pure aggravation annoyed Madison even more. She truly felt disgust in her veins; she was through trying to make her fiancé into the perfect mate. She kept telling herself to either accept him for who he was or walk out the door, but for some reason she couldn't do either of the two. She just couldn't seem to build a tolerance for his non–Prince Charming attributes, yet she wasn't prepared to walk away from all she had built with him. It was definitely a catch-22, no matter how she sliced it.

Madison suddenly decided she was going to get out of the house and go to the mall, one of the few things that put her in a good mood. She threw on some black leggings, with a tan shirt that was long enough to cover her butt, and then pulled on her UGG boots. Her hair was pulled back in a ponytail, and although she wasn't spruced up, she looked cute without trying. She said nothing as she passed Jamahl, who was still stationed on the couch. She noticed that he looked at her while she was putting on her coat, but she knew he had too much pride to ask where she was going.

It was a Saturday afternoon, which meant it might be a bit crowded at the mall, but the way she was feeling, she figured it would beat sitting alone indoors. She was hoping Jamahl thought she was running off to meet her secret lover. At times, she really wished deep down that she had a lover. Her midnight-blue BMW was sitting in the driveway in desperate need of a wash, and Madison jumped right in. She put on her seatbelt and drove off, waving to her gorgeous neighbor Mitchell as she passed. *Damn, if he wasn't married and I didn't live down the street from him with Jamahl* . . . she told herself again for the millionth time.

She was only five blocks away when she realized she had left her cell phone at home. She sat at the stop sign for a whole minute, wondering if she should go back, but she decided against it. As though she weren't addicted to her CrackBerry, Madison kept driving. It took everything in her to keep going, but she wasn't in the mood to go back to that house and see Jamahl's happy-go-lucky expression. He had this ability when they fought, to carry on like there was nothing wrong; meanwhile she would be smoking out of her ears. By the time she reached the mall, and stepped inside to her shopping heaven, she forgot about her phone. She walked right toward Nordstrom, ready to get lost in the scent of new clothes, shoes, and accessories.

Madison perused the floor and looked at the different racks of clothes. She had her eye on all things bright, it seemed—her last few shopping trips, she had brought home colors that stood out. Madison was ordinarily a black, white, gray, and navy girl, but lately she was loving bright colors from the whole Crayon box. It was actually making her enjoy shopping even more because she knew she wasn't buying things the same or similar to something she already owned, and even if the item *was* similar to something she owned, she knew she didn't have it in that color. She walked around the racks and took her time pulling things off to get a better look. It didn't take long before the sight of a pine-green shoe and another paisley shoe caught her eye. She went straight to the woman behind the register to ask for both shoes in her size and then sat down to wait.

She looked around the mall at all the people whisking by. There were mothers with their strollers, and young girls with their friends and other ladies with their husbands. For a split second, Madison got lost in their joy. She wondered to herself which she would rather be: a mother, a young girl, or a wife. She was a thirty-six-year-old woman, and still there was so much she hadn't experienced. Some days she felt left out—behind in life. She often felt regret that she had chosen a career over motherhood and a more settled lifestyle. Motherhood was pretty much out of the question; the job was so demanding she felt she would be a horrible mother. Her career definitely called for some sacrifice. Yet Jamahl wasn't looking to marry someone who couldn't commit to their home, let alone him. Madison knew exactly what she wanted on most days, but others, she didn't.

She was thinking about how great she would feel as a mother or a wife. She thought about what she was missing in her own life. It wasn't until the lady returned with her shoes that she remembered that being any of those ladies would likely not afford her the opportunity to just come to the mall on a lovely Saturday afternoon with no kids in tow, like she could, and shop without any regard for someone else or the "responsibilities of life." So, at that moment, she realized that she would rather be just who she was—a young, single, not lonely, successful woman with no children just yet. She knew that with all great things comes sacrifice, and she had chosen hers long ago. And when she tried on that pine-green shoe and strutted across the floor to the mirror, she was that much more assured that she was living the right life for her.

Madison had both pairs of shoes in a shopping bag and was making her way out of Nordstrom and on to the next store when she started to feel better about everything, including the tiff with Jamahl. All the women passing her appeared miserable suddenly. They were either struggling to look at something while watching their child or they were trying to hurry as their husbands rushed them along. Madison, on the other hand, was taking her precious time trying on everything she felt would look great on her at her high-powered job.

Chapter 5

He was taller than he looked on television, and his smile and flawless skin weren't the result of air-brushing for the magazines: he was gorgeous. As soon as Madison looked up and saw him walking toward her, along with two familiar faces and two strange ones, she put on her friendly face.

"Hey, Maddie, this is Johnny Polytics, our new artist on Intheloop Records. Johnny, this is Madison, the program director," Kristin, the Intheloop rep, said.

Madison was dressed in dark blue, fitted skinny jeans and a navy-blue-and-white Akademiks T-shirt.

"Hello, there," Madison said as she reached out to shake Polytics's hand.

"Nice to meet you. I really go by Polytics," he replied.

"Nice to meet you as well," Madison said.

"Thank you for supporting the new record so heavily," he said.

"Thank *you* for making a hit—that's what we

play here at Drama Ninety-Nine, so it's my pleasure."

"Well, thanks for considering a hit so early on before the rest of America caught on."

"Again, no problem. I've been doing this for quite some time. I know a hit when I hear one."

"Well, that's good to know. I may have to find a way to get you on my payroll to have you sit with me in the studio and pick my hits."

"Whoa," Kristin interrupted. "Let's not make those jokes, especially not in public or so loud."

The three of them giggled, but Polytics didn't take his eyes off Madison, not even for a second.

Polytics had the hottest single on the East Coast airwaves. There was no secret that all his prior success on the street underground level was about to pay off big-time. Every time you opened a magazine or turned on your television, you saw his face or something about him—never mind that one of his songs was played on the radio every thirty minutes. He was large in stature, and his celebrity status had escalated overnight. It was no coincidence that one of his first stops as an established success would be Drama 99 FM. This radio station was where all artists wanted to be if they could.

Everyone passing Madison's office recognized him instantly but tried not to stare. Not that you couldn't notice him—he had an attention-grabbing physique and aura, and the fact that he was dripped in diamonds didn't make him any more low key. Madison didn't feel that comfortable as he eyeballed her, and decided she should put an end to their powwow. He was fine, and under different circumstances, she would have turned on her flirtometer, but this wasn't the time nor the place . . . or the person.

"So you are going to do an interview with our afternoon radio queen?" she jumped in.

"I thought you were doing the interview," Polytics said with a grin.

"Oh, no, not me. I sit back here and run things, and the talented Miss Ivy does the interviews."

"Oh, that's too bad. I thought we were going to get the chance to chat it up and get to know each other better."

"Well, we will have plenty of chances for that behind the scenes," Madison said.

"I'd like that," Polytics said.

"Well, off the air, rather," Madison said, realizing that "behind the scenes" didn't sound so great.

"Gotcha," he said.

People from the department were walking around not too far away from them, picking up faxes and going from office to office, but it was as though Polytics didn't even notice. He was totally giving Madison his undivided attention. Kristin cut her eyes back and forth between the two of them to see if she could pick up a vibe, and Madison noticed that her own responses weren't helping the matter any. She almost couldn't help it. His charm and swagger were turned up to the trillions, and she didn't want to back down. She had to force herself to snap out of it and just begin to walk away.

"Well, first things first. We need to take care of business, and you guys have to be on air in less than five minutes, so how about you go back to the studio and get settled?" she said as she headed back into her office.

She didn't even look back at Polytics, and she hadn't given any fair warning that she was about to make an exit. She had to take control of the situation. She knew Kristin would get the hint and know where to take him.

"OK, we'll see you in a few," Kristin said.

Kristin and Polytics headed back to the studio together. A few of the station staff were in their path and quickly moved out of the way. If there was one music business rule most of the staff grasped and lived by, it was the "don't be a groupie" rule. It didn't matter how much you loved the person's music or talents, you were not to stare and be a nuisance to the celebrities. So to avoid looking like they were paying Mr. Polytics any mind, they scurried out of his way, almost pretending they didn't even know who he was.

Once he walked away, Alexis looked at Madison and then looked away.

"What?" Madison laughed with a full-fledged smile on her face.

"Nothing," Alexis replied with an equally obvious grin.

"Whatever," Madison said. "Y'all folks need to get your minds out of the gutter."

"I didn't say anything," Alexis said as she turned away and began typing on her computer.

Alexis wasn't sure if Madison was joking or a bit upset—it was hard to tell with her. Madison was moody; at certain times in the day she was mad cool, and then at others she was just an absolute bitch. Alexis decided to act like she hadn't seen any of that flirtation because the last thing she wanted was her name in the middle of any he-said-she-said.

The "industry," as it was often referred to, had an unspoken code. The code was that everything was to be kept a secret, especially from those not in the industry. As Jay-Z stated in one of his hit songs, "It's a secret society, all we ask is trust, and within a week, watch your arm freeze up." Most people obeyed because it was the world they were privy to; it was a privilege to be appreciated. People dreamed and died to be a part of the music business, so, for most, once you were in, you weren't to take it for granted. Yet there was more than enough gossip to go around—way more than what actually became public knowledge. The industry was filled with sex, drugs, and rock and roll—literally. There really was no code of conduct, and that was why there was a scandal every way you turned—enough to write a book.

Alexis wondered if the people on the outside knew that the industry wasn't all it seemed, if they would still want in so bad. If they knew that hanging with the stars and having access to some of entertainment's most glamorous events meant nothing at the end of the day, would they still envy her for being in the industry? If they knew that dealing with a bunch of egos and the fraternity mentality of the industry could make you want to stab someone, would they still spend their entire careers trying to get a job among the business?

Madison was back in her office by the time Polytics got off air, and she was hoping he and his escorts wouldn't make their way back into programming, because she didn't want another awkward moment. She was able to roll with the punches, but not in the middle of her department in front of her staff. Behind closed doors, she could show him she wasn't one of the little girls he was used to impressing. Moments passed, and there was still no sign of Polytics, so she figured he had gone ahead to his next business stop. She continued looking through the *Billboard* magazine to see what songs were climbing the charts and didn't notice at all that Jocelyn, the new music director, had stepped in.

"Maddie," she said.

"Yes," she said as she looked up.

"We are going to have a little problem. Trait's record is number one on the *106 & Park* countdown, and it's playing heavy on the station down the dial."

"So what's the problem?"

"We may have to get on this record, but if we put it in now, are we going to look late?"

"Who said we have to put it in because other people are playing it? We are Drama Ninety-Nine—we play what we play, and we decide what's a hit."

From the look on Jocelyn's face, Madison could tell she wanted to say something else but was hesitant to challenge her.

"Listen, Jocelyn, that is not a problem. If we decide to play it because we think our audience will like it, we will play it."

"OK," she said as she began to head out of the office.

Madison felt a little bad that she'd been a little

rough on her, but she knew she had to teach her how things worked in the New York market. Jocelyn had only been there for a couple months and was still caught up in the glitz and glamour of the New York market. She was talented and knew radio, but Madison had been trying to get her to see it was not going to be as easy as it had been in Philadelphia. Prior to her being hired, the acting music director, Keith, had been keeping things in order for Madison, but he hadn't been completely ready to take on all the responsibilities of the job, so Madison had brought Jocelyn on board. So although she didn't mean to come off like a witch, she knew she had to keep grooming her. Besides, Madison hated that she called her Maddie—she was her staff, and she didn't want her getting that comfortable.

One thing Madison's position called for was leadership and management skill, but as a woman it also called for fear. As a woman she was tested way more than the men in her position were, so Madison had to constantly keep her law laid down so people knew not to mess with her. She didn't like to always be labeled the ball breaker, but she knew that was how she kept her staff under control. The fact that Polytics had made her vulnerable in front of everyone didn't help, so she had to quickly erase those thoughts; a little ball busting was a quick and easy way to do so.

Chapter 6

"I'm getting married," Hannah said.

Reyna heard the words, but she took a minute to respond. Her mind computed it, and instantly, she felt happiness, jealousy, anger, joy, sadness, and fifty other feelings all at once. She was happy for Hannah—God knew Hannah deserved some happiness in her life—but Reyna couldn't help but wonder why she herself wasn't engaged yet. What in the hell was taking her boyfriend so long? She had been with him way longer than half the married couples she even knew. It was times like these she wondered why she was still dealing with his crap. Then again it was times like these that reminded her why, because if she ever wanted to walk down the aisle anytime soon, she couldn't waste time starting over with some new guy. Dang, her options sucked, and she knew it, and for that matter, so did her boyfriend. She wished she had the guts to just say to hell with it and leave his ass for making her wait so many years for him to pop the question. She worried deep down that by the time he did, she would have so much resentment in her heart, it wouldn't be quite the fairy tale anyway.

"Congratulations," Reyna blurted out as if that had been her sole thought and reaction.

"Thanks. Jerry asked me yesterday while we were at dinner."

"Aw, how sweet!"

"I love the ring, too. He did a great job," Hannah replied.

Laughing, Reyna said, "Well, that always helps the proposal."

"Yeah, girl. You are next, I'm sure."

Reyna hated that fake sympathy—she saw right through it. That was an "I expect you to be jealous" comment. Thing is, what Hannah didn't know was that Reyna didn't want to marry just anybody like Hannah or a lot of her friends did, she wanted to marry the man she loved and had been with for nine long years. She didn't envy Hannah's engagement, because Reyna knew she herself couldn't have told Jerry yes—if she were Hannah—after all the dirt he had done to her. So at the end of the day, Reyna preferred to wait for her man to propose than to have to settle like a lot of people. At the end of the day, that was Reyna's bright side. She felt as though she truly did have that rare true love she barely saw in most relationships, and she was happy that Michael hadn't ruined that yet.

Once she got off the phone, Reyna instantly realized how hard she had been on Michael. After she'd gotten home from Wal-Mart the day of their argument, he had apologized and explained that he hadn't meant it the way it had come out. The very next day he'd bought the dual hampers and added his-and-her hooks in the closets. When she came home from work, he'd had a candlelit dinner waiting. She really never did tell Michael how much she appreciated him, and she knew she could be a bit overbearing. She knew they shared something more special than most couples, including the newly dating and married couples. She wanted to stop holding against him the fact that he had his own agenda—how could she blame him when she did, too? Of course, she would have been happier if their two agendas were perfectly aligned, but she knew she couldn't fault him because they weren't.

Some guys didn't propose just to propose and then still cheat and act single. Some guys didn't wait until they were old, had nothing left to offer, and then propose to the one girl who had invested so much in them they wouldn't mind going ahead and marrying them. Some guys took marriage seriously, and Michael happened to be one of those guys. He wasn't going to rush into marriage, because he knew he wanted a lot of things to be right before he did that, and Reyna didn't want to hold that against him. At least, that was how she felt today at that moment—she just hoped she could remember this feeling next time she thought of her wedding day or saw that gorgeous engagement ring she had been waiting for.

Reyna took out her phone and dialed Michael.

"Hey, babe," she said once he answered.

"Hey, Rey," he replied.

His tone didn't have as much excitement as hers, but that was OK—she felt like she'd just had an epiphany.

"Hey . . . I just wanted to apologize to you."

"Apologize for what?"

"For giving you such a hard time when you were just being honest."

Michael didn't say anything, as though he was fishing for a setup.

"I know we have been having a rough time lately because we haven't been seeing eye to eye. I do feel we need to figure out how to compromise more, and you need to be more sensitive to my feelings, *but* I, too, need to do the same."

"OK, I feel you," Michael said.

Reyna wasn't going to let his demeanor discourage her efforts.

"Really, Michael, I know marriage isn't everything. I also know there are empty marriages all over this world, and there are cheating and disrespectful spouses everywhere you look, so, obviously, vows and a ring don't make a couple special. What two people share—the history and the love and the common goal to stand the tests of time— are what make a couple special, and that's what I want."

Something must have registered because suddenly Michael opened up some.

"Rey, no one said we won't have the marriage and the kids. We will. I just don't see why that is most important. I have seen a lot of my fellas move too fast and mess up their relationships. I know that what we have is forever, so there is no major rush. We still have a lot to accomplish and figure out before we go adding more to our plates."

Reyna was tempted to challenge him and state how marriage wouldn't make things any different, but maybe even better. Instead she chose against it. She knew they had different points of view on this, and it was about time she heard his view with an open mind for once.

"I understand," she limited herself to saying.

"We will get married, and when we do we are going to have a fabulous life and grow old together. My architecture firm will be established by then and will have gone public; you will have a permanent position at the hospital. We will be more stable to sustain the house we want and support the children we want. I just want us to do this right."

Reyna thought to say, *This is right. Let's just start this great life now. Why wait? My eggs won't last forever. Tomorrow isn't promised.* Instead she held her tongue and remained silent.

"You deserve the best, and I just want to give it to you. We are still young. We have time. Let's just enjoy this time we have now, and when the rest of our life together unfolds, we will enjoy that, too."

Reyna had to admit that the things Michael was saying were quite convincing. In many ways she knew if and when they had been married for several years with some noisy kids running around, she would miss the days of spontaneity and less responsibility. She was being like the preteen girls who just couldn't wait to grow up, and then when they were twenty-nine wished they could have back some of those years of carefree youth. She took what he was saying, and knowing she had been that preteen girl at one point, reminded herself why she had called in the first place. She had called because Hannah's bragging actually had made her appreciate what she had even more, and she wanted to tell him that.

"I like how that sounds, baby. That's why I called. Hannah is getting engaged—"

"Hannah?" he asked before she could finish her thought.

"Yeah, Hannah," she replied with a giggle.

"Didn't the guy she was with, like, get some other girl pregnant a few months ago? And, wait—didn't she just say she was pregnant by someone else a couple weeks ago?"

"Yes and yes," Hannah replied, not feeding into where he was going with his recollections.

"Wow, OK. Let's bet how long that will last."

"That's not nice. I'm not going to do that. They have just as good a shot as anybody."

"Yeah, sure. If they do last, they will not be happy. She barely has a career, and they have had way too much damage already. It won't be wedded bliss, I bet you."

"I'm not betting, but I am going to end this conversation. It's not nice."

Michael laughed. "OK, if you say so. I know you are thinking the same thing, but you just don't want to be mean because that is your friend."

"Yup," she replied.

Reyna eventually ended the phone call, and, surprisingly, she felt extremely optimistic about her future with Michael. She wondered how, with so many issues with her friends and family and her extremely demanding medical career, she managed to make Michael her main priority. She knew it had to be a woman thing, the whole biological clock thing, but still she felt so weak sometimes for allowing him and their life together to consume her. All the "strong, single sisters" told her to put herself first and not put no man that high on a pedestal—and every other sisterhood quote ever made. The thing Reyna had to remember was that not only were those sisters single, they were looking for Mr. Right constantly. They tried to act as if they were setting their standards high and were comfortable being single, so there was no rush, but that wasn't the case when they were out at clubs or home alone complaining. So Reyna paid them no mind; no woman or man really wanted to live this life alone, and she was no exception.

Chapter 7

It was his first day back on air since the prior week, and DJ KD had a mouthful. As soon as he cracked the mic, he blew up, so much so that he didn't introduce himself or give the station call letters. The first thing he did was clarify that the story Tryme had been spreading all through the media was false.

"Tryme, that's all you can do is try, but you will never succeed, not over my dude." Vice, the board operator, didn't know what the proper protocol was when a jock threw a tantrum over the airwaves, but he stood with his finger close to the dump button just in case.

"That fake thug came up in here thinking he was running things. Nobody tells me what to do—I do what I want to do. You need me, I don't need you. Your team should've told you you were overstepping your boundaries, but they didn't let you. They let you step into the ring for a nonwinning battle. You mad at me 'cause I didn't want to play your wack records. Then you tried to try me—and you got your ass beat! Then you want to go on the radio and say you did some damage—negro, please! Get the incident report from the police— the police that got called on me! You can spread whatever lies you want—but I'm here every night— you will never get the last word."

KD was just filled with anger. It was bad enough he had been off the air for days, but he had been itching to respond to clear his name, and it showed. Vice finally signaled to him that he had to wrap up for commercial, and because no one played around with ad time at Drama 99, KD cut it short and took a seat.

As soon as he made sure the sponsors were well into their sales pitch, Vice looked over at KD.

"You alright?" he asked.

"I'm good," KD replied.

"You just blacked out live."

"He better be glad I didn't see him last night at that album release party. It would've been round two."

Before KD could turn to see what had caused Vice's expression to change so rapidly and drastically, he heard the voice of Madison ripping through the doorway.

"Are you out of your damn mind?" she said.

KD looked up to gather his response, but he didn't think quickly enough.

"Do you think this microphone is your personal diary for you to vent your personal issues?"

"No, I was just—"

"It's not. You keep your drama and bullshit off my airwaves, or you will not be on them again, are you clear?"

"Madison, I was just responding to all the stuff being said. My listeners want to hear my side."

"Don't try to make this about your listeners or good content—this is about your ego."

KD started to contemplate if he should have just left well enough alone.

"His record label just called, and they are pissed off. You are trashing their artist on the air, and they just had him up here to give an interview," Madison continued.

"Is that what this is about? Kissing some label's ass?"

"No, it's about not wanting added drama spoken over the air—"

"We can't speak of any drama at Drama Ninety-Nine FM?"

"Real funny, KD. I'm not in the mood tonight. Unless you want Vice finishing your show, I suggest you relax."

"I *am* relaxed. I just don't understand why I can't speak my mind just because the record label is upset. I don't work for the record label."

"Yeah, well, you work for me, and I said cut that shit out."

Madison exited on that note. She was well aware KD was one of her top DJs, so she wasn't trying to take him off air any longer than he already had been, but she wasn't in the mood for added drama.

KD was just as pissed off back in the studio. He was sitting in the swivel chair playing with the pen in his hand.

"We are back on in sixty seconds. You ready to rock?" Vice asked.

"Yeah. I was trying to tell you that you was blacking out and to be easy, but then I seen her out of nowhere," Vice said as he adjusted the levels on the board.

"You was saying to relax because of Madison or the investigation?" KD asked.

Before Vice could respond, he was silencing KD and counting his fingers down from five.

"WDRD, it's your boy, KD, bringing you the drama like I do each and every day. For those of you just joining me, I just let the tristate know that nobody's favorite rapper, Tryme, is a fraud, but due to music business politics, I am going to say no more about it."

Vice looked over at KD, shocked that he had made that stab at Madison over the airwaves like that, but he turned back away quickly in case KD decided to redirect his aggression. KD continued with some more banter about the music world and some of the drama within it before he got into some regular entertainment news.

Although KD and Vice expected Madison to appear back in the studio, she didn't. She was sitting in her office trying to get her stuff together to get the hell out of there and wondering why she had her behind still in the building that late. By the time KD was on air, she was well into overtime hours. She knew that the on-air staff that came to work after she was gone felt a little more free to take risks. She knew KD was shocked to see her pop in the studio, but she was more pissed that he had made his slick remarks on air even after he'd known she was listening. It was a good thing for him, though, that she was in no mood to care. The station was consuming all her energy, and on this particular night she was ready to throw in the white flag.

An hour had gone by, and Madison was home and dressed in her comfy pajamas. Her hair was wrapped up, and she had her red and blue scarf tied around her head. She was all ready for bed and went into the family room to spend some cuddle time with her man in hopes to take her mind off the stressful day at work. When she walked in, he was sitting on the couch with the remote in his hand. He wore a pair of gray sweat pants, and his hairy chest was exposed through a saggy wife beater. He didn't look up or acknowledge her when she walked in, but she just continued on her way to sit beside him. Once she plopped down next to him, he looked at her.

"Damn, do you have to jump down so hard?"

"Jump? How do you jump down, Jamahl?"

"Never mind," he said and turned back to the television.

Before he'd just annoyed her, Madison had wanted to rest her head on his shoulder, but he had just diffused that feeling with his attitude.

She sat there for a few moments looking at the sports news he was watching. A few moments went by, and no words were exchanged. All Madison could think was, *what happened to the generic welcome-home questions? What happened to enjoying spending some quality time together? What happened to us?*

"So, no 'how was my day'?" she asked.

"I was watching something," he replied.

Madison bit her bottom lip to prevent from speaking too quickly because she knew it wouldn't be very nice. She didn't want to argue, but his unpleasantness was pissing her off quite fast.

"How was your day?" he asked with an obvious hesitation.

"It was fine, Jamahl."

"So why did you ask me to ask?"

"Oh, my gosh, are you serious?" she said as she turned to look directly at him.

He just looked back at her.

"Did it hurt you to open up dialogue with me?"

"No, but I am saying you acted as though you had something to say, when really you just wanted me to say something."

"I didn't act like anything. I just asked you why you were sitting here speechless like I didn't just come home and join you on the couch."

Madison knew where this petty bickering was headed, so before he gave his counter she got off the couch.

"Never mind, Jamahl, enjoy your alone time. I am going to bed."

Jamahl made no attempt to change her mind; he just watched her walk down the hallway toward the staircase.

Madison reached her bedroom and was beyond annoyed. She sat on the side of the bed and rubbed her toes on the plush maroon carpet in her bedroom and tried to let her blood pressure drop some before she turned on the television. She told herself to shake it off and start a new day—the last thing she needed was to go down her Jamahl-gets-me-sick road. Once she got into bed, she hit POWER on the remote. A familiar tune filled the room. It was Polytics's new video on BET. Madison felt guilty, but watching him shirtless and rubbing on all the young video chicks was clearing her mind and cheering her up. Even though she knew everything about that was wrong.

Chapter 8

Naomi hadn't called home to her parents in a few days. She had been so caught up in work she kept missing the window of time to just call and say hello, and her parents were not up on the texting game yet. She had just made it back from work, and she promised herself that she would call home tonight. It seemed as if she had left some of herself behind in Texas. She was very close to her parents; she was their only child, and prior to moving to New York, she had barely gone a weekend without seeing them.

Several times, when Naomi was home in bed, she wondered if she ever should have left Texas. She'd gone to college for broadcast journalism, and working in the big city of dreams was like a fantasy she never really expected. That was why, when she'd actually gotten a callback from the record label, she hadn't wanted to pass up the op- portunity; it hadn't taken much for her to get up and go. Well, not much hesitation aside from her boyfriend, Charles. She and Charles had been together since high school, and as far as she knew, they were getting married as soon as possible. However, after a lot of thought and his support to take the job in New York, Naomi had decided to go for just a few years and come back home to Texas with a great résumé and a lot of contacts. Naomi was able to speak to Charles more frequently than to her parents; she and Charles spoke via text throughout the day and on the phone sometimes at night when her parents were already in bed. Those were the times she had time to talk on the phone for hours with him. She was wishing she could speak to her mother and father even half as much.

Within the first thirty minutes of being home, Naomi was dressed in her pink flannel pajamas and big puffy socks. She turned the channel to BET to watch the latest videos as she stuffed some potato chips in her mouth. She was in no mood to cook, so she had already made up her mind that she was going to make some ramen noodles when she got hungry. Besides, expensive dinners were not in her budget—having to pay New York rent was pretty much all Naomi could afford for the most part. She stuffed in two to three chips at a time as she watched the new video by Brian Mc Knight; she loved her some Brian, like most ladies.

After she was temporarily filled with potato chips, she put the bag down and finally called home.

"Hey, baby," her father said as soon as he heard her voice.

"Hey, Daddy," she said in her little-girl voice.

"How's my little girl?"

"I'm good, just tired and working an awful lot."

"You're doing a lot of overtime?"

"Not every night, but I work some nights until about eight or nine PM."

"How are you getting home on those nights?"

"I usually take the train. On some nights I can get car service."

"Why aren't you taking car service every night? I don't want you out there late at night like that on the train."

"Trust me, Dad, I would rather take the car service, but with the budget cuts and all, they don't let us take them all the time."

"Oh, well, on those nights, you go home at a decent time. I don't want you traveling that late on the train. It's dangerous."

"I know, Dad, I will try."

Naomi expected her parents to do the whole safety-training speech. Every time she called home, they went through all the dos and don'ts of living in the city.

"Is Mommy around?"

"She's at the grocery store, but I know she wants to speak with you. You're gonna just have to call her back."

"OK, should I just call her cell phone?"

"You can, but if she's shopping, she probably won't be able to talk to you the way she would like."

"OK, no problem."

"What are you eating for dinner tonight?"

Naomi knew if she told him she was eating ninety-nine-cent soup, he would object to her lack of nutrition and vegetables.

"I'm not sure yet. I'm going to cook something though."

"OK, baby girl. Eat and then call your mother back after nine thirty."

"OK, Daddy."

Once Naomi hung up, she stood to go make her little broke-man's dinner. She wasn't all that hungry yet, but she knew the later she waited, the closer to her bedtime she would be eating. She was only a whopping one hundred thirty-five pounds, but she wasn't trying to get in the habit of eating late and becoming a cow. She learned quick that skinny was very "in" where she worked. She did want to take a minute to call Charles first, so she figured she would give him a call while the water boiled. She was dialing his number when she did a double take at the television screen. Tyreek was in the new Polytics video. Tyreek worked with Naomi, and she saw him almost every day at the office, so she was surprised to see him on her television. She hung up the phone and began to watch the video closer. In Texas, people you know and see in real life didn't just appear on TV.

She watched clips of him dancing. Naomi had been sitting on the edge of a brown and cream armchair in her living room, but as she became more intrigued by the video, she began to sit back. Tyreek was five-eleven with broad shoulders. He was brown skinned with shoulder-length dreads and close-shaved facial hair. Naomi had noticed his good looks before at the office, but the more she saw of him on her television screen, the more attractive he became to her. She didn't notice it at first, but she was wearing a slight smile on her face as she saw him profiling and interacting with the other people in the video. She hardly ever got a chance to speak to Tyreek, but she knew he was a pretty big deal at her company. Watching him on her television made her feel honored just to be in the same building with him every day.

Naomi had one good girlfriend from back home who lived in New York, but because she worked so much, Naomi didn't get to see her as much as they had anticipated. Still, when it came to the person she relied on to chat it up with, it was still Devora. She wanted Devora to get a glance of Tyreek before the video went off, so she quickly called her. Devora answered on the second ring.

"Hey, are you home?" Naomi blurted.

"Yeah, why?" Devora asked.

"Turn to BET—hurry, hurry!"

"What? I have seen this. This is the new Polytics video."

"I know, but you see that guy with him in the gray hoodie?" Naomi asked.

"Yeah, who is that?"

"That's my coworker Tyreek. He's a cutie, I think."

"Uh-oh . . . someone has a crush," Devora teased.

"No, I just think he's cute, and I wanted your opinion."

"He *is* cute, I agree. You guys are cool?" Devora asked.

"No, not really," Naomi answered.

"Well, if you think he's cute, try to get cool with him and see where it goes."

"No, I still have my baby Charles at home," Naomi said.

"Charles—many-miles-away Charles?"

"Yes, but it's not his fault I moved here."

"Well, who knows what Charles is doing while you're gone? It won't hurt you to make a friend," Devora said.

"You know I'm shy. I'm not trying anything," Naomi said.

"Well, you better toughen up. New York men don't wait around for shy."

Naomi knew what Devora meant. Still, she knew she wasn't on Tyreek's level. Tyreek probably had a slew of girls, and if they looked anything like the girls he was dancing with in the video, Naomi didn't feel she stood a chance.

Chapter 9

Monday morning everything was as usual at the radio station—except the midday jock wasn't in yet. Madison was running around trying to see if he would be there in time for his shift, which began in five minutes. No one could get him on the phone, and he hadn't reached out to anyone. For all anyone knew, he was oversleeping in a deep coma from the fun night out the station staff had had the night before. She'd told him to leave more than once because he needed to be at the station on time regardless. He never did listen to her, and it looked like—just as she predicted—the evening and his drinks had taken a toll on him.

"Alexis, go to the studio and ask someone from the morning show to fill in for his shift until he gets here," Madison said to her assistant who was sitting at her computer.

"OK," Alexis said as she stood to walk to the back.

Madison went into her office. She hated starting off her work weeks on a bad foot. She began checking her messages and getting settled in. The third message was from Neil, manager of Polytics. He was inviting Madison to Polytics's album listening party that Wednesday night at the Hit Factory. Madison penciled down the information, erased the message, and continued on. By the time she was done, she saw Alexis's head bopping down the hall toward her.

"OK, Citrus is going to do it," Alexis said.

"Great, thanks."

Alexis turned toward her desk to sit back down. Madison then thought about how Citrus had the tendency to be on the wild side.

"Alexis, call him and let him know to tone it down some and stick to the music scheduled—no slipups!" Madison yelled.

Madison went back to what she was doing. She finished responding to some e-mails and returning some calls. Before she knew it, it was a quarter to twelve, and the "New Music at Noon" was about to begin. Madison finished her coffee and walked back to the studio to make sure Citrus understood which songs to play in this segment. She made her way back and on the way glanced up at the picture of Polytics's album cover on the wall. She remembered the conversation they'd had when they met and how she'd wondered if Kristin thought she was flirting. She thought about it all of forty seconds until she was standing in the studio doorway trying to get Citrus's attention. The "on air" light was off, but he was prerecording some breaks for his weekend show. After he saw Madison standing there, he quickly finished his sentence, wrapped up, and hit the STOP button. Madison informed him what the rules were for the show and showed him the list of songs he was allowed to choose from for the next thirty minutes. Citrus expressed his understanding of the rules, and Madison went about her business. After spending a few moments in a colleague's office, Madison made it back to her office. Coincidently, as soon as she walked in, she heard Citrus introducing the next new song of the day, Polytics's upcoming single. Madison could only chuckle on the inside.

Just as she sat back in her office chair, she noticed that SoundScan had been sent over, and she instantly opened it and began to look through the report. She got lost in the data, looking at nationwide sales versus New York sales, etc. She took notes on some of the albums and singles she wanted to discuss with her programming staff and placed some sticky notes on the report. Just as she was wrapping up, her assistant came into her doorway.

"Jamahl is on the phone," she said.

"Thanks," Madison said and immediately picked up her phone receiver. "Hey, babe."

"Hey," he replied. "I was calling to remind you we have that dinner Wednesday after work."

"Oh, yeah, for your cousin's graduation. Yes, I remember. I'll meet you there after work."

"OK, that's fine."

A moment went by, and neither of them said anything.

"Is that the only reason you called?" she asked.

"Well, that and to say hello. I didn't get to see you or speak to you much yesterday."

"That's very true. I did miss you. We should do dinner later tonight. What you think?"

"Sounds good to me," Jamahl replied.

"OK, call me when you get off. We can go somewhere around here."

After they finished making their plan, Madison hung up and went back to her computer. She began drafting her e-mail to her staff regarding the SoundScan reports and the points she felt they should discuss in their meeting tomorrow. She decided she was going to make another cup of coffee to get her a quick boost of energy. She went to the kitchen, made her cup of coffee while chatting with some of her colleagues, and blew on her hot cup to cool it off on her way back. It was already close to two o'clock by the time Madison took a seat in her office—half the day was gone. She was well aware she wasn't leaving at exactly five o'clock anyway, but she was happy to see that the business day was almost over.

"Madison, Neil is on the phone," Alexis announced.

"OK," Madison replied. She sipped her coffee and then answered the phone. "Hello."

"Hi, Maddie, it's me, Neil. I was calling to put you through with Polytics. He wanted to speak with you."

"OK," Madison replied.

"Hold on one second."

Madison's mind wondered what this could be about and how Polytics had some nerve to have someone call her for him and expect her to hold.

"Madison?" Polytics asked.

"Yes, this is she."

"Hi, how are you? So sorry to have you on hold. I

just didn't want to call and cause any excitement with your assistants or whoever."

It was as if Polytics had read her mind.

"Oh, it's no problem."

"Well, I was calling because I wanted to personally invite you to my album listening session this Wednesday."

"Oh, yes. Neil left me a message this morning."

"I know, I told him to. But I wanted to call and invite you myself and let you know how very disappointed I would be if you didn't make it out."

Just as Madison was about to say of course she would be there, she remembered her reminder call from Jamahl a few hours prior.

"You know what, Polytics . . . I do have another engagement to attend, but—"

"Oh, no. Don't make me postpone it just for you. I really want you there."

Madison blushed slightly; she didn't want him to notice she was actually a bit flattered. "I was just going to say I will figure out how to do both."

"OK, great. I will be looking out for you. I won't let them press PLAY until I see you in the building," Polytics said.

"Bet."

Madison still was a bit uncomfortable speaking with Polytics because they hadn't formed enough of a relationship for her to tell exactly how he was coming at her, so she decided to wrap up the phone call on that note.

"So, I'll see you then."

"OK," he said.

"OK, bye."

Madison hung up before he could interject with anything else. She felt like he was surrounding her. Because of his music, his pictures, and his calls, she felt like he was all she had been able to think about all day. Now she was trying to figure out how she was going to keep her commitment to attend his album listening event *and* the dinner with her fiancé. It was absolutely normal for her to attend an album release party or a listening party, and there was no reason this one should be any different. She was starting to wonder if she was making something bigger out of this than it was.

Chapter 10

Sereeta used her key to open the door to Corey's home; she saw two of his cars in the driveway, and she wasn't sure if he was there or not. She was coming by to get his bags ready for the next few games on the road, and she had to be done within an hour and back to the stadium to put his press suit in the cleaners.

As soon as she stepped indoors, she noticed the place was a mess. She looked around and noticed pillows from the couch on the floor, the magazine rack knocked over, and chairs and cushions all over the living room. She figured Corey had had company over the night before, and she hadn't been invited. She walked farther into the house and noticed some articles of clothing in different parts of the house. *How wild did the party get that everyone forgot stuff behind?* Sereeta asked herself. She left everything right where it was; her job duties didn't include being a maid, so she wasn't about to create any expectations on his part.

She walked through the living room and the

family room and made her way up the staircase. As she reached the top of the stairs, she spotted feet and legs in the bathroom ahead. She stopped at first, thinking it was Corey and not wanting to surprise him while he wasn't fully dressed. Having heard her steps, the person poked his head out of the bathroom door, and Sereeta realized it wasn't Corey. It was one of the guys from his team, but Sereeta didn't know his name—he didn't play that much.

"Hi, there," the guy said.

"Hi," Sereeta said as she slowly took a few more steps down the hall.

"Darnell," the guy said.

"Excuse me?"

"My name is Darnell. What's yours again?"

"Oh, Sereeta. Nice to meet you . . . again," Sereeta said, trying not to show her discomfort.

Lemme find out Corey is with that down-low stuff, Sereeta thought. She was mad she had stumbled upon this guy brushing his teeth in the bathroom after having spent the night at Corey's house. This was one of those big secrets that would be hard for Sereeta to pretend she didn't notice. Although Sereeta was definitely uncomfortable, Darnell didn't seem to be the least bit bothered by her presence. Sereeta continued past the bathroom and down the hall toward Corey's bedroom. The door was cracked a bit, and Sereeta could see that one of the lamps was on inside. Once she pushed the door open, she instantly noticed a half-naked woman lying in the bed. Sereeta jumped.

"Oh, I'm so sorry," Sereeta said.

"Oh, no problem," the young lady said as she pulled the sheet over her body.

Sereeta didn't know if she should leave or continue with her assignment.

"You came to join the party?" the young lady asked Sereeta after she noticed she wasn't leaving the room.

"Excuse me?" Sereeta said.

Just as she was waiting for the lady to respond, she heard a voice coming from the other side of the room.

"Who are you talking to, Kyleea?" said a young lady coming out of the master bathroom.

Sereeta looked her up and down and noticed she was in a robe—looked like it was Corey's robe at that.

"Oh, hi," the chick said.

"Hi," Sereeta said.

"I'm Bianca," the girl said.

"Hi, I'm Sereeta. Corey's personal assistant."

The girls giggled.

"Aren't you lucky," Bianca said.

"I guess," Sereeta said. "I'll be right back. Can you excuse me?"

Sereeta stepped out and down the hallway. Darnell was still in the bathroom washing his face. Sereeta put it together now; Darnell wasn't ashamed of being caught in his boxers in Corey's house because there were plenty of women to go around in the Cox mansion.

Sereeta took out her phone and called Corey.

"Hi, Corey, I'm sorry to bother you, but I just got to your house to pack your bags, and you still have guests in your bedroom; I'm not sure if I should do this later."

"No, no. Tell them to go downstairs to the living room, or have Darnell get them out. I need my bags here on time, and I need my suits here now; the on-site cleaners can't take the players' clothes for same-day service after one PM."

"OK," Sereeta replied. "So just ask them to go downstairs?"

"No, tell them. Listen, Sereeta, you got to get that stuff here. There's no time to be shy."

"OK," Sereeta said.

A bit angered by the fact that Corey was getting a bit smart, especially when he was the one having orgies in his house, she headed back into the bedroom.

"Bianca, Kyleea . . . I'm sorry, but I have to take care of some things in here. Would you ladies mind sitting downstairs for a while or going into the guest bedroom for now? Darnell is out there."

"Who is Darnell?" Kyleea asked Bianca.

"The one I was with—Corey's teammate," Bianca answered.

"Oh." Kyleea giggled as she scooted off the bed.

The two of them took their time as they began to gather some of their things and head out of the bedroom.

"Thank you, guys. When I'm done you can come back up."

Sereeta didn't bother to see where they went—downstairs or into the guest bedroom. All she wanted to do was pack Corey's bags and get out of there. She didn't even want to know exactly what had gone on last night between Corey, Darnell, and whoever else was over.

Sereeta began packing some tracksuits and jeans out of Corey's drawers and closets. He had instructed her before as to what exactly he liked to pack for road games and how much of everything. This was only his second trip she had packed for him, but she already had a grasp on what she was doing. She took the three pairs of 7 For All Mankind jeans out of the closet and placed them in his bag, tucked everything to the side, and closed the bag. She filled the front pouch with his socks and wristbands, put his boxers and wife beaters on the other side, and zipped the bag completely closed. She grabbed suits and things off closet hooks and then headed downstairs with his bag and clothes in hand.

Once she got midway down the stairs she began to hear the giggle of one of the females. Sereeta rolled her eyes and continued down. She reached the living room and saw one of the girls lying on top of Darnell, kissing his neck with her left hand in his pants. The other young lady was sitting close by with a big grin on her face. Darnell looked over and saw Sereeta standing there.

"You finished up?" he asked, speaking over the girl whose face was buried in his neck.

"Uh, yeah," Sereeta said.

"OK, tell Corey I'll lock up and be at the stadium in an hour."

"OK, will do."

The lady stayed in action during their exchange of words, as though Sereeta's presence had no effect on her little porno movie. Sereeta turned away and headed toward the door; neither girl said good-bye, and neither did she. Sereeta was grown, so it wasn't as though she was naive that things of that nature actually happened for real— and not just in the music videos and movies—but to witness it firsthand just threw her for a loop. She had to ask herself what these chicks were doing that to themselves for—they couldn't possibly understand how gross they looked. Sereeta wondered sometimes if *she* was the one missing something— maybe they were the smart ones, and she was the dummy. Besides, she was the one working like a slave to earn her check when all they had to do was open their legs.

Sereeta hopped in the Suburban Corey had provided her for the day. The driver turned back and said, "To the stadium?"

"Yes," she replied. She instantly pulled out her cell phone. Within a few moments, Reyna was on the other end. "You wouldn't believe what some girls are willing to do just to be in these guys' presence," she blurted out as soon as Reyna said hello.

"What are you talking about?"

"I just left Corey's house, and these chicks were in there with his teammate, and it was just disgusting."

"What were they doing?"

"Well, while I was there, not so much, but last night and before I got there, who knows."

Before Reyna could inquire more, Sereeta's phone beeped. Sereeta looked at the phone and saw it was Corey.

"Hold on," she told Reyna. "Hello?" she said to Corey.

"Hey, you on your way here?" he asked.

"Yes, I will be there in about fifteen minutes."

"OK, great. I am also going to need you to book two flights."

"OK," Sereeta said as she pulled out her pad.

"Both from JFK to Cleveland—one for Bianca Watts, and the other for Kyleea Jones. If you need any of their information, call Darnell at the house—he will have it."

Sereeta couldn't believe what she was hearing.

"OK, I'll get right to it," she responded.

"Alright, I will see you soon," he said.

Sereeta hung up and clicked back over to Reyna. "Girl, I have to go. I have to go book flights for those two skanks I was telling you about."

"Huh?"

"Yeah, I guess they want them to continue pleasuring them when they get to their next game in Cleveland. So let me go book these flights before he calls me with something else."

Reyna laughed. "OK, talk to you later."

Sereeta took the airline number out of her BlackBerry and called Darnell to get the ladies' information. She had already told herself she wouldn't talk directly to the chicks—she didn't want any part of what was going on.

Chapter 11

The high-waist jeans and button-up top were far from the most fashionable outfit in the place, but Madison felt confident. Her gold stilettos and exposed cleavage added the touch of sexy she needed, and she was good to go. She walked around the room looking for Polytics or Neil to let them know she had arrived, but neither of them were anywhere to be found.

The room was huge, almost resembling a giant Manhattan loft. Off to her left behind her was a large glass wall that separated the room from the studio. From the open area you could see directly into the studio where all the equipment, speakers, and microphones were. There were a few couches and tables scattered along the wall, and there was a bar in one corner of the room. It was a new studio Madison hadn't been to yet—most of the listening parties she attended were at Sony Studios. She wasn't surprised that Polytics would want to use the new and "exclusive" Hit Factory studio for his listening event.

Madison was happy she had managed to keep

her commitment with Jamahl and still make this event as well. She had accompanied Jamahl to the dinner, but she just let him know she had to leave early "for business." At times like these she was thankful he was usually understanding about the fact that she mixed work with pleasure so much. Not that Jamahl could really complain, as many times as he had left her out to dry at an event or something.

She went toward the back hallway where a couple people were standing. She spoke back to the few familiar faces that shouted, "Hey, Madison," as she walked by, but she felt no one was worth stopping for a formal greeting. She made her way toward the back and noticed a crowd of people in the studio. Madison glanced around to see who was inside. She recognized a lot of label executives and press people. After a few seconds she caught eyes with Polytics, who was already looking back at her. He smiled to let her know not only did he see her but that he was happy to see her. Madison smiled back.

Within seconds he was making his way toward her—he along with several people's attention were heading her way. Madison remained calm and still, but for some reason she was feeling nerves in her stomach. She was definitely not used to feeling nervous—she usually made people nervous. When he stopped in front of her, she looked up at him with a smirk.

"Hey there, sexy, I'm so glad you were able to make it," he said as he reached over to hug her.

"No problem."

"As promised, the party is waiting on you. I didn't play one song yet."

"Well, I don't have a lot of time, so let's get to listening."

Madison was doing a pretty good job of playing it cool, but on the inside she was trying to monitor her every word and action. She didn't want to give off the wrong vibe or make any mistakes that could imply the wrong thing.

"Let's," Polytics said. He took Madison's hand to direct her to the studio control area.

Madison was taken aback by the hand holding, and she instinctively grabbed her hand back. Polytics stopped in his tracks to see what the reaction was about. Madison felt the discomfort from the attention they were attracting.

"I can walk," Madison said when she saw his perplexed look.

"OK, *sooorry,*" he replied.

Madison bucked her eyes at him to signal *Well, go ahead.* He began to walk again, and they continued down the hall to the studio. Neil, along with a few other people from the label and management, were already sitting inside.

"Hey, there, Maddie!" Neil shouted as soon as he saw Madison walk in.

"Hey, Neil," she said as she gave him a hug.

"Aren't we looking hot. Big plans tonight?" he said.

"I am coming from a dinner," she responded.

Madison was hoping he would leave the topic alone, so she instantly began to make her rounds around the room to say hello. Once she was done greeting everyone with a hello or a hug, Polytics pulled out a large cushy chair for her to sit in. She quickly glanced around the room to see if anyone reacted to Polytics's chivalry—if that was even what it was. She started to wonder if she was the only one overanalyzing anything. Polytics could have just been messing with her that day, and here she was acting as if they were ex-lovers or something. She began to feel stupid, like she was playing herself for even thinking that all her paranoia or discomfort was necessary. Polytics could have any girl he wanted—he was at least five years her junior, and he was probably not interested in a program director from New York when he could have an exotic video chick every day of the week.

Madison finally managed to calm down and relax. She sat back in the chair, finally enjoying the moment and the sucking up that came with her job. A few moments later, Polytics's new single, "Broken Rules," was playing through the oversize speakers in the studio. Madison looked through the glass to see the crowd's reaction. She liked to use this as a part of her decision making to see if a song was a radio-friendly track. Madison and the others could see clearly all the guests and staff working the event outside the studio control room, and everyone watched how they received the music they were hearing. Heads were bouncing along, and feet were tapping; one or two people were even rapping along. There were also those cats who had gotten ahold of a leaked record from the Internet or were heavy enough in the music business to get an early copy, and they wanted the room to know they were "ahead of the game," so they rapped every word very hard.

"This beat is hot. Who produced this? Dr. Dre?" Madison leaned over and asked Polytics.

The music was loud, and it was hard to hear over it, but Madison had leaned over close enough to hear his response.

"No. Actually, it's this new cat I mess with. His name is Elly," he replied.

"Oh, OK. Sounds like a Dre beat."

They were basically yelling over the track, but their voices were completely drowned out by the music, so they had to get pretty close.

"Yeah, I have heard that before. This track is about how I don't care what the rules say—when I want something, I am going to go after it."

Madison had been watching the crowd with her ear close to Polytics's mouth, but as Polytics spoke those words, she could feel that he was staring directly at her. Madison turned to verify, and sure enough, he was looking her dead in the eye.

"Are you trying to tell me something?" she asked.

"I'm not a big trier. I'm more of a doer."

Madison gave him a look. For a moment she forgot about not wanting to show any interest. After she'd convinced herself he wasn't obtainable, subconsciously, she must have become intrigued by the challenge. Before she could reply, the music faded out, and the next track began to slowly fade up. With the music lowered, Madison wasn't willing to speak for fear of being overheard, and she found this awkward silence the perfect chance to brush off what he was saying.

As the volume got louder, she kept looking at him out of the corner of her eye. Last she looked, he was still looking. The new track came on, and it had an R & B hook. *Oh, brother,* Madison thought. The words *"I enjoy the moments that are shared by we, because when I'm doing you I am doing me. All that sex-iness on top of me, I now know the definition of ecstasy"* Madison wanted to comment on, but she didn't want to open that can of worms. Instead she just sat there, swaying her head to the music like most of the people on the other side of the glass were.

"So how do you like this one?" Polytics leaned over and asked her midway through the song.

"I like it. It's different. I like how you have the Caribbean undertone to it."

"This one was for the ladies. I have a lot of hard songs—I wanted to do something a little softer."

The music was loud, but Madison could've sworn he had damn near seductively whispered the word *softer.* "Yeah, I think it's best you mix it up when you're a new artist so you don't turn away any particular audience."

"Exactly," he replied as he turned away.

The next track began, and Madison began to ask herself just how long she would stay and what could be her most tactful exit. She was uncomfortable for sure, yet the last thing she wanted to appear as was weak and impressionable. Madison had been around the block, and she knew the games men played. She knew it wasn't impossible that there was a bet going around, possibly between Polytics and his people. The last thing she wanted to be was some test or topic of some mix-tape record.

A couple tracks went by with no real conversations. People were just bobbing their heads, tapping their feet, and rapping along to the familiar songs. Madison got comfortable and was enjoying the album. She had to admit Polytics was a talented artist and had a bright future ahead of him if he played his cards right.

"So what you think?"

"I think it's a hot album. You have quite a few single options, and that's always a good thing."

"What you think the next radio record should be?" he asked.

"I hate to give that advice because then you think I'm obligated to play it." Her look with her words told him she was well up on all the tricks.

"Not at all, nothing like that. I just figure who better than the queen of radio to help choose my next radio record."

"Well, technically, I would be choosing your single—most songs that make the radio will have a video and promotion to support it."

"Understandable. Now, which record do you think that should be?"

"How about I take the album home, listen to all the records, and tell you which I think should be your singles?"

"I like that idea. Can we do that tonight?"

"I didn't say *we* would take it home, I said *I* would take it home."

"Honestly, I'd love a detailed critique of all the songs, along with why you choose the singles you choose."

Madison just gave him a look. He was asking to come to her house, and she wasn't sure just how to take that.

"I'm not sure about all that. I don't mind giving you the feedback, but I'm not too comfortable with you coming to my house."

"I respect that," he said.

Madison could sense that he wasn't feeling her shut down, and although she wasn't trying to be cold, she just felt that—considering his tone—the decision was best. "How about we go back to the station and go through the album there?"

"Cool, that's fine with me. I wasn't trying to get in your bed or anything."

Madison blushed, a bit embarrassed by his comment.Was it all in her mind, or was he interested in her?

"No one said all that, but my place is a little personal. This is business."

"Whatever, yo."

Madison sensed his street side showing; she was surprised he had actually gotten a little attitude, as though he hadn't understood where she was coming from.

"You want to do this or not?" she asked. She was a bit intrigued by this guy who didn't seem intimidated by her in the least bit. But at the same time, she wasn't trying to let him get their relationship twisted. He needed her—she didn't need him.

"Yes, I said we can do that. As soon as this is done, you want to just ride over together?"

"Sure, why not?"

Within the next thirty minutes, a lot more guests had begun to show up. Polytics got on the microphone and announced that the album had two more tracks to be heard. He thanked everyone for coming, informed them it was unlikely he would be around when the event was done, but he would be having a platinum party very soon. The crowd laughed at his blatant cockiness and applauded him for all he had accomplished thus far.

Some people, realizing they weren't going to get a chance to meet or chat with him, began to gather their things. Polytics and his crew began to chat about the plans for the evening, and Madison began to gather her things as well to head out.

"Where are you going?" Polytics asked as he noticed Madison preparing to go.

"Uhh . . . home," Madison said with a sarcastic undertone.

"I thought we were going to the studio to listen to my album."

"I heard you guys making plans, so I figured you changed your mind."

"No, planning for after our session," he said.

"Oh, OK. I can spare an hour or two."

Polytics continued to make plans with his team as to when and where he would meet them later that night. Madison checked her voice mail as she waited for Polytics to finish up. Once she finished, there had been no message from Jamahl, so she hung up and looked around to see where Polytics was. When she turned around, he was signaling for her to come over. Madison *slowly* walked over to be sure to eliminate any idea he might have had that he was in control. Once she arrived to where he stood, his security team escorted them out the back entrance.

Once downstairs, she saw a black Suburban parked in front of the studio. There were some fans standing a few feet away, screaming his name, and a couple guests from upstairs stood by watching them. Polytics, Madison, and one of the security men got in the vehicle, and the other people stepped away. The security guard sat in front with the driver, and just Madison and Polytics were in the backseat. Once they pulled away from the studio, Polytics told the driver where to go. Madison just sat back and looked out the window, wondering what she was doing alone with this man, knowing how unclear things had been since the day they'd met.

"You OK?" Polytics asked a few minutes into the ride.

"Yes, I'm fine."

"Well, I know that, but are you feeling OK?"

"Wow, I can't believe you used that corny line on me."

They both laughed.

"I'm just saying you seem distracted."

"Nah, I'm cool. Really."

"OK, because there is no need to be nervous around me. Nothing will happen that you don't want to happen."

Madison looked at him, shocked that he would say such a thing, but she giggled and turned away before a conversation began that she didn't want to have.

She had been in the business for all these years and dealt with several celebrities—she knew very well that this wasn't an issue of being starstruck, but she couldn't put her finger on what it was. Something about him kept causing her to look away and be soft-spoken—almost on the verge of shy. She didn't like feeling so uneasy and vulnerable, but there was a piece of her that kind of liked what he was doing to her. His attention made her feel a little excitement inside, though she was trying her damnedest to ignore and deny it.

Chapter 12

The Suburban had big, beige, plush leather seats and a mini refrigerator down below. Madison had been in a million of these, but she always enjoyed the ride each time. It was better than a limousine or a Maybach or any of the other flashy means of chauffeured transportation, in her opinion. She liked how it was discreet but luxurious; it signified importance but it wasn't flashy.

The radio was tuned to 99.1 FM, and Madison listened carefully to see if KD was keeping it short and sweet. Of course he wasn't, and Madison could only sigh to herself that she had to speak to him once again. As she sat there listening carefully and critiquing his every word, she felt Polytics tapping her leg.

"So tell me more about yourself," he said.

"What is this, a date?" Madison asked.

"Damn . . . you are so mean."

"No, I'm not. I'm very nice, actually."

"You always have some smart response. I was just asking you a question."

"I was only kidding. I'm not mean—you're just sensitive."

"Oh, good one. Whatever, Miss Madison, you're real funny."

Madison was trying to hide that she was still blushing. She felt like a schoolgirl having her first conversation with the coolest boy in school.

Moments later, they pulled up to the station. The driver and the security guard discussed things Madison couldn't hear, and then the driver got out and opened Madison's door. They both stepped out of the car and into the building as security followed them. Once inside the lobby, Madison stopped at her own security desk to get them both checked in. Once they had their security badges, they headed up to the ninth floor. Martin, a security guard who secured just the ninth floor, seemed surprised to see Madison back at the station. He looked thankful that he hadn't gotten caught sleeping on the job. She liked that—keeping everyone on their toes. The studio was around the corner, and though she was tempted to go tell KD about his long talk break, she decided to head straight toward her office.

At some point when the security guard had been checking them in, Polytics and his security had had a quick conversation that had led to his security guard waiting behind. It seemed as if the guard was going to chill with Martin. Madison waved her key card and unlocked the door that led to the office. She and Polytics made their way back to her department without saying much of anything to each other. It was so late at night, there was no one still in the office except probably some cleaning staff taking out the garbage. Polytics looked around at all the platinum record plaques hanging on the wall outside of her office as he waited for Madison to key into her office.

Once the door was open, she turned on the lights, and they stepped inside.

"You can take a seat," she said.

He sat down on the plush leather couch across from her desk and began to look around her office. She walked around and sat in her chair.

"Pass me the CD," she said.

Polytics reached in his pocket, pulled out a CD with a clear cover, and handed it to her. She placed it in the CD player behind her desk.

"I appreciate you taking the time out to do this," he said.

"No problem," she said.

"Just goes to show that you are a real special person. You don't owe me shit, but you're looking out. I really like that about you."

"Aw, thanks," she replied as she hit PLAY.

A few seconds later, the sounds of a harsh beat began to seep from the speakers in every corner of her office. Polytics's lyrics began to consume the beat, and it wasn't long before both Polytics and Madison were bopping their heads. Madison used the remote by her keyboard to turn the volume down some.

"Now, this one I like. The beat demands your attention, and your flow is different on this track versus the others," she said.

"I was thinking about making this one my next or third single," he said.

"I think it definitely should be a single, but you

may want to make one of your tracks with an R & B hook your next single. As we discussed, you have to build your ladies audience."

Just as Polytics was about to respond, there was a knock at the door. Madison leaned over and pressed PAUSE on the remote.

"Who is it?" Madison yelled.

She couldn't depict who belonged to the muffled voice on the other side of the door. She was guessing it was KD, Polytics's security, Martin, or someone working late trying to find some other human life in the office. She walked around her desk to open the door. Standing on the other side was the five-three cleaning lady with garbage bags in her hand.

"I needed to get your garbage," she said.

"Sure, I'm sorry," Madison said as she moved out of the way.

The little lady entered the room and began removing the filled bag of garbage and bringing it to her cleaning cart outside Madison's door. As she did what she needed to do, Polytics looked around the room at all the platinum- and gold-record plaques hanging on the wall addressed to Madison Cassell of WDRD. He read each one, checking out all the details.

"Do all the artists send you a platinum record?" he asked.

"Not all, but most. The ones whose music I have played."

"Well, I'll be sure to send you my platinum record next month."

Madison giggled.

The woman had replaced the garbage bag with

an empty one and finished what she was doing. Madison waited and began to close the door behind her after saying good night.

"How are you so sure you're going to go platinum?" she asked.

"I just do. My album is hot, and my singles have been the biggest club songs all month."

"Well, I'm happy that you're so confident and so excited, but it's happened before."

"What has happened before?"

"An artist looks so promising, and then their career flopped."

"Oh, no—that won't be me."

"OK. Well, if you are so sure of yourself and your career, why do you have me up here late at night to get feedback?"

"Because I wanted you up here late at night," Polytics said as he moved toward her in one movement.

Madison was thrown completely off guard, but before she could try to gather her thoughts, Polytics's strong hands had the back of her head, and his tongue was roaming around in her mouth. She felt his other hand stroking her back, and though her mind was telling her one thing, her body was enjoying every second of it. Madison couldn't remember the last time she had been kissed so passionately, if ever at all.

She finally placed her hand between herself and Polytics to make some room between them. As soon as he backed up enough to look her in her eyes, he reached back in with his mouth. This time while he kissed her he picked her up and walked toward the wall behind her. She could feel her body release endorphins; she seemed to just get weaker and weaker. Madison knew this was all wrong, but there was no doubt that it felt all right. He had her pinned against the wall, kissing every bare part of her body he could reveal as he removed her shirt and pulled her bra strap down. Madison just gasped for air as she took huge breaths, her body reacting to the shock and euphoria. It seemed that it happened in one action, that Polytics had removed her jeans and had her legs wrapped around his waist, thrusting her. Madison knew it hadn't been one motion, but it was happening so fast she couldn't find the time to think. She wanted to stop because she knew there was no turning back, but the heated moment was so unbelievable she didn't want to stop it and ruin everything it could be.

His shirt came off, and Madison ran her fingers all over his sculpted body as she grabbed, pulled, and scratched for more. He was so built and so large she couldn't believe that all of him was wrapped around all of her. He was surely good at what he did because there was no time for Madison to think—it was as if he had put her in a trance. She had gone from his waist to pinned against the wall to bent over her desk chair to the edge of her desk and back to his waist. By the time they were done, twenty-eight minutes had gone by, and Polytics was just finishing what he'd started. They were both breathing heavily, and Madison couldn't look him in the eye. It was like waking up from a dream—not wanting it to be over but in shock that it had even happened.

Madison had changed clothes in her office before, but after all the years of working there, she had never been in that office stark naked until now. She began to pick up her clothes and slowly put them back on. Polytics began to get himself dressed as well. Neither of them said a word as they caught their breath and dressed themselves. It was as though they had silently agreed somewhere along the way that this was going to happen, so there was nothing to discuss. The longer the silence settled in, the more Madison realized what she had just done was so risky and crazy she was in disbelief that she had let it happen. She began to wish it really had been a dream and it wasn't an actual reality that she had just finished having sex with a rapper—a rapper whose song she played on the radio constantly. She was well aware what kind of implications and drama could come from that reality. If only she were dreaming, it could've been the best dream ever, with no consequences to pay. This was looking like the real reality here: she had just had sex with Polytics. It was real good sex, but it was definitely something that could ruin her career, so as mind-blowing as the experience had been, it was beginning to lose its excitement.

"This stays between me and you," Madison said as she put her shoes on.

"Of course."

"I don't normally do this," she said.

"Right, so it was just something special about me?" he asked.

She just looked at him. "I guess you can say that."

"Well, that makes me feel awfully special," he said.

She was trying to remain composed and not let him see how uneasy she was. Although she was trying to speak calmly and appear unruffled, she could tell her mannerisms and fidgeting fingers were giving away just how frazzled she was.

"This is so embarrassing to ask now, but what is your real name?"

He chuckled. "Clarence."

"Nice to officially meet you, Clarence," she said.

Madison found it in her to find the humor in the situation. She had to admit, regardless of how unethical or tacky the sex was, it was worth every 1,680 seconds. She didn't feel right critiquing his album after that; she just wanted to wrap this night up before anyone knocked on the door or saw them leaving together.

"I guess it would be best if we listened to your album some other time," she said.

"That's fine, it *is* getting late," he said.

"Besides, you're going platinum either way. You don't need me."

"Of course I need you."

Madison turned back to see that Polytics looked serious. She had only been kidding, but maybe he hadn't seen her smile. Instead of acknowledging his tone, she checked to make sure they were both fully dressed and presentable and opened the office door to leave. She grabbed her purse off the door and turned off the lights. Polytics walked out behind her and closed the door.

"It will lock automatically?" he asked.

"Yes," she said.

"I'm going to need the key to your office—one

of the privileges of being your favorite rapper," he said.

Madison caught the humor, but she couldn't laugh. She was almost hoping they could just walk and not talk and pretend he hadn't just had his penis inside her and his tongue down her throat. Hearing him speak of it only made her more uncomfortable—it made all the voices inside her head speak louder and louder. So she tried to ignore them, and she ignored him.

Chapter 13

Sereeta lived in a quaint little apartment in the heart of Harlem. She loved her apartment, but it wasn't until she began making the salary that Corey was paying her that she was able to really hook it up. She had been to IKEA, Target, and Bed Bath & Beyond once every weekend for the past month. She didn't even know that buying stuff for a living room and kitchen could be just as much fun as clothes shopping. She had finally realized she was becoming addicted to decorating and interior designing; she was wondering if she should make it a side hustle.

Corey had left town for the day and had let her know she wouldn't have to work for two days. She was so relieved to get a break; she could just stay home and reorganize her closet and install this wardrobe organizer she had purchased last weekend. She knew it was a bit pathetic to have days off with no one to share them with, but she was becoming content with the lifestyle she had. She had a few guys in her phone book who she was intimate with from time to time, but one or two had a girlfriend, and the others were only looking for fun and nothing serious. Most times she could call them when she was in need of a good time as well, but she had long ago gotten tired of the games. She didn't like the feeling of being used, so she didn't answer their calls or hang out with them unless she wanted them. It was easier to feel like she was using them than face that they were using her. So, on most occasions, she didn't have anyone to go on dates with or spend days off with.

She had been up and at 'em for about two hours when Reyna called. She let Sereeta know she was coming over and would be there soon. Sereeta didn't mind, because Reyna was one of the few people she would allow in her apartment when it wasn't clean. She had a thing for keeping a presentable home; she was very organized and meticulous. Her attention to detail was one of her strengths as Corey's assistant. She began to change into something a bit more presentable—instead of the underwear and wife beater she had slept in the night before. She threw on a pair of green leggings and a T-shirt. She had no plans on leaving the house today, so there was no need to look fabulous. She even left her head scarf on—she figured she would rather her wrap be fresh for when she was going somewhere.

It was about one o'clock when Reyna showed up. The doorbell rang two times consecutively, and Sereeta jumped off the couch to open the door. When she opened it, Reyna was standing there looking like a sad puppy.

"What's wrong?" Sereeta asked.

Reyna stomped over to the couch. She plopped down on the brown microfiber love seat.

"What's wrong?" Sereeta repeated, following behind her.

"I hate my job, Michael and I are fighting, I need to lose, like, ten pounds, and I am miserable," Reyna blurted out.

"Someone sounds like they're experiencing PMS," Sereeta said.

"You sound just like Michael. Oh, my gosh."

Sereeta laughed as she pulled a couch pillow into her chest and scooted back in her seat.

"Don't brush off all my problems just because I have my period," Reyna said.

"I am not, but you just tend to dwell on—and create—the negative when you are going through this time of the month. I am trying to tell you not to be so hard on yourself. It's just hormones."

"It's not just hormones. Our fighting is real."

"Chances are you are fighting because you are being hormonal," Sereeta said, laughing.

"No, I am mad at him because he is going away with all his friends next month, and he and I haven't been away in years."

"So plan a trip with him for later this year; then that issue is resolved."

"No, he won't have that many more vacation days left to fit in another weeklong vacation, so we would have to go for a long weekend, and why do I have to get the short vacation and his boys the long one?"

"It's not as if you have been asking to go away with him, and you guys did go to Hawaii before."

"I did mention it once or twice, but he always

said, 'We will look into it,' and 'we' never did. And we went to Hawaii, like, three years ago. Besides, the real problem is that he didn't want to go with me, or he would've planned something. But he is all excited about going away with his *boooys*," Reyna said.

Sereeta started to giggle. "I understand your point, but no need to fight over it. Plan a trip for the top of next year that is a week long and look forward to it and let this be over with."

"I want me and you to go away together next month," Reyna said.

"Next month?"

"Why? So when he goes away you can go away, too? Don't be so petty and obvious."

"No, so that when he is away I won't be home pissed off. Instead I can be on vacation, too, having a good old time."

"If you are serious or still feel this way when your period is over, let me know," Sereeta said.

Reyna picked up a toss pillow and threw it across the room.

"Stop that. I'm just irritable and have cramps. I'm not having an out-of-body experience," Reyna said.

"What did you have in mind, Reyna?"

"I don't know. Maybe Vegas for just an extended weekend."

"OK, I have to speak with Corey about it and let you know."

"You sound like he's your man," Reyna said.

"No, I mean I have to see about getting off and all that," Sereeta said.

"For a weekend?"

"I work weekends, too, remember. There are no set days that I do or don't work."

"That sucks."

"Well, it's not that bad. I usually get two days off, separate or together, and some weeks I can get three or so off if he has an away game and doesn't ask me to come or do anything back home."

"You have to travel with him to away games?" Reyna asked.

"No, just once so far, but he needed me to arrange a meeting while he was in LA, and he wanted me to purchase some things from Rodeo Drive and be at the meeting with him."

"Well, what about vacation days?"

"I'm not sure how they work yet. That's why I have to talk to him about it."

"It's a very unorthodox job," Reyna said.

"Indeed," Sereeta replied.

"So how do you get paid?" Reyna asked.

"His accountant deposits my check in my account every two weeks, so I get direct deposits just like you."

"Oh, OK. That's cool, at least."

"What do you mean, 'at least'? I love my job," Sereeta said.

"Because you get to flirt with a bunch of rich black men—who wouldn't love that?"

Sereeta laughed. "It's nothing like that. It's just free and flexible. Even when I'm working, sometimes I feel like I'm off—I don't have a boss over my shoulder watching me most of the time. I can always fit my errands in throughout the day. He gives me pocket money, which I guess is called petty cash, to run the errands and stuff and pay for things—he always tells me I can keep what's left over, so a lot of days lunch is on him, and I come home with extra money," Sereeta said.

"Sounds nice, but is it challenging? What do you do on most days?"

"Whatever he needs—errands mainly, but he also has me make and return calls for him, arrange meetings, keep his locker at the stadium organized and kept up," she said.

"They don't have staff that does that?"

"They do, but he likes me to bring certain things from his house on some days. Like, he wants to wear certain things after the game if he's going somewhere, so he will have me bring it to the locker beforehand if he isn't leaving from home. Stuff like that."

"Boy, is he spoiled," Reyna said.

"He's just rich, that's all."

"Aw, look at you defending your man."

"Knock it off. He is not my man. I wish my man had it like him."

"You don't have a man," Reyna said.

Sereeta started laughing, and so did Reyna.

"You know what, this is why you and Michael are fighting now—because you are an evil bitch when you are bleeding," she said.

"Whatever. I am just saying stop playing around. He is single, and clearly you are the lady in his life," Reyna said. "You don't have a man, so why not?"

"I am the assistant in his life, Reyna, that's it.

Why not? Because I work for him, and I need my job."

"When you become his girl, you won't need a job, 'cause then your man will be balling," Reyna said. She had lifted her arm in the air and pretended to make a basketball shot.

"You are such a nut, and I hope you know that," Sereeta said. "There won't be any of that going on. I am not trying to lose my job for the groupie seat and be assed out—literally."

"If he hasn't made a move on you yet, he likely doesn't see you as a groupie. He respects you. See where it goes—maybe this can be a little love story. Usher married his stylist," Reyna said.

Sereeta got off the couch. "I'll be back. I'm going to fix something to drink."

"Oh, did the conversation get to you? You are in denial that you have a crush on your boss!" Reyna yelled after her.

"Not at all!" Sereeta yelled back. "I'm just thirsty!"

In the kitchen, Sereeta poured herself a glass of AriZona iced tea. She stood there and then took a step, absorbing the conversation she was having with Reyna—which she wanted to stop. She didn't even want to put those thoughts in the air. It was hard enough remaining totally professional with a man who oozed confidence and was rich as hell and could buy her anything her heart desired. Hell, yeah, he was a catch. Still, she knew her chances of being with him were almost impossible, and she didn't need any girlie emotional feelings clouding her judgment. She couldn't afford to lose her job, and she knew that if she started flirting with him, he might get turned off and fire her. So unless Corey proposed or something, she was going to continue to act like he was a seventy-five-year-old, broke, hideous creature, and that he was the last thing on her mind.

Chapter 14

"*I*'ll *murda dem, I'll murda dem*" blared through the speakers in the office. The CD in the stereo belonged to Random—he was a new artist on the label. Naomi had heard one or two of his mix-tape songs in the past, but this was her first time hearing this new song. He had been signed to their label for more than two years now, and they were finally dropping his album. He was a major project for the label because they had put a lot of money behind him, and they were hoping for big sales when his album dropped. There were a lot of people hoping to prove themselves with this project— a lot of marketing and promotions people, that is. Although Naomi was the new girl in marketing, it was even obvious to her who was trying to cut whose throat and who was trying to prove to the bosses that they were next in line to shine.

Her boss and a few other coworkers were huddled around the stereo system getting their first listen of the record. The stereo was in the wall in the center of the department's floor; there were a table and several chairs right in front of it. It was a setup perfectly designed for meetings where music needed to be heard. The staff didn't hold as many meetings there as they would've liked because it was such a disturbance for all the assistants sitting a few feet away in their cubicles. However, the staff usually held their music priority meeting every Monday right there in the middle of the floor. People from other departments would just walk up and listen and chime in. It was a cool concept that stemmed from the VP of marketing saying he wanted an open floor meeting to invite all ideas into their marketing plans.

From her cubicle, Naomi couldn't get a clear view of everyone sitting in front of the stereo, but she kept peeking over to get a glimpse of Tyreek. He had come down to listen to the track as well. He was in A and R and worked on the ninth floor, but he usually made his way to the marketing department at least once a day to do some dealings with Max, this guy who sat a few cubes away from Naomi. Today, however, Tyreek was just down there to hear the feedback on the record. When Naomi saw him sit down, she figured he was the A and R on Random's album; otherwise he probably wouldn't have come down. He was dressed in blue jeans, a Rocawear hoodie, and some Timbs. His dreads were pulled back in a rubber band, and his facial hair looked a little scruffy. He was totally masculine and grungy, but Naomi was still so impressed by everything about him.

This gathering to listen to Random's album was happening because the song had just landed on the VP's desk and was hot off the press. The VP had a strong belief that the first impression of a song could have a make-it-or-break-it effect, or it could be one of those songs that had to grow on you over time. Some artists didn't have that time; some artists didn't get the continuous airplay or the video exposure. Some artists had one shot and one shot only to impress a DJ or a programmer, so the VP liked to have a lot of ears give their opinion on that moment. The usual procedure after listening to a new single was the following: shortly after, they would meet, listen again, critique it, and then decide all the angles they could take when promoting it. They would decide which radio stations across the country would play it and then get to delegating who was to start the promotion of the record and who else would do what else.

Naomi wished she could sit in on those meetings because they looked so interesting, but she had been present for only one. Her boss had told her that after the other assistant came back from maternity leave in a few weeks, she would be able to go to the meetings, but right now, because staff was limited, they needed someone on the other side of the door. Naomi could hear the song from where she sat, and she definitely thought it was a good record. She bopped her head along lightly and tried to understand all the lyrics. She had always been a hip-hop and R & B fan, which was why she knew her job would be enjoyable for her. The song had a hot beat, and Random had a real unique flow; Naomi thought for sure there was a place for him on the radio. She knew what he looked like from his press shots, so she knew he was a good-looking, tall guy the girls would like.

After the song ended, most of the people who had been listening filed into the VP's office. They were going to list all the song's selling points, like who the producer was and anything else that would get it more press and publicity. Naomi saw them all walking into the office, and she buried her head back into the files on her desk, placing them in chronological order. As she turned to clear off some more space on her desk, she heard a voice. She turned around, and it was her boss.

"What did you think of the record?"

"I liked it a lot actually. The beat was different, and the hook was catchy," she replied.

"What did it make you think of?"

"It made me think of dancing at a club, honestly."

"Cool, thanks," she said and walked away.

Naomi was surprised she had even come over and asked her opinion. She was pleased that Tiffany actually valued her opinion, and although it was a small thing, it had Naomi feeling real good on the inside.

She went back to her mundane task—that she hoped would fill up at least an hour or two of her day. She was updating the files and packaging older documents to be put away in the file storage closet. She glanced up on occasion to check her e-mails and texts, but for the most part, she kept her head buried in her files.

Kevin walked up. "Boo," he said.

Naomi jumped, startled by his presence. "Oh, my gosh, you scared me."

"That's what I was trying to do," he said.

"Meanie. What do you want?"

"Nothing, just came to check on you and see if you wanted to get lunch later," he said.

"Sure, how about two PM?"

"Why so late?"

"I had a big breakfast," she replied. "But one or one thirty is fine."

"OK, see you then," he said. "And I hope you have a cute coat or something because you definitely didn't check out the fashion chic channel this morning before you left."

Naomi glanced down. "Forget you . . . what? I wanted to be comfortable."

"Well, brush your hair before we head out. I don't want to be seen walking with Ugly Betty."

"How mean are you?" she said.

"Lata."

Naomi knew he was playing, but she was also a firm believer that there was truth to every joke. She caught her reflection in the computer screen and finger-combed her hair back; it was already in a ponytail, so there wasn't much more she could do. After a while she just brushed it off—besides, this was who she was every day, and Kevin had no right talking.

Almost an hour went by—it was close to noon, and most of the department was still in the meeting about Random's single. Naomi's boss had stepped out for lunch, and a few others had left the room as well. Naomi had been busy answering phones, sending and responding to e-mails, and working on the filing project she had started that morning. A few phone calls had come in, but she had only taken messages because she was pretty confident that none of the callers were VIP enough to interrupt Tiffany for. That list Naomi had created with the VIPs had been coming in handy. Only once did she need to intercom Tiffany to see if she wanted the call, and that had been Hollywood. This time around, Tiffany had said to tell him she was in a meeting and that she would call him back. Naomi had been furious because Tiffany had had an attitude as if Naomi never should've interrupted her in the first place. *If I would have told him that on my own, I would have gotten yelled at,* she told herself as she hung up the phone.

When Naomi saw her boss leaving, Naomi said nothing to her at all. Some days Naomi just wished she had an office she could close the door to and not have to see Tiffany at all. She pretended to work as she discreetly watched her boss exit the department. Knowing she was gone, Naomi sat up at her computer and logged on to her Facebook account. Excited to see that her red notifications icon read *14,* she began to look through them. One of her guy friends from Texas had written on her page I miss ya, come home soon. Naomi smiled and began to write back. When she was home she hadn't paid that boy no attention in school, but she had to admit she missed him, too. She missed all her people from back home, and she missed not feeling out of place. As she was typing back, I miss you, too. I'll be home for the holidays, she noticed Tyreek exit the office in which the meeting was being held and walk in her direction. She instantly glanced at her reflection in the computer screen again to see how she looked. Remembering what Kevin had said, she knew she wasn't looking like she belonged on the cover of a magazine, but she wanted to at least look presentable. By the time he reached her cubicle, she had already smoothed her hair down and licked her lips.

"Hey, is Max in today?" he asked Naomi.

"Yes, but he went down to the art department," she replied.

"OK. Can you tell him Tyreek came by?"

"Sure."

Before she could say any more, Tyreek walked back to where he had come from. Naomi watched him walk away and felt a bit disappointed that she couldn't keep his attention any longer than a few seconds. She understood that they hadn't really gotten to know each other yet—the extent of their conversations was usually a few words or a question and answer. Still, she didn't get why he couldn't just take a second to ask how she was doing or ask her name, even. In her opinion, guys always took a second to say at least a few words to most girls. Naomi had seen Tyreek on many occasions laughing and chatting it up with girls who worked there, flirting as well, so she knew he wasn't some antisocial, quiet guy. She felt under par, knowing he didn't care to even be cordial with her. *Damn, am I that far from his league that he couldn't even acknowledge me?* she thought.

Once he was out of sight, she looked back at her Facebook page profile picture. She was attractive, but she didn't highlight her attributes. She wore loose-fitting clothes that covered her 34-C breasts and her size-six waist. She kept her hair pulled back in a ponytail most days, and she wore no makeup at all, aside from lip gloss. She had light brown skin with jet-black hair and brown eyes. Back home in college she was considered one of the pretty girls at her school. She'd had a boyfriend, but on a regular basis there were different guys trying to talk to her. Even though she'd turned the guys down because she was madly in love with Charles, she enjoyed the attention because she hadn't gotten much of it in junior high and high school. Her confidence level had skyrocketed in college, but ever since she had moved to New York, she felt overlooked and unattractive. Most of the girls in New York City were pretty, fashionable, and bubbly. In comparison to them, Naomi was no triple threat.

As she stared at her profile picture, she started to think about her high school days when she wasn't that popular. Looking at her picture, she realized she looked pretty much the same as she did back then, give or take a few things. She began to wonder if she just simply wasn't all that attractive. It didn't make her feel any better that Tyreek had just treated her almost like she was invisible. Something wasn't working in her favor.

Because her boss was out to lunch, Naomi decided to make a quick call to Devora.

"I don't know why it seems like he just looks right through me," Naomi said.

"Well, do you guys have a reason to speak, or do you try to start a conversation?" Devora replied.

"You know I'm not going to try to start talking to him. I wouldn't even know what to say."

"You ask a question, that's the best way. Ask

about something to do with his department or his job—that will at least get the ball rolling, and most likely he will want to brag about himself."

"Yeah, well, he comes over to me to ask me about where one of my coworkers is, but then he just runs right off after getting an answer. No 'thank you,' no nothing."

"Maybe he was just in a hurry."

"Yeah, he's always in a rush, but I just want to at least get to know him a little."

"You sound so young, like he's a crush from eighth grade."

"It's just I've been here for seven months already, and I have no male friends, and it would be nice."

"Why him?"

"I guess because I work with him. There are no other options, and I think he is cute."

"That's a good enough reason," Devora replied, laughing. "Well, for starters, try to consider some other options as well, just in case he's out of your league."

"Devora!"

"What? I'm just saying, just in case."

"Yeah, yeah. Well, I guess you coming out with me this Friday then."

"I can go out with you, that's fine. I don't want you looking all desperate around your office trying to get that boy's attention, I know that for sure."

"Shut up, ain't no one looking desperate. I just said I wanted to get to know him."

"Well, maybe it's time you start making yourself more noticeable," Devora said.

"What is that supposed to mean?"

"Like wearing different clothes, changing your hair—you know, catching up to New York trends around here. Tyreek is probably accustomed to a certain type of girl. You can at least try to step up your game some."

Naomi looked down at the purple knit sweater and Mossimo jeans she was wearing.

"Well, then, I guess you're going shopping with me this Friday."

"I guess you're going to pay me for all my services rendered," Devora replied.

They both laughed.

"Good-bye, crazy," Naomi said. "The Wicked Witch of the East will be back soon."

"Lata," Devora said.

Naomi hung up and got back to work, sorting through the SoundScan files. SoundScan was the report of all the albums sold for the week; it was released to the industry every Tuesday, and careers were made and lost because of this report sometimes. At the end of the day, no matter how many bottles got popped in a video or how many Bentleys were driven to the clubs, album sales were all that really mattered. A part of Naomi's job was extracting all the sales figures for all the urban artists and keeping them in a spreadsheet alongside the information on the amount of spins that week. The promotion department where Naomi worked dealt with the artists' visibility and popularity. Her department promoted the music to radio stations all across the world in hopes of getting records played, and they arranged in-store signings and other events and opportunities to help make the artists more popular. Naomi enjoyed her job; although she wasn't a big part of the program yet, she believed that, in time, she could be.

She sat there, doing her work and randomly thinking about Tyreek and all the other cute guys she worked with who never paid her any mind. She wasn't sure if Devora was right about her needing to update her look—all she knew was that she was tired of spending all her nights and weekends alone at home. She wasn't sure what she was going to do, but she knew she had to make stronger efforts to get some attention. Just the thought of talking to Tyreek made her nervous. What should she say to a guy like him? He was a mover and shaker in the business. He seemed like the type of guy who was interested in only money and power—two things Naomi knew nothing about. She knew if she was going to try to find the courage to speak, she had to take advantage soon, because to her understanding he traveled a lot with the artists, so she would have only limited amounts of time to spark a conversation with him. She was definitely not skilled in the area of catching a man, and definitely not a man this far out of her league. She had realized less than a week after she'd moved to New York that the pace of things was also way out of her league, especially in the music business. She had never had a chance to learn the ropes or adapt to the pace, but she was tired of being a fish out of water. She knew if she could get Tyreek's attention, she could finally begin to make her time in New York a lot more interesting.

Chapter 15

KD sat down on the edge of the office chair as though he had no intention to stay long. Madison had scheduled a meeting with him, and she hadn't told him what it was about, but she was pretty sure he knew it was regarding his incident with Tryme and getting arrested. She wasn't in the best of moods on this particular day, and everyone knew on days like this they shouldn't push her buttons.

She was wearing some gray fitted Joe's Jeans with a long-sleeved white and black Baby Phat top—it was one of her favorite shirts because on the back, in small print, it said DIVA ON BOARD. She was wearing her flat gray boots, and her hair was pulled back in a ponytail. She was dressed down, enjoying a casual day at work, but just because she was dressed casually didn't mean she wasn't taking care of business.

"Sit back, take off your jacket, stay a while," Madison said as she leaned back in her chair.

"I have another meeting after this. Is this going to be long?"

"Well, about as long as you make it. We need to cover some things. If you cooperate and I get what I need by the end, you will make your meeting."

The look on KD's face meant he wasn't interested in that response, but instead of challenging her, he just removed his navy blue flight jacket. Underneath he wore a white and navy blue Alador & Smith shirt with some True Religion jeans and construction boots. KD had one of the biggest names in radio, and he was well paid and very well respected. Good talent was hard to come by, and he knew this, so although he worked for Madison, he was also well aware of his worth at the station.

"Listen, KD, I am not trying to bust your balls in here, but I am just a bit fed up with having to talk to you."

"What I do?" he asked.

"Well, for one, this getting arrested situation. This station doesn't need any more drama surrounding it, no pun intended."

"That wasn't my fault—he came at me, and I defended myself."

"You do know that self-defense is only justifiable when you match the force."

"What are you talking about?"

"If he used his fists, you can defend yourself with only fists. Once you picked up a weapon, it was no longer self-defense because he didn't have a weapon. You upgraded the level of force."

"Yeah, my lawyer told me something like that."

"Well, this is likely to carry on a bit longer if he chooses to press charges."

"I am working on getting the charges dropped.

Besides, I heard he is going to anyway because he knows this is a horrible look for his career," KD said.

"Exactly. You can't be on air threatening to ruin his career and never play his music. We are supposed to play songs our listeners want to hear, not just the ones by the artists you get along with."

"I didn't mean it like that. I am just saying how he going to be rapping about being all hard and he pressing charges over a fight? He is getting killed in the streets right now, so he was going to drop it for that reason, not me."

Madison laughed. "Well, that's very true. I thought the same thing, but I figured he was trying to get a few moments of fame in all the entertainment news reports."

"Yeah, he may have been, but he realized how it backfired."

"Well, I just wanted you to know how to handle it discreetly. The business department gave the tapes the police were asking for. Lucky for you, the tapes didn't catch everything, but it did show some stuff. I don't think you have much to worry about, but I just need you to be easy for a bit."

"No problem, I'm over it. People is talking, he is looking like a herb, I am done with it. He will drop the charges if he knows what's good for him, and if not, I have a very well-paid attorney. I'm not all that concerned," KD said.

"OK, well, then good. Let's talk about the other thing I have you in for."

KD looked at her with his eyebrows raised.

"Your talk breaks—they are too long, and you—"

A beeping noise came from her phone; she looked over, and it was her intercom. "Hold up," she said to KD. She answered the phone.

"You have a call from someone who says it is very important. He said you know who it is, but he won't tell me," Alexis said.

"You know better than to call me with this nonsense. If he doesn't give a name, he must not want to speak with me. I have to go."

She hung up the phone and looked back at KD. He was just shaking his head.

"You are so hard on that poor girl," he said.

"Come on now, how is she going to expect me to get on a call without knowing who it is? For all I know, it's some unsigned rapper trying to get my ear about radio spins, and she's trying to put them through."

KD's bass-filled laugh filled the room.

The beeping sound started again. Madison answered it. "Yes, Alexis."

"It's Clarence," she replied.

Madison froze. A piece of her wanted to take the call just to see what he had to say, but she knew she shouldn't talk to him in front of KD. Besides, she didn't want him calling her at the station making things look too comfortable between the two of them. She knew Alexis might have recognized his voice, so his secret-admirer game he played was not helping anything. She knew she might be paranoid—maybe no one would notice anything. It wasn't as if she didn't have a lot of artists as associates and friends. It was just that if this even raised one eyebrow in the industry, and it got out of control, she could lose her job. Polytics, on the other hand, would be a multiplatinum-selling artist.

"Tell him I am in a meeting and I will call him when I am done," she said.

She hung up the phone and could see that KD was glued to his BlackBerry, pushing buttons. She was glad because she figured he wouldn't ask any questions; she only prayed he didn't know Polytics's real name because she didn't feel like having to come up with an excuse for avoiding his call. When artists took the time to call personally, it was very rare that she didn't take the call. That is, if she wasn't fucking them, of course.

"An important call from Clarence? Who is that, a secret admirer?" KD asked as he looked up from his BlackBerry.

Damn, he was paying attention, she said to herself.

"No, just a colleague," she replied. "But back to what I was saying . . ."

"Yeah, I have been cutting my talk breaks a lot. I will have Vice give you an air check," he said.

"Yes, I will need that. I will also need you to give me your topic points before each show—e-mail them to me."

"Give you my topic points? Are you serious? I don't know my topic points in advance. I just talk."

"That's the problem, you just talk."

"You are killing me. You can't actually expect me to send you topic points before my shifts."

"Alright, well, how about this? You work on keeping your talk breaks under three minutes, keep your beef off the air, and cover the relevant entertainment news, and I won't need the topic lists . . . but

I will want air checks for a month straight to make sure you are working on it," she said.

"A'ight, that's fair."

"OK, so then we are done. You can run off and make your next meeting," she said.

KD pulled his jacket back on.

"Alright, I will see you later, boss lady."

KD headed out and left the office door open behind him. She looked over at her phone for a second, contemplating if she should call Polytics back, but instead she turned around and began checking e-mails. She was tempted, but she didn't want to give him the idea it was OK to call up to the station. She was hoping that despite what had happened between them, things could remain business as usual. Her concern was that maybe this was just wishful thinking, and maybe he was the wrong guy to take this risk with. So far, it didn't seem as though he was playing his cards right.

Chapter 16

The job was still considerably new, and it hadn't come with a handbook, but Sereeta was learning quickly that at times she was meant to be seen and not heard. The ballplayers were used to carrying on with their regular course of business regardless of who was around or where they were—at least, that was the impression Sereeta had. In the first couple weeks she had been introduced to everyone as Corey's assistant, and since then they had treated her like a teammate. They spoke freely in front of her, changed in front of her, and several times acted as if she weren't there. Sereeta couldn't help but wonder if Corey was supposed to give her a 101 on what to expect with the job because it seemed like an adventure each day.

She reminded herself that this was a job. She wasn't going to get emotionally attached to anyone in her work because it would only backfire. She also realized it was best that she mind her own business as to the things going on around her.

Being around the girls, the drugs, the plotting . . . Sereeta felt as if she were a fly on the wall. It seemed just because she worked for Corey Cox, people didn't care what they said or did in front of her. It made her extremely uncomfortable, but the more time that had passed, the more she was getting used to it.

It was a Thursday afternoon, and there was a home game that evening. Sereeta showed up at the stadium early to get Corey's clothes from the cleaners and swap out the clothes in his locker. She was dressed in blue jeans and a white T-shirt with a short black knit cardigan over it. She'd had a late start and hadn't put much effort into her outfit for the day, but like most days she still looked casually cute. She was hoping it was early enough in the day where she would barely see anyone while she was out and about and that she could get back home at a decent time. Some of the assignments Corey had given her to do for the week consisted of things she could do from home as well, such as a few phone calls and recording some of the ESPN footage.

She pulled out the access card Corey had bestowed upon her and swiped it to access the locker room. When she walked in, she could hear voices coming from deeper in the room. The locker room had a lobby area, a few lounge areas, and the location with the lockers and seats. When she passed the main lobby area, she could see that a few of the players were sitting around shooting the breeze. They all gave relaxed hellos and went right back to their conversation. Sereeta greeted them in return but continued to Corey's locker. At first,

Sereeta paid them no mind, but as she leaned inside Corey's locker, she began to pay attention to what they were talking about.

"Nah, Shorty was official," Lonnie said. "I saw her when she first got to the hotel."

"Oh, you saw her?" France asked.

"Yeah, the brown-skinned one with the fat ass, right?" Lonnie replied.

"Yeah, she came back up to the room with me," France said. "I had to get Tyrone and Nate to go back to Nate's room. My brother Mark had bagged her friend, so he took her to Tyrone's room. As soon as the coast was clear, this bitch wasted no time. She just dropped to her knees and started sucking me off."

Sereeta was able to tell that he was telling a story about some girl he had met a couple nights ago and taken to a hotel. They were huddled around in the locker room like they were sharing ghost stories on a camping trip. France went on to tell them how they'd ended up smoking marijuana and all the things the girl was willing to do and did for him. Sereeta was moving along as if she wasn't paying attention, but although the locker room was spacious, when it wasn't crowded, voices traveled. So even though she could pretend, there really was no way they could think she didn't hear them. With the tabloids paying thousands for great stories, she would've thought they would be more discreet with their business. It was almost as though they were daring her to say something.

The players weren't supposed to smoke marijuana, especially not during the season, and here these guys were talking about it like it was nothing.

Sereeta couldn't tell if they trusted her that much or if they were just too stupid or didn't care. It wasn't the first time one of them had said something in front of her that—if she'd wanted to make an easy and quick few thousand dollars—she could've shared with the tabloids. They were damn lucky Sereeta was trying to keep her job and didn't want to get blackballed from the sports world, because she knew quite a bit about the players' secret lives. She had met a couple of their mistresses; she knew a lot of their tricks as to how they kept their secret lovers secret and all the ways they met the girls and everything. One thing Sereeta learned was these men talked just as much in their locker rooms as women did at nail salons.

She had zoned out of the conversation for a while—that is, until she heard them talking about Corey.

"Nah, that bitch Flash bagged was bad, too. Don't get it twisted," France said.

"She was a'ight, the Spanish one?" Mike said.

"Nah, she was black. She was, like, caramel complexioned, five-five; she had some big-ass titties," he said.

"Oh, yeah!" Collins said, jumping out of his seat like he'd just won on a game show. "She was bad as hell."

"Yeah, she was leaving the restaurant when we was through eating, and she was trying to get his attention. At first, he wasn't even checking on her, and I was like, 'If you don't bag, I am'—she was definitely a ten," France said.

For some reason Sereeta began to feel her heartbeat racing. She wasn't sure if she was angry or jealous or just nervous to be overhearing some-thing about her boss. She felt like she knew Corey better than all of them. She worked with him al-most every day; she saw him when he was upset, tired, happy, energetic; she knew all sides of Corey. She was pretty sure some of them knew him pretty well as well, but she felt like they downplayed her relationship with him. If they had any respect for her, they wouldn't be talking about him so freely, but, then again, it wasn't like they were insulting him. She couldn't tell why she was getting upset, she just felt weird hearing about some girl Corey had bagged on the road.

"He is always like that, though—he be letting a lot of good ones get away," France said.

"Remember last season when that girl was danc-ing on him all crazy in the club—she was trying to fuck him on the dance floor, and all he did was walk away," Lonnie said.

"She was cute, too—a little skinny, but cute," Collins said.

"Nah, even worse than that was that time those girls were in front of the hotel rooms, and that Spanish broad took her panties off and handed them to him and he just gave them back. We were on the road for like four nights and he didn't smash nothing the whole time."

"He just seems real picky or real focused," Mike said.

"Focused on what? He isn't married. He doesn't even have a girlfriend," France said.

"Focused on the game, on his career. And he does have a girl, I thought—that brown-skinned joint from where he's from," Mike said.

"I don't know, but if so, that shit isn't worth all that. She isn't even here."

"I respect him for it, but sometimes I be like, 'Damn, man, you not going to hit that?'" Collins said.

"Yeah, if we didn't know any better, you would think he was gay," Mike said.

They all began to laugh. Just at that moment Sereeta dropped her purse, and a bunch of her items and some change fell out. She quickly squatted down to pick up the contents from her bag.

"Don't worry, your boss isn't gay," France said.

She looked up and saw France standing a few feet away, looking down at her.

"Huh?" she said, pretending she didn't know what he was referring to.

"You was over here listening to us talking about your boss? Flash is our boy—we are just clowning on him, so you can relax. Over here dropping shit," he said.

Sereeta finished putting her belongings in her bag and stood up. She grabbed Corey's athletic bag and headed toward the door. She could hear France laughing and saying something to the guys, and she just assumed they were talking about her. She was so embarrassed and so angry. She was happy to hear that Corey wasn't such a pig like the rest of them, but having to find out that gossip at the cost of being embarrassed . . . She wasn't sure it was worth it. Besides, the girlfriend at home clearly had his heart. She didn't know why she cared anyway.

Chapter 17

The night after Sereeta got back from the locker room, she wanted to tell Corey what had happened. She even started to but then changed the course of her conversation. She wanted him to know how France had treated her, but she realized she didn't want to ruffle anyone's feathers. It was awkward enough at times being around the guys—she didn't want to make it any worse by being labeled a tattletale. She also didn't want to tell him what the guys were saying about him. Corey seemed like a pretty laid-back guy, but for all she knew he could have an uncontrollable temper.

Sereeta didn't want any problems. She was thankful that things had still been going pretty well with the job; she had gotten the hang of her duties and begun a pretty smooth routine. Corey seemed pleased with her work ethic and style, and they seemed to mesh well. He still wasn't very talkative with her, but she didn't mind so much. It seemed as if he'd had a bad experience in the past getting too friendly with his employees or something and was trying to keep it professional. Most of the time when the two of them were alone, they sat in silence or they watched television in the car or listened to music. He didn't seem to care too much about her life outside her job or what her thoughts were about her job. He had a job for her to do, he expected her to do it, and he didn't seem to expect much more.

Sereeta didn't mind their lack of friendship mainly because it kept her on her toes. She was always eager to get her job done efficiently because she didn't know what to expect from him. She knew it was probably best they kept things this way so that there were no blurry lines as to what was what, and there were no drunken nights after partying where something could happen between the two of them. There were times when she wondered if he didn't like her, especially when she would see him on the phone laughing and seeming so happy, and then he would hang up and just be quiet around her. Over time, though, she figured if he didn't like her, he would have let her go a while ago.

Corey told Sereeta to drop off at his house the clothes he had asked her to pick up at the dry cleaner's. He would more than likely be gone by the time she got there, but she wasn't staying long either way. She then had to run to the mall and purchase another iPod for him and some Bose headphones. As far as she knew, that was all he needed her to do for the day, but most days he would call her at the last minute to let her know something else had come up, so she wasn't getting excited about a free evening just yet.

The funny thing with her job was she was never

technically off the clock. There were days she
would have to do things for him till ten o'clock at
night, but then there were times she was off for
three days straight. She liked the flexibility; she
loved not being confined to a desk or an office;
she enjoyed being able to shop and travel and get
paid for it. She knew most people thought her job
was cool because she worked for such a rich person and got to hang out with all these rich ath-
letes, but the best part about it had nothing to do
with who her boss was.

She sometimes wished she could have the same
job but work for a woman. She didn't mind working for Corey, but being around so many men all
the time was just intimidating. It didn't help that
most of them didn't have all that much respect for
women, so on top of having to hear stories she
didn't care to hear, she had to be subjected to
some of their egos. One of the team managers referred to her as "Corey's groupie" once; another
time, a teammate had asked her "When Corey is
done, can I be next?" On both occasions, Sereeta
had ignored it, almost as if she were walking down
the street and would never see these people again.
Yet in this situation she saw them all the time.
Corey actually spoke to the manager about what
the teammate had said. She hadn't been the one
to spill the beans—she didn't want to start any
drama and risk having Corey rethink hiring her, so
she let it be. In the end she was happy he had
stood up for her.

When she reached Corey's house, his driver was
waiting outside to bring him to the stadium.
Sereeta walked up to the doorstep and noticed the

door was cracked open. She slowly pushed the door open and walked inside. At first, she didn't see Corey or any of his belongings. She walked farther inside the house and closed the door partially behind her, as she had found it. The brown and cream runner carpet that led from the doorway into the living room was a bit crooked, she noticed. She bent down to straighten it up. Just as she went to stand back up, she heard footsteps. Corey was walking toward her.

"Hey, are you a bit early?" he said.

"Just a bit. I finished up at the stadium and came straight here."

"Why don't you drop my things upstairs and ride over with me?" he said.

"Back to the stadium?"

"Yeah, watch the game. Chill for the night. I'll put you in the skybox."

"Uh . . . uh . . . OK," she said.

"You can invite a friend to meet you there, if you like."

Sereeta had been working for him for quite some time but hadn't yet really enjoyed any perks—at least not any that people expected her to get. She'd had a few drop-offs and pick-ups by limos and a few free NBA T-shirts, but nothing really special. Sereeta was beginning to think he just wanted her to see that this was a job and not recreational. This was the first time he had offered to do something this nice for her, and she was beyond excited.

She ran upstairs, dropped off his things, and headed back down to the truck where Corey waited. She stepped inside the car, and Corey looked over at her; he looked less scary tonight for some reason.

"Thanks," she said.

"No problem. You work hard, so you deserve a night off."

"I appreciate that," she replied.

"Tell your friend their pass will be at will-call."

"Oh, yeah," she said as she pulled out her cell phone.

She began to text Reyna to let her know the plans and see if she could join her. Once she finished the text, she placed her phone in her lap and looked out the window. The radio was tuned to Drama 99 FM, and Corey was bopping his head slowly to the new Ludacris song playing. As usual, the car ride was a bit quiet, aside from the music and the muffled sounds from the street outside.

Once they got to the stadium, Sereeta followed Corey through the players' entrance.

"You are going to be sitting in the box with the other players' guests, their families, and friends."

"OK."

"You can leave and come back if you would like—you will just need this pass," he said as he handed her a square-shaped pass that read SKYBOX #12 on it.

"I will more than likely be here to the end."

"OK, and your guest's pass and ticket are at will-call under your name, but I just remembered they are going to ask for ID, so you can either go down and meet him at will-call or I can call and have it switched."

"It's not a him," she said.

She didn't know why she cared to correct him,

and she was just as unsure why he was willing to go through all this trouble for her.

"Well, he—she—whoever," he said as he kept walking.

"You can change the name to Reyna Benton. I'm not sure exactly what time she's getting here."

"No problem."

They continued down the hall and could hear the noise and voices from the announcer speaking and the fans in the stadium. After a few moments they reached an elevator. There was no one standing by the elevator except a security guard. Once they reached it, the guard used a key card to open the doors. Sereeta followed behind Corey as they entered the box. She had to admit that having Corey Cox escort her to the skybox felt surreal; she was trying not to show her excitement, but she was definitely feeling it.

Once they reached the top level to the stadium, they stepped off the elevator. The floor was carpeted, the lights were dim, and the people were dressed up. They looked more like the guests at a social mixer and not fans at a basketball game. There were bars along the back wall and waiters walking around with hot plates. Sereeta just followed behind Corey down the corridor, passing box after box. As they walked, different people pointed at Corey, and some spoke, and he quietly spoke back. As she glimpsed inside some of the skyboxes, she noticed white men in business suits, a few young black kids, and a few well-dressed ladies. She tried to figure out how all of them had gotten their tickets and who they were. She felt special knowing that everyone knew how she'd gotten hers and who she was—well, maybe not who she was, but who they thought she was. She had to admit it felt awfully nice being Corey Cox's special someone, even if just for one night.

Once they reached Skybox #12, there were a few others sitting down. Corey walked in, and everyone stood up to greet him.

"This is Sereeta, everyone. She will be joining you this evening. If she needs anything please take care of her."

Sereeta stood there in amazement. She wasn't his "assistant" tonight, she was Sereeta, and he had asked that whatever Sereeta needed, please take care of it. She felt her heart drop at his kindness; he looked more appealing to her than he ever had. She wondered if she was dressed up enough to play the part. She hadn't planned to come to the game, let alone to be in the skybox as Corey's date, so she wasn't dressed the way she would've planned to. She had on a gray turtleneck tunic and some leggings with some black flat boots. She was carrying her black Gucci bag, and her hair was in a bun with a bang. She looked casually cute, and she guessed she looked good enough for Corey not to clarify that she was only his assistant.

"Hello, Sereeta," the folks in the room said.

"Hi," she said as she stepped closer to Corey.

"Sit wherever you would like. Save a seat for your friend, and I'll see you later tonight or tomorrow," Corey said as he moved out of her way so she could head toward the seats.

"Thanks, Corey, I appreciate everything," she said.

"No problem," he said as he walked off.

That was typical of Corey to show no emotion. Despite how sweet he had been by doing all this for her, he had walked off with no more than his signature "no problem." Somewhere in her imagination she imagined him kissing her good-bye and holding on to her hand until he couldn't hold on anymore. That would be just the ideal ending to the night, but it was just a thought. There was nothing whatsoever between her and Corey, and she didn't want there to be, and he had made it very clear that neither did he.

Once he left, she began to watch the pregame festivities. The people looked so far away from where she sat, she couldn't believe these were considered VIP seats. She noticed the big screen directly in front of her and began to watch from there. Reyna had texted her a while ago when she was in the car and said she was going to be heading to the stadium within fifteen minutes or so, so if Sereeta calculated correctly, Reyna would be there before the game started or early into the first quarter.

Sereeta looked around the room subtly to see if she recognized anyone, but no one looked familiar. There were two guys in their midtwenties, a woman maybe in her forties, and two white men in their thirties dressed down in jeans and sneakers. There was nothing that gave away who any of these people were, but because Corey had said it was the box for friends and family of the team, Sereeta figured these people were just that. One of the guys in their twenties approached Sereeta as she looked around the box trying to see everything inside.

"Hi, my name is Mark," the young man said as he sat down.

"Hi, Mark," she replied.

"My brother plays for the Knicks."

"Oh, that's cool. I'm a guest of Corey's."

"Yeah, I know. I was here when you guys walked in. I wasn't stepping on any toes."

Sereeta just smirked at him, not knowing what else to say and not wanting to admit that she was just his assistant.

"Oh, OK. Well, enjoy the game," he said as he put his drink in his other hand.

"You don't have to run away," Sereeta blurted out as she noticed Mark standing up.

He looked back at her to examine her facial expression. Sereeta was trying to remain relaxed and not let him see that she was a bit uncomfortable and nervous.

"You sure?" he asked.

"Yes, I'm sure," she said, throwing him her sexy smile.

She realized she had wanted him and others to think she was Corey's special girl, but she quickly realized how letting Mark walk away was just stupid. Here she could be meeting the man of her dreams, and she was letting him walk away so she could give off some false impression of being with someone she wasn't. Even crazier was that he could easily find out that she was just his assistant. She decided to stop living in fantasy land; Corey was gone somewhere in the locker room, and she was sitting alone. Mark was a handsome guy, and she could use the company until Reyna showed up, at least.

"I don't want any problems with Corey Cox."

"Trust me, there won't be any problems with him. Maybe the girl you meet in here next game, but no problems with me."

Mark seemed shocked that she had said something so bold. He started to laugh and put his hand over his mouth to contain his reaction.

"Don't worry, it's OK. It's nothing like that between me and him."

"OK, I was about to say you are a tough cookie."

Sereeta just laughed and looked out toward the court to see what was going on.

"And for the record, I'm in this box quite often, and you are the first lady Corey has ever brought up here."

Sereeta looked at him to see if he was being serious, and then she turned away when she realized he was. She didn't want him to spot the flutter her heart had just made. She sat there thinking what the hell was wrong with her that she was even thinking this way all of a sudden—she knew she had to stop these thoughts before she got herself in trouble or lost her job.

"He has only been playing in New York for a few months, and besides, I work for him. I am his personal assistant."

"Oh, really?" Mark said.

"Really, so don't go starting any rumors."

Mark just laughed. "You know I was."

The announcer began to announce the players as they exited the locker room and made their way to the court floor.

"You will be here alone?"

"A friend of mine will be meeting me soon, I hope."

"You're trying to get me beat up in here," he said.

"No, it's a girlfriend of mine. I'm single, Mark. I'm not trying to get anyone beat up."

"Well, that's good news."

"What's good news?"

"That you aren't trying to get me beat up and that you are single."

"Good news for you or for me?"

"For me and hopefully for you."

Sereeta liked this guy's swagger. He was six-two and brown skinned with a mustache and light goatee. He had a low fade with a part on the left side, dark brown eyes, a narrow nose, and full lips. He was definitely good-looking, but Sereeta was digging his carefree personality.

It was well into the first quarter before Reyna showed up, and by then Sereeta was realizing that she would've been just fine if she hadn't made it at all. It was like a perfect first date with Mark; they were laughing, talking, watching the game, and having a good time.

Reyna walked in and looked twice as nervous as Sereeta had before she'd met her new friend. Sereeta gestured to catch her attention and signal her over by her. Reyna walked up and stood over Sereeta and Mark. They both looked in her direction, but no one said anything right away. Reyna was dressed real cute; she had on some fitted 7 jeans with black knee boots and an orange Kani Ladies top. She stood there with an awkward smile, wondering if she was intruding on a private conversation. Sereeta looked up at her with the same devilish smirk and recognized Reyna giving her the eye, indicating her curiosity as to the identity of the cutie she was sitting with.

"Mark, this is my friend Reyna. Reyna, this is Mark," Sereeta finally stated.

"Nice to meet you," Mark said as he reached out his hand to shake Reyna's.

"You as well," she said.

"Take a seat," he said as he stood up.

Reyna hesitated not at all as she sat down in the seat he had emptied.

"I'll give you girls some alone time. I will be right over there for a while," he said as he gestured to the empty seat by another young man in the room.

"Is that guy with you?" Sereeta asked Mark.

"That's Nate's cousin. We aren't technically together . . . but we kind of are."

Reyna gave a look of confusion, but Sereeta continued to talk to Mark. "Why don't you and your friend come sit over here with us—you don't have to leave us alone."

"It's OK. Besides, I don't know if he wants to move his seat and all."

"OK, no problem," Sereeta said. "I just didn't want you to feel that I was done with you now that my friend has arrived."

"It's OK that you used me for company," he said jokingly.

"It's not like that at all; you are welcome to come back over whenever you feel like it."

Mark nodded his head with a giggle and walked away.

Reyna gave Sereeta one of her looks.

"What?" Sereeta asked.

" 'Come sit over here with us'? Is someone playing a desperate card?" Reyna said, looking at Sereeta out of the corner of her eye.

"Uh-uh! No, you didn't!" Sereeta laughed. "I was just trying not to be rude; he came over to keep me company when I was looking like Sad Suzie."

"OK, I'm just saying. You up here in the skybox trying to catch you some high-quality fish."

"Whatever, it's nothing like that."

"Yeah, OK, Desperado."

Sereeta just sucked her teeth and turned back toward the game. Corey was down there dribbling the ball up the court. He looked so miniature from where Sereeta sat until she looked up at the JumboTron and saw it zoom in on his face.

"That's your boss, right?" Reyna asked.

"Yeah," she said, never taking her eyes off him.

"He *is* cute."

"I guess."

"Don't try to act like you never looked at him that way," Reyna said.

"I don't. He walked me up here tonight; if you were on time you could've met him."

"He walked you up—like, personally escorted you? Ah, shit."

"Knock it off, it was nothing like that."

Sereeta knew she was fronting and didn't know why. The truth was that prior to tonight, she really hadn't seen Corey in that light. She had been more afraid of him than attracted to him. Even though she'd had a glimpse of temptation tonight, she didn't want to entertain the thought—not one bit. She knew Corey was an all-business kind of guy, and she didn't want to mess up her job in any way.

Chapter 18

Madison walked in the house and was stopped in her tracks by the darkened room and sweet scents. She slowly closed the door behind her and tried to take in the ambience of the room. There were dozens of tea-light candles everywhere all over the porch and living room. She didn't see Jamahl anywhere in sight, but she knew he was responsible for this, although it was so out of character. The sounds of Brian McKnight swayed through the air, and the smell of something tasty in the oven filled her nose. Madison was excited. No one had ever done anything like this for her before, and it was the last thing she expected from Jamahl Walker.

She saw a note on the table that read *Read Me.* A smile covered her face. She opened it up. *Go upstairs, take a shower, change into something comfortable, and meet me back in the living room in thirty minutes. Don't be late.*

Madison set the card down, tossed her purse on the porch chair, and headed upstairs. She could feel the butterflies in her stomach like she was a little girl. She didn't know what had caused him to do this for her—their anniversary and her birthday were months away. She got to the bedroom and saw a trail of rose petals leading to the bathroom. Madison stopped once again, just looking at each rose petal—some were red, some were yellow, and some were white. She began to wonder if this was even Jamahl's doings—had Polytics kidnapped him and planned this out, or was this a trick on her from God to make her feel guilty for what she had done with Polytics while her boyfriend was at home?

Initially, she was wondering where he was hiding. Was he in one of the bedrooms or in one of the rooms downstairs? Suddenly her excitement began to fade, and her guilt began to heighten. She undressed slowly as she thought a million things about how horrible she was. She kicked off her black ankle boots and removed her black slacks and blue and black cardigan. She took out a bobby pin and pinned her hair up. She couldn't believe that only weeks after she had resorted to sleeping with another man for some attention, Jamahl had decided to go do the most romantic thing he had ever done for her. *Damn,* she said to herself.

She almost wished she had a time machine to go back and fix her actions. She knew that what she had done had not only risked her job, but it had risked her relationship with the one man who had stood by her side through all these years. She knew she was no walk in the park—a lot of times she brought her job home with her. A lot of times she forgot that her title of *boss* was only at the office, and Jamahl wasn't her staff, so when she would talk down to him or treat him like he was beneath her, he didn't like it one bit. She knew it took a man with confidence to be with a woman like her. Not only was she strong-minded and out of control half the time, she had a hard time with any level of submission. It didn't help that she was surrounded by rich and famous men who most men would easily be jealous of and feel insecure about, and she made no efforts to comfort him. When she really thought about it, Jamahl was a good man to even still be dealing with her, let alone planning romantic nights. She knew it was messed up that it had taken her cheating on him and to come home to this for her to appreciate him.

She stood in the shower, washing away all her guilt in hopes of meeting Jamahl in the living room with a smile on her face. She stepped out of the shower and walked back to her bedroom. She didn't know if Jamahl was in one of the other bedrooms on that floor or if he was going to jump out and surprise her at any point. She was just hoping to clear her mind of all the negative thoughts and guilt so she could fully appreciate all he had planned. She put on a purple teddy nightgown; not really sure what he meant by *change into something comfortable,* she chose to go with what she thought he would like to see. She combed her hair down, lotioned up, and sprayed on some Smell Goods.

Madison looked at the clock and saw that she had three minutes to go before she would be late. She walked out of the bedroom and began to head downstairs. Just the scent of the food and the sight of the romantic candlelit scene below her was enough to put her in a good mood again. She stepped into the living room, where she saw the table set and a note on her plate. She walked over to the table and picked up the note. *Take a seat, enjoy the wine, and listen to the music. I will be with you shortly.* Madison smiled again. She pulled out the oak-wood chair and sat down on the soft plush cushion. There were two glasses of white wine on the table, a bouquet of roses in the center, and two tall dinner candles. Madison had to admit she couldn't have done a better job if she had set this up herself.

She sat back, resting her head on the tall back of the chair, sipping on her wine. She felt sexy in her nightie, sitting in the candlelight in the living room of her three-quarters-of-a-million-dollar house. A few minutes went by, and she heard a noise. She slowly looked over the back of the chair, but she didn't see anything. The song on the CD player changed to another, and Brian began to croon his song, "Never Felt This Way," one of Madison's favorites. She could feel the chill go up her spine. She was anticipating seeing Jamahl even more now, but she still couldn't see him. She could hear him in the kitchen, so she assumed he was preparing their plates. She rested her head back on the chair once again with her eyes closed, trying to sit patiently and let him take charge for once without trying to be the boss. She was realizing she liked how it felt. She just sat back, waiting for him to run the show. She took a sip of her wine.

A few moments later, she heard footsteps. She remained still with her head leaned back and eyes closed until she heard them even closer. She finally opened her eyes, and there he was standing in front of her. She didn't know if it was thinking all the lovely thoughts or just that the barber had hooked him up, but Jamahl was standing there looking fine as hell. He was wearing a wife-beater tank top and some black lounge pants. His full lips looked Vaseline smooth, and he just looked ready for loving—maybe it was the candlelight or the wine, but Madison wanted him. She was too horny to notice that the look on his face didn't match the mood of the night. He looked upset. She looked down and saw her work BlackBerry in his hand.

"What's wrong?" she asked.

"You tell me," he said. He extended his arm and opened his hand, passing Madison the work Black-Berry. She looked at it, and there was an e-mail from Polytics. I miss you, baby, when can I see you again. I have been horny all day thinking about you. Madison's mouth dropped open as she tried to think of something to say, but nothing was coming out.

"It was vibrating by your purse in the porch. I was going to bring it to you. I didn't know that I would intercept you and your boyfriend's plans," he said in an attempted calm tone.

"Jamahl," she said. "I know this looks crazy."

"Who the fuck is that?" he said, not paying her plea one bit of attention.

"Jamahl—" she said.

"*Who* the fuck is that!?"

Madison knew he was real pissed off. In most situations she would never allow him to talk to her like this, but in this instance—where she was dead wrong and she could clearly see that he wasn't playing at all—she knew this was not the time to get angry. Madison wasn't prepared to tell him the truth, though. She knew it would sound even crazier telling him it was Polytics, one of the biggest rappers in the game, hitting his girl on the Black-Berry saying he was horny. He would never believe it was innocent, so though she contemplated coming clean, she knew this was the time to lie.

"He's just some guy who works at a label who has been trying to holler at me. There is nothing going on, though," she said.

Madison was thankful that she coded the names in her phone—Polytics was entered in as "PC, Intheloop Records." She didn't like leaving people's full names or artist names in case her phone was lost or stolen. She knew some crazy teenager would have a ball just calling up Russell Simmons's house and Jay-Z's cell phone. She had been coding celebrity names for years, so she knew Jamahl wouldn't question the secret name—or he would wonder why a regular-label person was coded. Either way it didn't matter—she was calculating her story in her head, and she was damn sure sticking to it.

"When is he going to see you again?" he asked.

"I don't know, Jamahl. I hardly ever see him. I don't even know why he sent this," she said.

"Call him right now and find out why."

That caught Madison way off guard. She looked down at the phone and acted as if his request was no problem for her, but then she didn't know how to get out of that.

"He is my colleague. I don't want to make a scene here," Madison said.

"This isn't causing a scene. He just sent you a text that's crazy—he already caused a scene," he said.

Madison had to agree. Here they were in the middle of their candlelit house about to embark on an extremely romantic evening, and now they were standing there arguing over this e-mail. Madison's heart was beating; her shower was becoming irrelevant as her perspiration levels increased. She couldn't believe how fast the tables had turned. Moments prior she had been looking forward to one of the most romantic nights of her life, and now here she was on the verge of possibly getting caught in a huge lie and losing her boyfriend of six years. She wished that she didn't care, that she could put up her tough-girl wall and dominate this situation, but she couldn't. Something inside her was broken down; she was scared shitless and didn't know what to do.

"I am not calling him. This is silly," she said, rising from her chair.

"Then I will call," he said as he reached for her phone.

"No, you are not," she said and jerked the phone from his reach. "This is silly, and I can't believe you would ruin this beautiful night with this insecure nonsense."

She began to walk toward the staircase, knowing that her attempt at reverse psychology had a slight chance of working because it was the oldest trick in the book. She headed up the stairs, back to where she had tried to shake her feelings of guilt, only to revisit them full force. She was hungry, but she was just going to have to eat later because if she wanted to get out of this without being fully exposed, she was going to have to stick to her stance of being disgusted, disappointed, and mad. She was just hoping it was a matter of time before he would begin to second-guess himself and let it go.

Chapter 19

The restaurant was crowded by the time they got there, and if they hadn't known that most restaurants in the city were going to be pretty filled that night, they would have left. Naomi was out to dinner with Severio from accounting. They had spoken on and off for months, but after she had told him a few days prior that she was homesick, he told her he wanted to take her to this Texas barbecue place; without much hesitation at all, she obliged. She didn't know if it was supposed to be a date or if it was just a friendly night out, but she was interested in some company.

Severio was cute. He was about five-eight and brown skinned with a goatee and light brown eyes. He was a bit stocky but wasn't too built up, had nice skin, and had a beautiful smile—not that she was checking him out. She preferred not to consider it a date because she knew that technically speaking that would make her a cheater—because Charles was still supposed to be her loving boyfriend back home. They now barely spoke about much when they did get a chance to speak, and although she still missed him, she was definitely adapting to being without him. So even if just for the friendship, Naomi was glad that Severio had invited her out.

The waiter sat them down in the back in one of those tables a lot of people probably complain about. It wasn't as though the bathroom door swung open to hit them, but they were a bit too close to the kitchen and all the hustle and bustle. Even if they wanted to make a big deal about it, they knew they would end up having to wait quite a while for another table and would only hurt themselves, so they happily sat down and stayed put.

"I know these seats suck, but when you get your plate, you will feel like you're back home and will forget about where you're sitting anyway," he said.

"These seats beat sitting at home another night watching television," she said. "And I don't have DVR, so by the time I get home, there's nothing good to watch on television."

"So, you really just stay home all the time? I would think after moving here from Texas you would be like a tourist going to all the New York museums and crap," he said.

"I went to MOMA when I first got here, but once this job got ahold of me, I haven't been able to enjoy the city as much."

"You really need to take some more time to do it. This city really has a lot of great things to offer, and you live right here in Harlem, which is a great place to live."

"Yeah, that's what I hear. How Harlem is on the

rise and there are so many nice spots and events to attend."

"So why don't you go?" he asked.

"I don't know—no one to go with usually."

"A true city girl can roll dolo," he said.

"Dolo?" she said, scrunching up her nose at him.

"Alone, by yourself—you don't need anyone but your damn self to go out and have a good time," he said.

"Wow, I am definitely not there yet," she said.

"I don't know why. If you're home alone, why can't you go out alone?"

"I don't know. Something about being in public around a bunch of people hanging out with their friends or boyfriends or someone, and I'm just there all alone with no one to talk to. You start talking to strangers and eavesdropping on conversations," she said with a chuckle.

"What's wrong with talking to strangers?" he asked.

"I don't know, I guess I'm just not outgoing enough."

The waiter walked over dressed in all black. She was five-seven and light skinned with a short reddish-brown haircut like Rihanna. She was a pretty girl, but definitely not Rihanna pretty. Naomi wondered if Severio was thinking of things he would like to do to the waiter. She hated having a pretty waiter or bartender serve her when she was on a date. The young lady began to take their orders. Naomi didn't bother with the salad-ordering routine—she had come to a Texas-style restaurant to enjoy a good old Texas meal. She ordered barbecued chicken and ribs with macaroni and cheese and some potato skins. Her mouth began to water just thinking about the meal to come.

"You're going to eat all that?" Severio asked.

"I sure am," she said.

He laughed.

"I used to eat my mother's cooking every night back home. This is nothing for me," Naomi added.

"OK, well, I'm glad I took you here then," he said.

"So you are single, Mr. Severio?" she asked.

He seemed shocked at her bold and out-of-the-blue question.

"Actually I'm not, but my girlfriend and I are kind of on a break of sorts right now," he said, looking down at his fingers fiddling with the cornbread.

"A break or a breakup?" she asked.

"I don't even know myself—it's her thing. It's been close to two months, and I am real unsure as to what is going on with things . . . and with her."

Naomi wanted to ask more questions, but she was beginning to sense that this was a pretty soft spot for him, and she didn't want to pry if he wasn't comfortable talking about it.

"Well, I am in a similar situation," she said.

He looked up at her and tilted his head with a curious expression.

"Yeah, he lives in Texas, and we said we were going to try to do things long distance, but I don't think it's working out so well."

"Why do you think that?"

"In the beginning we talked and shared so much

that it was like obvious we missed each other like crazy. Now we go days at a time without speaking, and when we are on the phone, we have, like, nothing to say. It just seems like the love is fading and there is no more interest there. Maybe the distance is getting to us," she said.

"You don't seem all that hurt by it. Maybe you guys are just growing apart," he said.

Just 'cause I'm not pouting like you were? she thought. She pondered what he'd said and realized their adult lives may have made them different people or changed their priorities.

"I guess you're right," she said. "I did love him a lot—I almost didn't move here because of him. Now it's like I still love him, but I don't feel the same way I did."

"Does he know this?"

Naomi looked down at her plate. "No, he doesn't."

"Maybe you need to talk to him," he said.

"Yeah, maybe I do," she said.

Severio could see that Naomi was envisioning a clip of what she would say or what her boyfriend would say—from the look on her face, she had mentally left the table for a quick second. He wasn't sure what to say and was thankful when the waiter approached with their meals.

"Yummy, yummy," he said.

"Yes, no more talking now. It's time to eat," Naomi said with a smile.

She was kidding, and he knew that, but yet for the first few minutes of eating, they spoke only a few words. Naomi took this time to think if and when she was going to speak to Charles and what she would say. She knew things weren't what they should be, and if she didn't speak about it, there was a strong chance it would only get worse. She didn't want to end up seeking elsewhere for a man and have to cope with the guilt of cheating on Charles. She knew she had to figure something out . . . soon.

Chapter 20

It was a windy day—the kind of wind you can hear whirling through city buildings. Madison was walking down Forty-Second Street; she had hopped in a cab and asked to be dropped off on Forty-Second and Seventh. She wanted to spend her lunch hour shopping for a couple things for her weekend getaway to the Hamptons. She had left the station more than an hour ago, but because she was the boss of her department, and the general manager was out sick, she felt no rush to get back. She had spent the last twenty minutes in Sephora trying on makeup and new lip glosses when she realized she could be in there for hours if she didn't stop, so she headed to the register.

She bought two lip glosses and a nail polish and headed back onto the busy street. She walked for two blocks, pushing against the wind, heading toward the Victoria's Secret. She made her way through the crowds and began to hope that the store wasn't crowded the way Sephora had been. She had one more block to walk and was walking closer to the curb where less people were walking. Madison was so focused she didn't even notice the black Suburban rolling alongside her. She heard a horn a few feet away from her and jumped back, away from the curb. She looked back, trying to see why the horn was so loud and close to her, when she saw the black Suburban with tinted windows. Madison rolled her eyes and continued walking.

The Suburban pulled up, and the driver's-side window rolled down.

"Do you need a lift?" the driver said.

"No, I am fine," Madison replied.

"You sure?"

"I am sure. Can you drive along? You are kind of close to me," Madison said as she scurried along the curb.

There was a mass of people walking beside her, and she didn't care to weave her way through the crowd to get to the other side of the sidewalk. She preferred that this man move along so she could walk in peace.

"You are so stuck up," Madison heard a voice say.

She looked back and saw that the back window to the Suburban was rolled halfway down. She tried to see into the window but couldn't. Instead of trying to see more, she just rolled her eyes once again and continued walking.

"Damn, you are stuck up. Just because you run the biggest radio station in the country doesn't mean you have to act like that," the voice said.

Madison slowed down a bit to see who was saying this, though the voice was familiar enough. The truck had been following her very slowly, so Madison slowed down just enough to see in the back window. As she looked in, the window began to lower more, and then she finally saw the guy's face. It was Polytics with a huge grin like he had just succeeded at the best prank of the year.

"You was about to fight me?" he asked.

"No, but I was about to curse you out."

"I can tell—the look on your face seemed serious."

"I am not stuck up," she said, laughing.

Polytics opened the door. He was dressed in some baggy dark blue Rock & Republic jeans with a brown thermal and some brown construction boots. He had on a brown Gucci skully with a thick signature red stripe down the middle and some Tom Ford shades. He was damn sure looking fresh—dressed like a million bucks. Madison had to clear her mind to remember that this little charade with Polytics was only going to get her in big trouble if she didn't stop.

"Get in. Ride with me."

"How do you know I don't have somewhere to be?"

"I don't know, but I know you can get in for a second."

Madison looked up the street at Victoria's Secret and figured a ride back to work was worth the change of plans.

"Well, drop me off at the station, then, Mr. Prankster," she said as she stepped up into the truck.

Polytics scooted over to make room for Madison.

"To the radio station, Cliff," Polytics told his driver. Madison assumed that Cliff knew which radio station she worked for. He wasn't the same driver, and Polytics must have told him something for him to know which New York radio station to drive to.

"Where were you headed?" Madison asked.

"I just left the label, and I was about to head back home to chill for a bit."

"Where do you live?"

"New Jersey," he replied.

"Oh, OK."

"You're a city girl, right?"

"No. I live in White Plains. I moved from the city a couple of years ago."

"Oh, OK. I thought I heard otherwise."

"You need to update your sources."

He just laughed and looked out his window. Madison noticed the quiet moment and went along with it. She took out her BlackBerry and began to check her e-mails. When Polytics heard the clicking sound from the buttons, he turned.

"Speaking of, I need the personal numbers. I shouldn't have to go through assistants and my managers to get to you."

"Why shouldn't you have to?" she asked with a devilish smirk.

"I feel I earned the personal number," he replied.

Madison didn't even want to get into that conversation, so she just began giving him her number. He pulled out his cell phone to put the number in. Madison gave him just the cell-phone number—not only had he not earned the house phone number, Jamahl was home more often than she was, and she didn't want any more problems.

"So you are going to call me when—during the

spare two minutes you get here and there with your busy life?" Madison said after he put his phone back on his hip.

"I was hoping to call you so you can join me through some of my busy life."

"Through some of your busy life?" she asked.

"Like, come along with me and stuff."

"Are you crazy? Are you trying to create a tabloid cover story?"

Polytics laughed. "What's wrong with that?"

"Listen, I'm not trying to be a part of your publicity campaign."

"Calm down, I'm just kidding. We can hang out some without it being a big deal. My peoples protect my private life well; my business rarely pops up in the news."

" 'Rarely'? Didn't I hear somewhere that you were messing with that video girl from your first video?"

"Are you kidding me? That wasn't in the news. She wrote a book and claimed to sleep with everyone. That doesn't count."

"Well, either way, I'm not trying to be in that mess. I am really starting to think you don't understand how crazy things would get if people thought anything was going on between us."

"What do you mean?"

"Clarence . . . I program a radio station, and you are an artist. There is an extreme conflict of interest here, and serious claims of payola can be made. I could lose my job."

"How? We aren't doing anything wrong. What if we really fell in love—that's forbidden?"

Madison looked him dead in his eyes. She was shocked he had used the world *love*. If she was correct, she even thought the driver had looked in his rearview mirror to make sure he'd heard correctly.

"I don't know about falling in love and all that, Clarence, but I am assuming I would lose my job or never have to play another one of your records. Otherwise it will be a conflict of interest."

"A'ight, so no one will know."

"There will be nothing to know. What happened between us will have to be kept a secret from everyone, and it can't continue."

"So we can't hang out anymore?"

"I should never have let this happen," Madison mumbled to herself.

"What?" Polytics asked.

Madison could hear the strong tone in his voice and the attitude behind it, but she was angry as well.

"You have nothing to lose here, but I have everything to lose. Don't go making this some career move for you and then damage mine."

She had gotten herself all worked up. She couldn't believe Polytics didn't understand how serious this was.

"Career move? I don't know if you noticed, but my career is just fine. I don't need you or any stunt to enhance my career."

"You know what I mean—I wasn't trying to play you."

"Yeah, you were. You think I was just trying to rock with you to get a look out there. I can bag any chick I want—just because you're the PD at Drama doesn't mean you're the best look for me. I was feeling you and figured we could rock some, but I see that's not in our best interest, so no worries."

Madison was flabbergasted. She couldn't believe he had actually said that much or cared that much. She really had thought this was just about some mischievous sex—she had no idea he had thought more of it. It had been weeks since their romp in her office, and he had only called twice—both times Madison had been out of the office. It wasn't as if he had left urgent messages or sent roses or anything—why would she think a man like him was remotely thinking twice about her? She assumed he had hit it and accomplished his mission.

"I didn't mean it like that. What happened the other day . . . I don't do that. That's not my MO at all, so obviously I was feeling you, too. I just don't want us to get caught up and follow our hormones and not be rational," Madison said.

The driver turned down the avenue that led to the station; they were only a few minutes away. Madison knew the driver was getting an earful but was trained to mind his business and pretend he wasn't even there. He was doing a great job because Madison did almost forget he was there.

"It's cool, Madison, no hard feelings. Don't worry, I won't tell anyone what happened between us, and I'll figure out another career move."

"You really are going to run with that, Polytics? I just said I didn't mean it like that."

"Yup, I hear you. No problem."

Madison could tell that he was tight. She was a bit flattered, but she was even more surprised that he cared or was that sensitive.

The driver pulled up in front of the station.

"Thanks for the ride, P. It was nice to see you," she said as she gathered her bags.

"No problem. You, too. I will see you around."

Madison didn't even bother giving him a hug or kiss; it was obvious that he wasn't messing with her. She got out of the car, thanked the driver, and headed inside her building. She felt strange, emotionally stimulated, like she had just had a fight with her man. She was trying to ignore her thoughts, but she was liking the whole thing—having him feel the way he did, feeling wanted by him, and having the conversation she'd had. She liked having the control, and she liked having his attention. As she rode in the elevator, she realized she really was feeling him, and although she didn't want to admit it, the excitement of it all was a bit too much. She was starting to worry. What had she gotten herself into?

Chapter 21

It was Monday morning, and the office was quiet, and the lights were still dimmed. Naomi had made it to work ten minutes late, but most of her department was apparently even later. She went to her desk and logged on to her computer, trying to get her day started before her coworkers filled the department. She pulled the file with the BDS reports she had been working on the Friday before. She started punching data into the Excel sheet; she knew her boss expected to see it by the end of the day, and she was hoping to get it to her by lunchtime.

Naomi was so caught up in her work she forgot about her new look and the reaction her coworkers were going to have.

"Oh, my gosh, I love it," said Toya from down the hall.

"Thanks," Naomi said, running her fingers along her hair.

"It is really so cute," she said.

Another coworker, Simon, stepped out of his office.

"You cut your hair!" he shouted. "It looks so adorable on you."

"Thanks, Simon," Naomi replied.

"What did you get, a makeover? You look like a totally new person," Toya said.

"No, I just cut my hair and did some shopping. Nothing major."

Tiffany walked up to her cubicle. "Wow . . . look at you, little miss diva."

Toya and Simon laughed; Naomi just blushed.

"You have a whole new look over here. New York is finally rubbing off on you."

"I guess," Naomi said, not knowing what else to say.

"It looks good on you," Tiffany said. "Now everybody back to work." She walked off to her office.

Simon and Toya made some last comments before they walked off as well.

Naomi knew she looked different and was pleased that it was so noticeable because she was hoping that when Tyreek came to the department today he would react differently. She was wearing some two-hundred-dollar Citizens of Humanity jeans, a flowy see-through top from Forever 21, and some ankle boots with a gold trimmed heel. Naomi definitely loved her outfit and was loving her waxed eyebrows and layered haircut. She felt like a new woman.

Devora had taken her shopping and gone with her to get her hair cut, just as she had promised. At first, it was a disaster because Naomi found it absurd to buy clothes with such high prices, and Devora had told her she was hopeless, but eventually Naomi was able to invest in some staple items. After getting Naomi to charge some designer jeans and boots, Devora took her around to different boutique stores for cute tops. Once Naomi made it to Forever 21, she was in love—cute clothes for much more affordable prices. By the time she left, she had enough variety to keep up her new look for quite some time. Devora had tried to get her to throw out some of her old clothes, but Naomi wasn't ready to go that far.

Just as she began to get busy into her work, she looked up and saw an e-mail from her coworker Jared. She clicked on it. Someone has a secret admirer. She blushed and quickly replied. Who is that? she wrote back. Naomi returned to what she was doing, but her mind began to race about who Jared had been speaking about. *Is he speaking about himself? Is it Kassan who sits next to him?* She would've loved if it was Tyreek, but she knew that it definitely wasn't him. When Kassan had seen her earlier on the elevator, she had noticed he was checking her out. She wondered if it was someone who'd had a little crush from before she'd made her transformation. Really, she didn't care who it was—it was just nice to be noticed and attractive to someone again.

If I told you, it wouldn't be a secret, would it? Jared wrote back. Naomi didn't even bother to reply—she figured he would eventually tell her or give her a hint, and she didn't want to seem too eager. Maybe the Naomi from last week would have pressed, but this week's Naomi was sexy and in charge. She definitely felt good, and she pretty much knew she looked good. She might not have been video-girl-ready just yet, but she felt much closer to their level with her new look.

Naomi was of course hoping that Tyreek made his way to her department today; the truth was that when he had overlooked her last week, she'd found the inspiration for her makeover. She had put way too much thought into it, so she had already made up her mind that if she didn't see him by the afternoon, she was going to make her way to his department. Her last hope was that he wasn't out of the office, because that was just as likely. She knew she would have to aim for the level of *America's Next Top Model* every day coming to work, so it was only a matter of time when he would see her. She was just hoping that today would be the day, while her haircut was still fresh and she knew she had put her best foot forward for her debut.

It was around two thirty in the afternoon when Tiffany appeared at her desk with two folders in her hand. Naomi abruptly stopped what she was doing and turned around to fully face her.

"Hey, Miss New Booty, can you go through these two files and separate the content by album release?"

"Sure," Naomi said, laughing.

Tiffany handed her the folders and walked away. Naomi watched her strut back to her office in her Jimmy Choo pumps. Naomi knew they were Jimmy Choo only because Tiffany had shown them to her when she'd bought them on her lunch break a few weeks ago. The pumps were black and gray, and today Tiffany wore black jeans with a gray button-up shirt, revealing a little cleavage. Tiffany was an attractive, tanned Caucasian woman with a nice body and pretty face. She had long black hair with bangs, large breasts, and a thin waist. She also dressed fashionable and chic; with all the money she made, there was no designer she couldn't afford. She didn't have any children, and she had just gotten engaged a little more than six months ago. There was no question that Tiffany lived the life of the "traditional" New York diva. Naomi envied her; she envied how she seemed to have a complete grip on life and confidence in who she was. Although at times it was hard working for her, Naomi had to admit that Tiffany deserved and demanded her respect.

Once Tiffany was out of sight, Naomi quickly looked through the folders. She realized she'd forgotten to ask the "number-one assistant question," which was "When would you like this done by?" She figured she could go into her office and ask her or just tend to the assignment first and get back to her busywork after. Instead of having to go speak with Tiffany, she decided just to play it safe. Although she'd learned that the more face time with the boss, the better, for some reason Tiffany just made her nervous. Every time she was around her, all she seemed to want to do was end their conversation so she could exhale.

Naomi began sorting through the two files and using paper clips to gather the documents. Just as she drifted off into her world of business, she noticed a person in her peripheral vision. At first, she didn't look over, because she was in the process of looking over one of the papers in her hand. Then she heard the person speak to someone a few cubicles away, and she recognized Tyreek's voice. She instantly sat up and tried to get a glimpse of herself in the computer screen but couldn't see much; she rubbed her lips together to smooth out her passion-fruit lip gloss. From what she could see, it looked like he might finish with his conversation and head back out of the department without passing her. She wanted so badly for him to see her haircut and new clothes.

Out of desperation, she rose from her chair and headed toward her boss's office. She tried to remain calm and walk naturally without looking over at Tyreek, but she was hoping he was looking at her. By the time she got to Tiffany's office and saw Tiffany's two piercing eyes looking at her, she didn't have anything to say.

"W—what would you like me to do with the files when I'm done?" she stuttered but eventually got out.

Tiffany gave her a blank stare—the one that read *Did you really just say that?*

"What would you think to do with them, Naomi? Give them back to me, obviously," she replied.

Tiffany's tone alone just made Naomi want to disappear. Although she felt stupid and on the spot, she was hoping Tyreek hadn't heard her spoken to that way.

"OK," Naomi said as she hurried out of the office before Tiffany got even angrier.

As she walked back to her desk, she looked over to where Tyreek was standing. She didn't see him and felt instant disappointment. She had done all that and gotten yelled at for nothing. He might not have even seen her at all. Naomi sat in her chair. She tried to shake off what had just happened and go right back to work, but she kept thinking about Tiffany's tone. Naomi knew if she lost this job she would have to go all the way back home, and she had heard some horror stories about people getting fired from her company. She didn't want to come off as desperate for her job, but at this time in her life, she was. Just as she began to paper clip some papers together, she noticed someone walking toward her. She turned around, and it was Tyreek.

"I know Tiffany is hard on her staff, but we have all been through it," he said.

Naomi was trying to take in the moment all too quickly. Here was Tyreek, standing a foot or two away from her. He was talking to her, and he was sympathizing with her. Although she was mortified that he had witnessed that scene, she was flattered that he was trying to make her feel better.

"Yeah, I'm getting used to it," she replied.

"You'll survive."

"Thanks."

"I like your haircut," he said, nodding his head upward toward her hair.

"Oh, thanks. I just wanted to try something new."

"Well, I like it. The new do looks nice."

Naomi giggled at his little rhyme. "Thanks, I'm happy you approve."

That may have sounded like just a figure of speech to Tyreek, but if he only knew how much she really meant it.

"See you later," he said as he walked away.

Naomi wanted to say, What about my outfit and

my makeup? Do you like it enough to date me? Her mind was thinking a million things all while she watched him walk away. She was trying to reflect on the conversation while it was fresh in her mind. She was trying to determine if he had been flirting or just making friendly conversation. She had to factor in that he had come back just to talk to her and that he must have been pleased enough with what he saw to comment on it.

That was all Naomi needed to make her day. Tiffany snapping at her had put a little damper on it, but Tyreek had surely made it bright. She was well aware that he probably didn't know her name, but she was hoping that today could be the beginning of a connection between the two of them.

Chapter 22

They had talked about three times in the past week, and Sereeta was starting to dig Mark. When she left the skybox that night, they had all gone out for drinks. Rashard, the guy Mark had been sitting with, had ended up coming as well.

After being with Mark for less than two hours, Sereeta realized that Corey was becoming the man in her life. A single woman with no consistent male companionship, sporadic sex, and no real social life was bound to get lost in her job working for a young rich black man. Sereeta wasn't trying to unintentionally fall in love with Corey or anyone else in the business all just to be hurt. Mark, she figured, would be a great addition to her life; they had great conversation and seemed to vibe really well.

Reyna and Rashard seemed to get along, too—they also exchanged numbers before the night was done. Sereeta didn't have a chance to get the update on how the two of them were going, but she was pleased with the way things were going with Mark. They had made plans to go out that Friday, and Sereeta was thinking it was best she not invite Reyna and Rashard. She figured she should take a chance and see how they interacted with just the two of them.

It was Thursday night, and she was just leaving the stadium after picking up some paperwork from Corey's coach. She didn't have any plans, but she wished she had. For some reason she had a lot of energy and no desire to go sit at home and watch television. Sereeta didn't have a slew of friends, and the few she did have mostly had lives of their own or didn't live close by. Most nights Sereeta went to a local hangout alone, shopped, cuddled at home alone, visited a male associate, or just talked on the phone with Reyna or some other friend. Tonight Sereeta wanted to hang out *with* someone. Her money was right, she was looking good, and she knew that she was too fly to be cooped up in the house for yet another night.

The air was crisp, and crowds of people covered the city street in front of her. She wanted to mix right in with the crowds and walk among them with some sense of purpose as well. She was surrounded by some of the city's greatest fashion stores, but she had no desire to peruse the racks as she often did. She stood there for a while, just people watching and thinking about what options she had. She already had plans with Mark for the next night and didn't want to call him and try to hang out because she didn't want to come off as too eager. Reyna didn't get off any time soon.

Then she remembered that she had met a few of the other players' assistants and they claimed to hang out sometimes. Sereeta hadn't been interested in joining the NBA Assistants' Associations, but she figured most people hung with colleagues—why couldn't she?

She picked up her phone and dialed Debbie, who was Matt Camby's assistant and had been working with him for over three years already. Sereeta held the phone to her ear and waited for her answer. Sereeta had never used the number before, so she felt a bit awkward, but she knew it was silly to make a big deal out of it.

"Hello?" Debbie answered.

"Hi, Debbie, this is Sereeta, Corey's assistant."

"I know who this is—how are you, missy?" she said in a chipper tone.

"I'm good. I was just leaving the stadium, and I was wondering what you were up to. I was going to see if you wanted to go for some drinks."

"Isn't that funny—I'm here at Wish 26 bar with Tamara now. Why don't you come down and meet us?"

"Cool, where is that exactly?" Sereeta asked.

"On Twenty-sixth and Eighth avenues."

"OK, I'll be there shortly."

"See you then," Debbie said.

Sereeta hung up the phone and was happy that she had somewhere to go. Debbie was a cool girl, and she was so thankful she was receptive to Sereeta's call. She had met plenty of stuck-up people to know that the conversation could have gone sour. Tamara was Nate's assistant, and Sereeta figured there was a good chance she knew Rashard from the skybox, so Sereeta told herself to be sure not to mention anything. She just wanted to hang out and have a good time, not gossip or piss anyone off.

The cab she jumped in smelled like must and funk. Sereeta scooted over to the corner and cracked the window for some fresh air. She began to reapply her lip gloss and brush her hair back into the right form to fix the damage the city wind had done. When she finished and went to put her brush back in her purse, she noticed the red light blinking on her BlackBerry. She removed the phone from her purse to see an incoming text from Mark. Her lips formed a slight smile as she read his words.

I look forward to tomorrow night. Call me later. If you are free, let's hang out tonight, too.

Sereeta grinned and put the phone in her lap while she thought out her response. Why, less than fifteen minutes ago when she had been contemplating contacting him, had she convinced herself that she would look eager? He, on the other hand, had reached out, and it was sweet and charming. Sereeta had to admit she liked the idea of hanging out with Mark. She was feeling her outfit and felt like the city was hers for some reason, like she just owned the night and could do whatever and go wherever she liked.

I will be free in a couple hours if you want to meet up. I will hit you up then.

A few moments later, Sereeta was pulling up in front of Wish 26 and paying the cab driver. She stepped out and walked toward the main entrance. There were a few people smoking cigarettes and conversing outside in the front of the bar and a security guard standing by the doorway. She walked up to him, showed her ID, and continued inside the club. She skimmed the bar for Debbie and Tamara but didn't see any familiar faces. She made her way toward the back of the lounge but didn't see anyone still. She stood by one of the tables and took a few seconds to thoroughly scan the location. After looking in every possible area of the club, she looked down at her phone to see if they had contacted her. There was nothing from Debbie or Tamara.

She was pissed off. Was this some kind of prank or mean girl's skit? She began to walk toward the front of the bar to leave, while typing a text to the girls to tell them she was there and how uncool it was that they were not. She was too pissed to call them—she didn't want to argue. Even if they had left, they could have called her to let her know. She excused herself past the crowd by the bar, trying to make her way through. Just as she emerged at the other end of the bar, she heard someone call her name. She turned around and saw Debbie waving her hand in the air over the crowd. Sereeta made her way back through the same crowd.

"Hey, I was just about to text you and ask you where you were."

"We were in the bathroom, sorry," Debbie replied.

"Oh . . . duh! That's somewhere I didn't look," Sereeta said, hitting herself on the side of the head.

"Hi, Sereeta," Tamara said from the bar stool beside Debbie.

"Hey, Tamara," Sereeta replied.

"Take a seat," Debbie said as she lifted herself onto her bar stool and patted the one next to her.

Sereeta hung her purse on the side of the stool and sat beside them.

"What are you drinking?" Sereeta asked.

"Vodka and cranberry," Debbie said.

"The same," Tamara answered.

"I guess I will go with the trend here," Sereeta said as she flagged down the bartender.

After a second or so, the bartender made her way to their area.

"May I order a vodka and cranberry?" Sereeta asked.

"Sure," the waiter said as she walked her petite frame back down to the other end of the bar. Sereeta watched her make her drink; it was just a habit of hers because she learned early in her "clubbing days" to keep your eye on your drink at all times.

Sereeta found it so odd that all bartenders had such similar characteristics. For the most part, they were petite, bubbly, and attractive. She had always heard that the New York bars preferred attractive bartenders so they would be successful at flirting and selling drinks. Still, with all the bars in this city, she didn't see how the bartenders all fit such a similar mold, as if they were robots trained at some school or off-site location.

Once she received her drink, she turned to the ladies as she took her first sip.

"So, how long have you ladies been here?"

"About an hour before you called," Debbie replied.

"Oh, OK. Do you guys come here often?"

"Not often. We've been here a few times. Usually we try to switch it up, but Debbie and I usually hang out at least once a week," Tamara said.

"That's really cool," Sereeta replied, beginning to feel like a third wheel.

"You are more than welcome to come along. We just go have a few drinks, relieve some stress, recap our weeks, and stuff. This job can be pretty isolating," Debbie said.

"Wow, that is just how I've been feeling lately. I feel like Corey is my husband, and I have, like, one friend left in the world."

"Yeah, we know what you mean. Except it's the husband with none of the benefits to go along with it," Debbie said.

Tamara nodded her head in agreement.

"Matt is married, though, right?" Sereeta asked Debbie.

"Yes, he is, but that doesn't mean a damn thing," Debbie said.

From the looks of Tamara's snicker and pursed lips, it looked as if there was a lot more to the story—a story Sereeta was tempted to hear, but she wasn't about to ask any questions. Instead of probing, she simply responded, "I hear ya."

"Nate isn't married, and he's like a spoiled brat sometimes," Tamara chimed in.

"Corey is pretty laid-back, but he has me do pretty much everything for him."

"Well, they all want different things based on things they are particular about," Debbie said. "Like, because Matt is married, I don't do too many things at his home. He has a lot of deals and stuff he works with, and he has me handle a lot of business and marketing for him."

"Oh, that's cool. You attend meetings for him and stuff?" Sereeta asked.

"Pretty much—meetings, liaisons between his sponsorship clients, and stuff like that. It's pretty cool."

"I've been to a couple meetings with or for Corey, but usually he has me doing things at the stadium or his house."

"That's the thing—when you're an athlete's personal assistant, there are no set job duties. It's whatever they need personal assistance with," Debbie said.

Sereeta had told herself she didn't want to meet with the girls to exchange gossip, and she could see the three of them sharing already. She figured sharing job duties was harmless information.

"The hard part is just mastering your own limits because after a while you feel owned by them and you must begin to say no, otherwise they will take advantage," Tamara said.

"You have to remember they are young and rich— they become spoiled easily. They are not used to being told no. They have enough money to buy anything, including people," Debbie said.

Sereeta was just soaking it all up like a sponge. She felt like she was in church receiving a message. She had felt very similar at times but never looked that deeply into it.

"If I knew then what I know now, I may not ever have started fucking Matt," Debbie blurted out.

Sereeta damn near spit out her sip of vodka and

cranberry. She turned and looked at Debbie, who just looked back at her like "Yes, you heard right."

Tamara began to laugh. "I second that," Tamara added.

Sereeta placed her glass down and shifted her body more in their direction.

"Does someone want to tell me something?" she asked.

"Nothing to tell. Like I said, it's whatever they need assistance with," Debbie said.

Were they, like, prostitutes? How could they not hear how they sounded, saying this as if it were just normal procedure? Sereeta had been working with Corey for quite some time, and he had never even implied he wanted those services.

"How long have you guys been 'assisting' them in that way?"

"Matt told me pretty much up front. He said he was married, and from time to time when he was on the road he might need help relaxing and asked me if I was comfortable with that," Debbie said.

"With Nate, after a few weeks he asked me one day to come by his condo really late to work on some forms he had to fill out for the association. When I got there he had some friends over, we were drinking, and things led to his kitchen, where it got extra hot in there."

"Wow," Sereeta said.

"What? You haven't done anything with Corey?" Debbie asked.

"No, not at all. He is so respectable and quiet, we barely talk," Sereeta replied.

"That is surprising. It's been a while, too."

"Yeah, I never would've guessed that the players mix their business with personal pleasure that way."

"Well, you have to remember we are expendable. We come a dime a dozen. Women would love to have our job—we get paid good money to just help out a millionaire with simple stuff. They know that if we don't play along, they will find someone else who will," Debbie said.

"Well, with Nate, he's cool. I'm kind of like his tier-B girlfriend. He definitely takes care of me, so I'm not as bitter as Debbie here."

"Why are you bitter?" Sereeta asked.

Debbie just shot Tamara a look; she didn't look angry, but just as though she didn't agree with the term *bitter.* "I'm not bitter," Debbie said.

"She's with married Matt, so she's more like a secret mistress than a girlfriend. For me, it's nice. I'm single, I have nothing to lose. If I ask him to do something for me, he usually does. I sleep at his condo some nights and everything. For Debbie, it's always on the road at hotels—like there's no real bond between them," Tamara explained.

"Damn, Tamara. You don't have to make me sound like a prostitute," Debbie said.

"Well, at least Corey seems like he just expects you to be an assistant. You may miss out on the other perks from sleeping with him, but at least you won't get emotionally attached," Tamara said to Sereeta, ignoring Debbie.

"What perks?" Sereeta asked.

"They're just more willing to lavish you with gifts and the perks of being an NBA wifey. They don't want you running to the newspapers or writing a tell-all book either, so they're going to do their best to keep things flowing between you once you enter that domain."

"Interesting," Sereeta said as she took a sip.

"I'm sure you will be fine—don't let us scare you," Debbie said.

Sereeta just laughed a bit. *Scared* wasn't the word—she was actually a bit insulted that Corey hadn't tried anything with her. She wondered if he wasn't attracted to her or if he was just that disciplined of a guy not to mix the two. She was finding it hard to believe that he was that disciplined. She wondered if the girls thought that maybe she wasn't good enough for Corey. She felt insecure for a moment and wanted them to know he wasn't strictly business with her.

"He brought me up to the skybox the other night to watch the game," she said.

"Oh, that's nice. Which one, number twelve or eighteen?" Tamara asked.

"Twelve," Sereeta said, feeling in-the-know.

"That's cool. Wait until he gives you a pass for number eighteen—then you will really feel like you've arrived," Debbie said.

"What's that?"

"That's where the NBA wives and girlfriends watch the game when they aren't sitting on the floor or something. Number twelve is typically for colleagues, family members, and friends they don't really rock with like that," she answered.

Sereeta instantly felt stupid. Here she was trying to brag and still had to be put down.

"The players usually come up there afterward

to get them or to hang out for a bit before going home with them."

Sereeta quickly remembered how she'd felt the other night when she was hoping to see Corey after the game. She wondered if he'd gone to box #18 after the game, and she began to feel bad.

"It doesn't look strange for the assistants to be among the wives and girlfriends?" Sereeta asked.

"No, it's not just the wives and girlfriends. It's just like the VIP to the VIP, and most players have their significant others in there. So it doesn't look strange—they all know we work very closely with the players, so it makes sense. It's like when you're at a club and you're in VIP—and there is another VIP section where the actual celebrities sit. That's all," Tamara said.

That's all? Sereeta thought. Clearly it wasn't just "that's all," or they wouldn't be praising it. *Whatever. I am Corey's assistant, not his concubine. I don't need to be in box #18,* she told herself.

It was at that moment that Sereeta decided she was definitely hanging out with Mark. She figured she would rather have her own man than be a mistress or a tier-B girlfriend anyway. She picked up her phone, texted Mark, and told him to meet her at her place.

Chapter 23

Mark entered as if he owned the place. He was usually so humble and polite, but he seemed a bit more abrasive when he walked through the door and headed straight toward the couch without waiting for direction. Sereeta loved a man who took charge, but with Mark she was still trying to feel him out. The times they had spoken he was funny and charismatic but didn't like to talk much about himself. She was trying not to ask too many questions or seem too eager, because he gave off a vibe that he was the private type. She didn't mind that so much, but she was hoping he would eventually open up. She still didn't know his permanent place of residence—he referred to at least two places as home. She also didn't know much about his career or what he did in his free time. She still hadn't figured out which player in the NBA was his brother. Most people would brag and name-drop, but he hadn't brought it up since the first time he told her his brother played in the league. She was beginning to wonder if he had just lied about that to get some play.

"Hey, what's up, little lady?" he said on his way to the couch.

"Hey, Mister," she said back.

"We watching a movie? You cooking for me? What we doing?"

She loved his cute but cocky sense of humor. "We chilling," she replied.

He sat in the middle of the couch, so unless Sereeta was going to sit on another couch, she was going to have to sit fairly close to him. She was dressed in a pair of black fitted Victoria's Secret Pink sweat pants, a cut-off white T-shirt, and some fuzzy socks. She didn't want to be too dressed down in front of him because it was his first time coming over to her place, but she had been home for a couple hours and wanted to get comfortable. He was wearing a white T-shirt, jeans, a pair of Air Force Ones, and a Yankee fitted cap: the hip male's safe but cute outfit.

Sereeta chose to sit beside him on the couch— no need sitting a few feet away on another couch, as if they were in high school.

"A'ight, chilling works," he said.

"What, are you in a rush or something?"

"Not at all. I'm yours all night," he said. "Unless one of my other honeys calls me up. Then I'm going to have to bounce," he said with a big grin.

She reached over, grabbed a pillow, and swung at his chest.

"Shut up," she said.

"I'm kidding with you. I'm here for as long as you will have me," he said.

She had to admit she liked the sound of that, but she wished he meant it with regards to life and not just for this one night.

She jumped off the couch with a quick motion, like she had just got real excited about something.

"OK, great. Well, let me pick a board game we can play," she said.

"A board game?" he asked. "We can't just watch a movie or something?"

Sereeta giggled. "What, you don't like games?"

"I'm cool with games, but just not right now. I don't feel like thinking all that much, and I'm competitive, so I don't want to start no fights on our first date."

She laughed. "This is not a date."

"Right, and you are not one of my honeys."

Sereeta sat back down and placed her hands by her side.

"OK, OK, you win. We will watch a movie," she said.

She picked up the remote and turned on the television.

"Let me see," he said as he removed the remote from her hand.

"Excuse me," she said.

"After you were trying to play a board game, I don't trust your judgment anymore," he said.

Sereeta just laughed. She wanted to take the pillow again and hit him, but she opted against it. She had been told in the past by her exes that she hit too much. Sereeta was trying to ignore the little excited fireflies inside her belly, but she knew she couldn't ignore the fact that she was feeling him. There was something about him—it was as if she'd

known him for years. He made her feel so comfortable. He was secure in himself, and it didn't
hurt that he was fine, too. She liked his height and
built, and she was loving his almond-shaped brown
eyes and his smooth complexion. *I could definitely
see myself having a baby with him,* she told herself.
She knew she didn't want to jump the gun because
she was well aware that this could possibly not go
anywhere. That wasn't going to stop her from
wishing and enjoying it along the way.

He was surfing through movie options on the
movies-on-demand channel.

"Don't go picking no horror flick, trying to get
me to jump into your arms or anything," she said.

"Oh, you stuck on the old tricks. The new one is
to watch a chick, romantic, lovey-dovey flick and
then you get all emotional and sappy and vulnerable," he said.

"Damn . . . y'all are horrible."

"I'm just schooling you to the new game. You
still stuck in the eighties."

"I see," she said.

"Or the dudes you been messing with are lame,"
he said.

"The problem is I haven't been messing with
anyone. Lames would be better than nothing
probably."

"Oh, so you are just settling for me? I hope not,
'cause I ain't no lame."

"I am not settling—knock it off. I'm just saying I
haven't been dating," she said.

"Why?" he asked. "You're such a pretty girl, and
you're mad cool. You can't just keep yourself from
the world like that."

Sereeta laughed. "From the world? You're crazy."

"Nah, but seriously, why don't you date? Your last boyfriend beat you up? You were a lesbian before?"

Sereeta cracked up laughing. She remembered they said when a guy kept you laughing, the guy could tell you liked them, so she was really trying to contain her joy.

"You are so stupid, I swear."

"Alright, tell me. What is the reason?"

"Just working all the time," she said. "I have been a workaholic lately. Corey keeps me real busy. Then I enjoy, alone, the little free time I get, so I just don't go out much to meet anybody."

"So your last boyfriend wasn't a crazy ax murderer?" he said.

"No, my last boyfriend was sane and respectable. We just went our separate ways because he was fond of the ladies, I guess you could say."

"Mmmm. I know what that means. Sorry to hear that," he said.

"It wasn't a loss in my family or something. Geez. No need to say sorry to hear that."

"Hell, the way y'all females be acting when you get cheated on, it seems worse than a death in the family."

There was Sereeta laughing again. She wouldn't be surprised if he had counted all her teeth by now. She couldn't seem to help herself. Mark's wit was just too much for her. His mannerisms and characteristics were even funny—he made amusing facial expressions every time he said something.

"Pick a movie, damnit," she said.

She hit him with the pillow again.

"*Sooorry*. Did I hit a sore spot?" he said.

"You are just a nut, that's all."

Mark chose a movie from the menu and set the remote down. He sat back and extended his arm for Sereeta to lie back on him. She nestled under his arm and felt at home. She couldn't believe how nice things felt with this guy so soon. She was impressed that he hadn't tried to turn this visit into a booty call, or at least not yet, and he seemed just fine with cuddling up to a movie. Sereeta was hoping he was enjoying her just as much as she was enjoying him. She couldn't remember the last time she'd just hung out with a guy she was actually interested in and had that much of a good time from doing nothing. In the back of her mind, she was really hoping he could be her boyfriend one day. She just hoped that after she found out everything there was to know about him, she still felt the same way.

Chapter 24

It had been a long week, and to Madison there were still fifty things to do before the end of the day. It was Friday, and although the music meeting was usually on Wednesdays, the week was so crazy she had to reschedule it for Friday. The music meeting was where the programming department got together and looked over research to see which music was no longer hot and needed to come out of rotation. More importantly, the meeting was to listen to new music to see which songs should be added to the rotation. Some weeks the meeting took less than fifteen minutes, and others it took hours. It all depended on how much new music was out there and how many hits were already on the station.

This particular meeting, Madison was hoping to be in and out. She still had to meet with the sales team, take a conference call with the West Coast programmers, and try to leave at a decent time so she could go to a very important dinner with some music business executives. It was already one fifty-

five and she was regretting moving the meeting
from Wednesday. She had sent out an e-mail that
morning letting the department know the meeting would be held at two PM, and Madison had
put her work aside to get ready. When the hand
was on the two and there was no sign of her staff,
she instantly became annoyed.

"Hello!" she shouted from her desk.

Quickly, Alexis appeared in the doorway with all
the needed material in hand. As a part of Alexis's
assistant duties, she was responsible for making
the folders for everyone that contained all the research data needed for the meeting. Seconds later,
the rest of the department began to trickle in: Jocelyn, Keith, and one of the department interns.
Madison allowed the interns to take turns sitting in
on the meeting to learn the process, while the others tended to the phones and the department's vis-
itors. It was 2:04, and everyone was sitting in a seat
in her office; the door was closed. Madison was ir-
ritated, so she got right down to business.

"We don't have time to listen to a lot of music
today, so everybody pick your favorite song, and
we will listen to one song from each person."

She noticed a couple glances, but she ignored
them as she turned to her computer to open her
e-mail.

Jocelyn began giving the data on the songs in
rotations. As she went through each song and
where they ranked, Madison would call out whether
to leave it or remove it. Usually, this was something
that was open for discussion among everyone based
on other factors, but Madison was in no mood for
all that, and time was of the essence. By the time

they got finished with the power records, which were the songs with the heavy rotation, Madison could tell the room was a bit uncomfortable.

"Everyone OK? Any disagreements so far?"

The hesitation was extremely obvious. No one really wanted to speak up with the tension as it was. Eventually, Jocelyn spoke up.

"Actually, I think we should leave Fantastic Four in power rotation because it's still real big in the clubs and the video is just starting to rotate on BET."

"But the research says it was ranked fourteen out of twenty," Madison said.

"Yeah, but I think because it is fairly new and people are just getting used to it."

"So then why were we playing it so early?"

"I really wanted us to break this record because I think it's going to be a huge record."

"I am not playing a song that is testing badly as a power."

"OK, well, can we keep it in the B category and slow up the rotation?"

"That's fine, but if research isn't better next week, it's coming off the air altogether or going in very light rotation."

Everyone started jotting down the notes from the conversation. That was the first challenge of the meeting, and everyone knew that Jocelyn was hoping she wasn't wrong about the song becoming a hit. As the music director, her opinion of music was supposed to be her value to the position, and Madison thought it damn sure better be sensible if she was going to challenge the program director.

Once the notes were taken, Jocelyn continued going through the songs and their rankings with the audience testing and SoundScan, etc. Madison let the rest of the meeting flow as usual; she let Keith and Alexis make any comments about the songs and express their like and dislike for them. Instead of speeding up the entire meeting, she limited everyone's commentary by making final decisions quicker than usual. There were only two more categories to go through before it was time to play the new music, and Madison looked at her watch to set a goal to be done with the meeting by two thirty. Jocelyn went through the next category with ease; the next songs were researching about the same and were all new, so it was easily agreed to leave them in the same category for another week.

Just as Jocelyn was getting ready to start reading the next list of songs, there was a knock at the door. Madison gestured for Alexis to open it because she was sitting closest to it. Alexis stood and opened the door slowly. Once she saw a familiar face, she backed away so Madison and the rest of the room could see who it was as well. It was Kristin, the promotional representative for Intheloop Records.

"Hey, missy," Madison said. "We're in the middle of a music meeting. Give us, like, ten more minutes."

"On a Friday?" she asked.

"It's been a crazy week, so, yes, it's right now."

"OK, well, I was just bringing a visitor by to see you," she said as she waved her hand to someone.

Madison looked down at her watch and back up, and standing in her doorway was Polytics.

"Whassup, y'all?" he said, as he stepped in the room to give a pound to Keith.

"What a surprise this is!" Jocelyn said.

Madison looked at her to try to read if she meant anything by what she'd said. She wondered if Jocelyn knew, or if he had been flirting with Jocelyn, too. Hell, Jocelyn was the next best thing if his only goal was to get in the bed with someone powerful at one of the most powerful stations in the world.

"I see you guys are busy. I was just in the neighborhood, and we figured we would stop by."

"Lucky for you, Kristin has a great relationship with us, because we don't just allow artists to pop up—that's an extreme privilege," Madison said.

"Really? I can't get any special privileges?" he asked.

Madison felt her stomach melt. In her mind, she felt like the entire room could read through his subliminal message.

"Lucky Kristin is with you," she responded before her nervousness began to become too obvious.

"So because I'm privileged, can I sit in on the meeting to see how this works?"

Keith began to scoot over on the couch to make more room for Polytics and all his muscles. The entire room looked prepared for his participation, and Madison didn't want to be the bad guy—she damn sure wasn't trying to bring any extra attention to herself, so she just giggled and added no response. He made his way across the room to the couch and sat down.

"I'm going to go speak with Jasmine," Kristin said. "I'll be right back."

"You are welcome to stay, too," Madison said.

"No, these meetings make me too nervous and antsy. I'll return when it's over."

"OK, it will be over shortly," Jocelyn said as Kristin walked away.

Once Kristin walked out of sight, Madison didn't want to miss a bit, so she got right back to the meeting.

"So how are the songs in the G category?" she asked.

Jocelyn quickly fumbled through her papers to find the research. Once she found the information, she began to read out loud how the songs were testing. Madison tried to remain calm and natural despite the fact that Polytics was sitting a few feet away from her. She felt as though he was watching her every move, but she was trying to avoid eye contact. As normal as she may have appeared, she couldn't help but think about all that had gone down the last time the two of them were in her office.

As soon as Jocelyn was done with the current music, it was time to listen to the new music.

"Remember, we are listening to only four songs, so choose wisely," Madison said as she looked around the room to make sure everyone got her point.

There had been plenty of meetings in which the goal was to keep it short, but everyone always tried to squeeze in one more song, so she was reminding them today that it was four only. She was happy she had planned to do that because there was no way she wanted to sit through a dozen songs with Polytics sitting in on the meeting.

"Well, let's start with Tryme's new song 'Floating.' It's about time to get on this record," Jocelyn said.

She passed the CD to the intern and said, "Number seven." She said nothing more because the intern knew what to do. He placed the CD in the CD player and pressed PLAY. Madison instantly thought to herself that Tryme wasn't necessarily a friend to the station right now, but she didn't want to open that conversation with guests in the meeting. The room sat back and listened to the track. Jocelyn and Alexis bopped their heads a bit, while Keith and Madison just twiddled with their pens. Polytics tapped his foot and observed what everyone was doing.

When the song was done, the intern stopped the CD.

"What else is there?" Madison asked.

Keith replied, "I think Lotus's mix-tape record is something we should at least be spiking; it's catchy, and they are playing it in the club."

"This is radio, not the club," Madison said.

They had all heard that line before, so Jocelyn and Alexis just giggled that he had set himself up for that one. Polytics looked Madison in the eyes as if her assertive, bossy side was making him feel a certain way. She didn't know if it was a turn-off or a turn-on.

"I know, but as a hip-hop station, I think this record is one that adds to our credibility."

"I agree," Polytics said.

Jocelyn turned to look at Polytics, as did Alexis and Keith.

Madison was so tempted to flex her muscles on him to let him know who was in charge, but she wasn't willing to risk putting herself in the middle of a challenge with this man when she really didn't know what he was capable of.

"Put it in," Madison said.

"Put what in?" Polytics asked.

Madison shot him a look of shock. She knew damn well he had meant that in a perverted manner. She was very tempted to ask everyone to leave the room so she could talk to him, but she decided to leave it alone.

"The CD," Jocelyn answered as she handed the intern another CD. "It's the first track."

Madison looked at Polytics one last time to let him see how displeased she was with his comments. He gave her a smirk back, and for a quick second she really felt like she was being held at gunpoint and forced to comply. As she turned away, she caught him winking his eye. She looked back, and he turned away. He was playing cat and mouse right in the middle of the meeting. That was when she wondered if he was just flirting with her or if he was subliminally threatening her. Either way she knew she would have to talk to him when this was over. She couldn't remember the last time she had felt so defenseless.

The song began to play, and the room sat silent as they listened. They had all heard the song before, but this was the format to review all songs.

However, midway through, Jocelyn told the intern to stop the music. Even after the song stopped, no one spoke. Jocelyn sifted through some CDs and handed the intern one more CD. As he placed the CD in the player, Madison looked over and realized this hadn't been discussed first.

"What is this?" she asked.

" 'Rumors,' " Jocelyn replied.

Before Madison could reply, the music had begun playing. It took only a second for her to recognize Polytics's voice coming from her speakers. From the look on his face, he recognized it as well. Jocelyn turned around to see his expression, and his smile said it all. Madison wasn't sure why she got so angry, but she felt her heartbeat start to race. Madison didn't know if she felt that Jocelyn was flirting with him or was trying to get on his good side, or if Madison was just pissed that she'd chosen to play it without running it by her first.

"Turn that shit off," she said.

The look on everyone's face was the same. The intern quickly turned off the CD. Everyone just looked in shock and waited for her next words.

"Alexis, do you have a song you want to recommend for this week?"

Alexis was so nervous she didn't know what to do. Madison could feel Polytics looking at her, but she kept her eyes on Alexis.

"Um, I had one," she said as she looked through the CDs on her lap.

"What was up with that?" Polytics said.

"With what?" Madison asked. She looked right at him and asked the question in a strong enough tone to let him know, whether they had slept together or not, he didn't want to push her much further.

"Why my song had to be shit, and why you cut it so short?"

"We are not putting a record of yours in rotation with you sitting right here—it's as simple as that," Madison said. "And had Jocelyn announced the record like she was supposed to, I would've told her that then," she added, looking at Jocelyn. "I don't know what she was thinking."

Jocelyn's embarrassment was obvious, and even Polytics felt bad for her.

"I won't vote," he said jokingly.

"We are not voting on a record of yours with you sitting here. If people want to impress you, this is not the time," Madison snapped.

"Oh, is that what it is? You just want me all to yourself?" he asked.

Keith's eyes damn near popped out of his head when he heard Polytics's comment. Alexis looked at Madison to see her reaction. It was like a tennis match—everyone was looking back and forth at the two of them, watching the offense and defense.

"Could you guys please excuse us?" Madison quietly and calmly asked as she looked around the room at her staff.

Alexis, Keith, the intern, and Jocelyn began to gather their things and exit the room. Every last one of them wished they could stay so they could see the fireworks about to take place. Keith closed the door behind them.

"You have a lot of nerve getting an attitude with

Jocelyn for being nice to me when you don't want anything to do with me," Polytics said right away.

"Is this some type of joke to you? Do you not understand what you're dealing with right now?"

"Is that a threat?" he asked.

"No, it is a serious question."

"I know you're acting real funny," he replied.

"Clarence, you can't mix what happened between us with business like this."

"Stop calling me Clarence, if we keeping this business."

Madison was sitting in her chair, and Polytics was sitting on the blue leather couch by her desk. He had one arm on the back of the couch, and his legs were spread wide open—his position expressed just how comfortable and cocky he was. As though none of this meant a big deal to him, like he had not a care in the world.

"Polytics, I can't take back what happened between us, but I regret it ever happened, and I am asking you to leave it in the past."

"Wow, you regret it ever happened?" Polytics said as he stood up.

He walked over to where Madison was sitting; she kept her eyes on him the entire time. He stood behind her, and as she tried to turn around to see why he was behind her, be bent over and began kissing her neck. Madison backed away some.

"Polytics?" she said as she put her hand between him and her.

He pushed the back of her chair to swivel her around so she was facing him.

"You are going to lie to me and tell me you didn't enjoy it," he said as he knelt down.

He placed his hand on her shirt and began caressing her breast. Madison's hormones began to whisper little voices. The danger of it all seemed to provoke her even more, but she knew now was not the time.

"Polytics—no!" she said as she pushed his hand away. "What happened was great, but it will be a regret if you are going to hold it over my head forever."

"I am not holding it over your head, I just want to continue getting to know you."

"What you just said in front of my staff was totally unacceptable."

"I am sorry," he said.

"I don't think you are; I think you are trying to control me with the fear that you may tell."

"I wouldn't do that. Let's just say I can't stop thinking about you, so I didn't approve of you ending it the other day," he said as he moved closer to her.

"Clarence, this is my career. You *can't* play like this. As much of a fantasy as this all may be, I'm not a risky artist, I am a professional businesswoman. I can't take chances like that."

She moved her chair back a few inches.

"You were a risky businesswoman the other day," he said.

"I know this, Clarence, but I didn't expect you to act so childish about it."

She could tell he didn't like that from the look on his face. He looked her dead in the eyes, and his tough-guy exterior elevated.

"Ain't no child up in here—you better get that straight," he said.

Madison could tell by his eyes that she was being introduced to the serious side of him, a side she had rarely ever seen from an artist in all her years. Artists feared her, worshipped her in the hopes that she would support their careers and make them famous. Artists didn't yell at her and threaten her. She was in shock.

"Listen, this is getting too far. Let's just discuss this after hours. My staff is outside waiting to finish this meeting."

Madison tried to stand up, but Polytics stood in her way.

"I am a grown-ass man—there are no little boys in this room. I was feeling you, and I acted on it, simple as that. What happened happened—shit was good. But that doesn't mean my career is going to be affected by it. You play records, and you aren't going to overlook mine because we fucked."

She could feel his breath as he enunciated his words. He was standing only a few inches away from her with both his feet planted wide apart. She had to admit she was a bit frightened, but Madison wasn't one to back down to anyone.

"Excuse me," she said as she pushed past him.

She walked over to the door and opened it.

"You can go now. I need to finish my meeting with my staff," she said as she held the door open.

Polytics could see Alexis glancing in the office from her desk, trying to get a peek. He stood there for a couple seconds, and then he began to walk out. Madison kept her eyes locked on him the entire time so he could get the message that she wasn't easily intimidated. As he walked by her, he stared her down until she was out of sight. Once he walked out, she summoned Alexis to come on in.

"Let's go, guys, back to business," she said loud enough for Jocelyn to hear it in her office, Keith in his cubicle, and Polytics walking down the hall.

Madison wouldn't let her staff think she'd gotten punked. Respect was a big deal in this business, and without it, one's demise could approach very quickly. She had worked too hard to rise to let this new artist, getting his first glimpse of the spotlight, ruin that. She knew this ordeal wasn't over, but at this very moment she knew she wasn't adding any of Polytics's records this week and possibly not for a while.

Chapter 25

"**I** slept with him," Naomi said into the phone.

"*What?!*" Devora shouted.

Naomi ran her fingers through her hair and shook her head—she had done this at least four times already. She closed her eyes and put her face in her hand and just watched the dark. "I know, I don't even know how I feel about it."

"Wait, pause. Rewind. What the hell happened?"

Naomi stripped off her leggings. "I don't know, it all happened so fast."

"You have had your makeover for less than a week, and already you are a totally different person?"

"I know, don't make me feel worse," Naomi replied as she placed the leggings she had just removed on a pile of clothes in the chair.

"Did you forget you had a boyfriend back home?"

"Did you forget I just asked for you not to make me feel worse?"

"What happened, Naomi?" Devora asked, clearly curious about the details.

It was Saturday morning, and Naomi was sitting on the chair in her living room. She had just gotten home less than twenty minutes ago—and hadn't been home since the day before when she had left for work. Usually she liked to unwind before hopping on the phone, but today she needed to talk to someone.

"Well, last night was Weezy's party to celebrate his album going platinum, and I went with my coworker. When I got there, Tyreek wasn't there—he showed up, like, an hour and a half later with Weezy. . . ."

"Why didn't you invite me?" Devora interrupted. "You owe me for my makeover skills."

"My bad—I had no intention to go until my coworker begged me to go with her."

"You know you was going so you could sniff out compliments on your new look."

Naomi glanced across the room into the mirror. She still had remains of last night's makeup on her face. Her hair was still pretty intact—at least, the finger-combed parts. "Really, I mean it. I wanted to just go home and relax."

"Yeah, yeah. So go ahead."

"So when Tyreek got there, he was at the table for a while. I almost forgot about him by the time I saw him by the bar later. We started talking, and he invited me to the afterparty at Weezy's suite at the Gansevoort."

"Uh-oh," Devora said, like she was watching a scary movie and the dumb blond girl had just walked into the dark, abandoned house.

"I know, uh-oh is right," Naomi said. "I thought about not going and sneaking out early, but it was less than thirty minutes later that he came and tapped me to leave."

Naomi made her way to her bed. Her chest rose for a millisecond before it went back down again; she was breathing short breaths, and she could almost hear her heartbeat. She was feeling so much anxiety from all her thoughts and fears. It was the same way she had felt when she was sitting in Tyreek's hotel room, and yet she was still shaky hours later.

"Oh, he was focused. That new haircut must have really worked," Devora joked.

"Yeah, and I was wearing those liquid leggings we got and a short sweater."

"With what shoes?"

"The peep-toe ankle boots."

"Ah, shit! Let me find out you were in there killing 'em," Devora said.

"Anyways . . . so my coworker wanted to leave, too, so we all walked out. Tyreek said I could ride downtown with him. I felt so uncomfortable the whole ride, and I was thankful there were a couple of other people in the car."

"Enough—get to it. How did you end up playing 'ride 'em cowboy'?"

"At some point during all the noise, drinking, and partying at the suite, Tyreek came up to me and asked me if I would mind walking with him to his room down the hall."

"Uh-oh," Devora said again.

Naomi couldn't even laugh this time because in retrospect she knew she should have known better. She threw her body on her bed and lay flat on her back as she looked at the chipped paint on her ceiling. What bothered her was she had subconsciously decided to put her morals aside and dance with the devil, despite the fact that her man back home had called her twice while she was at the party, and she had told herself she would call him when she got home in a quiet environment. At that time she hadn't imagined she wouldn't make it home until the next morning.

"When we got to the room, he was sifting through a bag for a while, and we started talking. The conversation led to more conversation, and then that conversation led to us making out, and then the making out led to . . . ya know."

"Wow! Well, was it good?"

"It was . . . good, I guess. I was so nervous I was hardly into it."

"Well, that's normal."

"I was a little tipsy, so it helped, but I was so nervous."

"So what made you do it? That must have been some great conversation."

Naomi laughed a bit. "I don't know what made me do it. He just made me feel so sexy."

"Well, that's a good enough reason, I guess."

"I guess," Naomi said.

Naomi lay on her bed, reflecting on all the things that had taken place in the past week and everything that was to come. She was dressed only in her sweater and underwear, and she had no intent of getting changed any time soon. Naomi was realizing that the worst part about the whole thing was that she didn't feel overwhelmingly ashamed—she only felt a little guilty. There was no denial; even she had to admit to herself that that was a problem. It was as though she was becoming heartless.

Chapter 26

"It is nothing like I expected," Sereeta said to Reyna.

"What do you mean?" Reyna replied, not looking up from the magazine. Reyna and Sereeta were at the nail salon on Twenty-Seventh Street getting pedicures. They had decided to spend some time together doing something they had both planned on doing anyway this Saturday afternoon.

"At times it's like men's balls are just everywhere, and no one seems to care that I'm standing right there. They talk so candidly and get undressed and do whatever. In the beginning, I didn't know what to do."

"Getting undressed?" Reyna asked.

"Yeah, whenever I'm in the locker room getting something for Corey, they'll just continue to change clothes, like I'm not there."

"Maybe you weren't supposed to be there," Reyna said.

"I would only go when Corey sent me in there or he was in there and asked me to come."

"Well, how about you let him know you don't feel comfortable going into the locker room when other players are in there?"

"Yeah, I probably will. I just didn't want to start complaining so early on. I'm not trying to lose this job."

"Yeah, true. Well, if you don't think it's that bad, I guess you can handle it."

"Yeah, I can handle it of course. It just wasn't what I expected."

"Well, look at the bright side—the job will keep you on your toes."

"Yeah, that's true."

Reyna glanced back at her magazine—right before a beige-skinned middle-aged man approached them holding a few pairs of socks in his hand.

"Socks for one dollar," he said.

"No, thanks," Sereeta said before he could say anything else.

"I'll take two pairs," Reyna said as she reached in her purse for some singles. Once she found the money, she picked out two cute multicolored pairs of socks from his bag. When she was done and had paid for them, the gentleman walked away. For a few moments neither of them said anything to each other. Sereeta watched the lady working on her toes to see if she was doing a good job, and Reyna looked through the magazine.

"But you know who is so cute?" Sereeta said out of nowhere. "Brian James. He plays center."

"Since when you know all this basketball stuff?" Reyna asked.

"I'm learning and asking my guy friends questions as I go. I figure I don't want to be working among them and not know diddly."

Reyna just laughed.

"But if you pay attention to any sports at all, you will see him at some point. He's real tall and brown skinned. He is fine, though."

"Listen to you—focus, missy."

"I *am* focused. I'm just saying," Sereeta said and sat back in her chair.

"If you say so," Reyna said.

"He's single with no kids," Sereeta said quickly before the topic changed.

"How you know all that?" Reyna asked with a chuckle.

"Let's just say I've been doing my research."

"OK, you better watch yourself, miss, before you become a sports story—'*Corey Cox's female assistant gets slain by teammate's wife,*'" Reyna said.

"Whatever. He is not married, and I'm not trying to do anything with him. I just said he was fine, that's all."

"Yup, well, I know what that means, coming from you."

"And what is that supposed to mean?"

"Well, as we all know, you like fine guys," Reyna said as she shot Sereeta a look that said *Don't make me explain no further.*

Sereeta was in no mood to dig a hole she couldn't get out of. Besides, she knew what Reyna was talking about. Sereeta had recently found herself in quite a few predicaments with some guys' girlfriends and had taken the walk of shame quite a few mornings after a one-night stand. She couldn't deny that she was a weakling for a cute smile, some pretty eyes, and a nice body.

The pedicure took another twenty minutes before they were finished up. Once they were done, they made their way over to a cute bistro on Thirty-Second Street. Once inside, they ordered iced coffees and pastries. Neither of them had to work that day, so they thought it would be nice to hang out more and enjoy a sunny day in the city. The plan was to catch a movie after the bistro and then dinner at San Fritos, which apparently had the best Spanish food on the West Side.

Midway through her cappuccino and a few bites of her brownie à la mode, Sereeta heard her phone ring. She glanced down and saw Incoming call from C.C. "It's Corey," she said as she looked back up at Reyna.

"You are off—don't start answering on off days, or it will get out of hand," Reyna preached.

"Yeah, you're right. I didn't get off until eleven o'clock last night. I just want to enjoy a day to myself."

"Exactly. When you are someone's personal assistant, it's easy to let their life become yours until you don't have one of your own."

Sereeta had heard that before, so it didn't take much convincing. She leaned back and took another sip of her cappuccino. Reyna began talking about Michael when Sereeta's BlackBerry began to vibrate on the table. It was a text.

Hey, I need someone to come with me on this trip. We leave in a few hours. If I don't hear back from you soon, I'm going to have to get another assistant to come with me. It's an important trip.

"Damn," Sereeta said out loud.

"What's wrong?" Reyna asked.

"That's Corey. He said he needs me to come with him on some trip today."

"On your day off?"

"They don't care about all that—their lives must go on. He said if I don't go, he'll just get another assistant to come with him."

"Does that mean he'll fire you if you don't go?"

"I don't think so, but I still can't risk having someone else do my job either, even if it *is* just for a day. What if he likes her better and gets rid of me?"

"Well, do what you gotta do," Reyna said as she bit into her pie. "When do they leave?"

"He said in a few hours."

"So you have to get up now and go?"

"I guess so. Let me call him back first." Sereeta dialed his number.

Reyna just shook her head. She was very familiar with working overtime; before she had started her own practice, Reyna had been a slave to the system. Still, she was mad she would have to end their lovely afternoon so abruptly.

"Yes, Corey . . . I will see you then," Sereeta said into the phone. As soon as she hung up, she looked over at Reyna and remained quiet. Reyna made a puppy-dog face.

"It's cool. Let's go," Reyna said.

"I know this is horrible. I'm like his little slave child," Sereeta said as she gathered her things from the table.

"No. Duty calls, girl. What you going to do?"

Reyna left a fifty-dollar bill on the table, which she knew was more than enough for their caffeinated drinks and desserts, but the waiter had been friendly, so she didn't mind leaving her a pretty hefty tip.

"I know, but, geez. I just want a day to myself."

"Listen, jobs are hard to come by. Especially one like you have, so just do what you have to do. We can always get together another time."

They pushed open the doors and felt the brisk air hit their faces as the noise from the busy New York City street dominated their conversation.

"Well, I have to run home, pack a small bag, and meet him at the arena."

"Where are you going?"

"He has some business meetings in LA. His driver is picking us up from there."

"Well, at least you get to go to LA for a couple days. It won't be all work."

"Yeah, that's true. We'll see. I'll call you when I'm done rushing and on the way to meet him."

"OK," Reyna said as she reached over and gave her girl a hug and kiss good-bye.

Sereeta scurried into the street to hail a cab. Within moments one was slowing down to pick her up. She jumped in, gave her address, and immediately started going through her bag for her Black-Berry again. Corey hadn't sent anything new. She would be at her apartment in Harlem in no time, so she decided to utilize the time the best she could. She scheduled Corey's dry cleaning to be ready for pickup when she got to the arena; she rescheduled her hair appointment; and she called her parents to let them know she would be away for work all weekend. With less than two hours to get to the arena, the cab arrived at her place.

Chapter 27

Sereeta had exactly twenty minutes to spare as she walked up to the players' lounge. She could see a couple people leaving as she walked down the hallway. When she was a few feet away, she could see Corey sitting on the couch. She walked in and noticed a couple of the other players sitting around.

"What's up, Reeta!" one of the guys said before Sereeta made it fully into the room.

"Hey, guys," she said to everyone.

She hated being the only girl in the center of all the guys and having all the attention on her. She was a confident woman, but being around all these successful men, who could have any woman they desired, just made her feel a bit insecure at times.

"So where you two lovebirds going?" Levon asked.

Sereeta looked directly at him to see whom he was talking to, and he was looking right back at her.

"Knock it off, niggah," Corey replied. "I have

some business meetings in LA regarding some sponsorship stuff."

"Word. Bradley set that up?" Levon asked.

"Nah, my agent. I should be back in, like, a day or two."

"A'ight, be safe, my dude," Levon said as Corey stood and grabbed his bag.

As he walked around the room giving his teammates a pound, Sereeta was still trying to make sense of Levon's lovebird comment. Did they not know she was just his personal business assistant, or was there no such thing?

Once he was done with his good-byes, Sereeta made a gentle wave in the fellas' direction and she said, "See ya, guys."

Corey headed down the hallway, and Sereeta followed behind. He was dressed in dark blue 7 jeans, a navy blue track jacket with a white stripe down the sleeve, and white Air Force Ones with a Yankee fitted cap. He had on his diamond necklace with the diamond basketball piece and had his three-karat earring in his ear. His haircut was fresh, and his facial hair was perfectly trimmed. She wasn't sure if it was the little joke Levon had made, but this was one of the few times she had noticed just how handsome and smooth Corey was.

When they made their way to the front of the arena, the driver was waiting outside the Suburban. When he saw Corey and Sereeta, he opened the door. He took their bags and placed them in the back while Corey and Sereeta got settled. She felt a little awkward for a moment; being his assistant at times did feel the same as being a helpful girlfriend.

"I'm going to need you to locate all the sneaker shops by the hotel we're staying at and all the ones that have at least fifty pairs of my sneaker in stock. Arrange a slot for me to make an appearance and then call the radio station and let them know which stores I will be at and at what times," Corey said.

Midsentence, Sereeta pulled out a notepad and started writing. Her little girlfriend moment passed right by once his boss tone reminded her girlfriends didn't get fired.

"What days and times are your meetings?" she asked.

"I have one this evening and one tomorrow at two PM, I believe. I may have another, but I'm not sure. I'll call Troy and see."

"Who's Troy?"

Corey looked at her as though she had asked the wrong question or was out of line to ask any question at all.

"Troy is my agent."

"OK, well, once I get the stores that are carrying at least fifty pairs and their locations, I'll schedule the times around your business meetings."

"OK, and I'll have some other stuff I need you to do. I want to make the most of my time there. I probably won't be back until the season is done."

"Not a problem," Sereeta said as she took some notes.

Her head was down when she felt the ride come to a halt. She looked up, and they were in front of a gate. She couldn't see to the other side of the gate, but she noticed the driver punching a code in a box outside the gate. She started to put the pad away, trying to see where they were. The gate slowly began to open, and she could see a large open area. As the car pulled into the gate, Sereeta saw three planes parked on the left of the vehicle, and one was pulled out directly in front of them. She looked over at Corey; he was looking out the window, too.

The Suburban pulled up right in front of the plane that was pulled out, and the driver put the car in park. Sereeta tried to remain calm, but she was starting to get excited. She wasn't sure, but it looked like they were taking a private jet to LA, and Sereeta had never even been in first class, let alone a private jet. The driver opened the door on Corey's side first and then made his way to her side. Once he had opened both doors, he went to the back to get their bags. There was a staircase in front of the plane. Sereeta couldn't help but think of the movie *The Bodyguard* as she saw the little flight-attendant men walking around this exclusive airport.

Corey took his bag from the driver, Sereeta took hers, and they headed toward the stairs. A young lady met them at the bottom of the stairs.

"Hello, Mr. Cox. How are you this afternoon?"

"I'm great, thanks."

"We will be taking off in less than fifteen minutes. Please watch your step, get comfortable, and we will be with you shortly."

Sereeta felt how strange it was that people didn't acknowledge her presence when she was with Corey, but she tried to understand that people probably didn't know how to greet her. Once she got more comfortable with Corey, Sereeta would ask him to introduce her so people wouldn't think she was just some groupie.

They headed up the plane stairs, and as soon as they reached the plane, Sereeta couldn't believe what she was seeing. The plane was gorgeous. A plush cream couch, butter-soft leather recliner seats, brown patterned carpet, dim lighting, and a fully stocked bar met her. It was just like all the planes she had ever seen on the video channels or in the movies. The same young lady from the stairs came, took their bags, and stored them away.

"Hello, my name is Sarah. If you need anything, just let me know," she said to Sereeta.

"Thank you, my name is Sereeta. I'm Corey's assistant."

"Welcome," Sarah replied.

Sereeta couldn't tell if she was just being paranoid, but it looked like Sarah's expression read "Yeah, right, I've heard every cover-up excuse in the book not to call yourself a booty call."

The pilot walked back to Corey and Sereeta, introduced himself, and then headed back to get ready for take-off. Corey sat down in one of the recliner chairs and turned the flat-screen television to ESPN. Sereeta was relieved that there was another television so she wouldn't have to watch sports the entire flight. Sarah had disappeared, and Corey and Sereeta were the only ones left. Corey kicked off his sneakers, pulled off his track jacket, and got comfortable in his chair with his white tube socks and white T-shirt. Sereeta was still sitting and watching everything in amazement. Just to see the lifestyle that money could buy . . . She was at that very moment loving her job.

The plane was soon in the air, and Sereeta was sitting in her chair watching *The Real World*.

"Get comfortable. It's at least a four-hour ride," Corey said.

"Gotcha," Sereeta said.

She kicked off her shoes and cuddled herself up in her chair.

"You should come watch sports with me so you can learn the business you're in," Corey said.

"Is that an order?" she said playfully.

"No, just a suggestion."

The quiet from the plane, the dim lights, and the gorgeous surroundings had Sereeta in a good mood and feeling less formal in his presence. So, without making it a big deal or getting nervous, she got up and walked over to the chair beside Corey. The flat-screen was on the wall in front of him, and he was watching *NBA Inside Stuff*. Sereeta wasn't a stranger to the sport, but she definitely wasn't up on all the stats and news.

"So, tell me more about yourself," he said as soon as the first commercial came on.

"Well, I have a dog that I had to hurry and schedule a sitter for today," Sereeta said.

"My bad for the last-minute notice—my agent was going to come, but now he has to meet me there. And I had forgotten all about the trip until last night."

"It's cool, I was just messing with you," she said.

"You hungry?" he asked.

"Um, I guess."

"Stop fronting. You know you are hungry. This isn't a date. You don't have to fake the funk," he said, laughing.

Sereeta started laughing as well. Corey pressed the button for Sarah, and within five seconds she was walking through the doors.

"Can we both have a hot plate, please?" he asked.

"Filet mignon or lobster and shrimp?" she asked.

"Filet mignon. I want a man's meal," he said.

She looked at Sereeta.

"I will take the lobster and shrimp—I guess the woman's meal," Sereeta said.

"You think you funny," Corey said. "I knew you were going to order the shrimp anyway."

"How did you know that?"

"Because filet mignon—that meat is probably too much for you to handle."

God damn. Sereeta hadn't expected that. It had been meant as an innocent joke, but she was no dummy. That meat comment had been as sexual as he could've gotten without being blunt. That was code for *a brother like me is too much for you.* Sereeta never would've thought a line like that would impress her, but sitting there on a private jet with this man, any line was bound to work.

"I'm a big girl," she replied.

"Mmmm, OK."

The reporters were back talking on *NBA Inside Stuff,* and Corey was back listening. Sereeta didn't know if she had misinterpreted his comment—if it hadn't been meant as a pass at all—or if the moment had just passed them by. She continued to watch the program, but her mind was a million places. All of a sudden, she was feeling moisture between her legs that was a sign of only one thing.

He is your boss, she had to remind herself. *This is a business trip.* She couldn't believe she had almost lost sight that easy—from a trip on a private jet and a menu with lobster on it, she had been almost ready to go against every rule she had made for herself. The number-one rule, of course, was no unprofessional behavior whatsoever with the boss.

Chapter 28

Corey had gotten up to go to the bathroom and by the time he reached the back of the plane, Sereeta was reaching for her phone in dire need of calling Reyna. Once she pulled out the phone, though, she saw the big red symbol indicating no service. *Damn.* She had forgotten that she was thousands of miles in the air. She sat there calmly and watched the television. She figured maybe Corey's absence was a good time to just get up and go back to where she had initially been sitting— pretend she thought TV time was over. At least it would put some distance between them, and she could try to cool off.

She walked back to her seat on the opposite side of the plane and began to pretend that she was fiddling through her bag so if he came out, it would look like she was over there for a reason and not just making a run for it. She fiddled until she heard the bathroom door opening, placed the bag on her lap, and sifted through it. Corey walked past her and went to his seat without saying anything. Within a few seconds she had pulled out her breath mints and lip gloss—she had to find something in her extended hunt. Once she applied some lip gloss and popped a breath mint in her mouth, she put her bag back down beside her and began to watch some more MTV.

"You done with your tutorial?" Corey asked.

Sereeta turned back and saw him watching her watch MTV. "No, not at all. This just caught my eye for a second. Here I come," she said as she lifted out of her seat slowly like she was intrigued by what was on the television screen.

She was kind of hoping that Corey would say, "Just messing with you" or "Never mind." No such chance. He patiently waited for her to come sit back down. It even felt as though he was watching her the entire time. She had to admit that although she was trying to prevent the situation from going anywhere, she was very flattered by the attention.

The NBA highlights were on, and Corey seemed truly interested in every play. She wondered why he wanted her to watch it with him so badly, but she figured she could just watch and learn as well. A whole ten-minute segment went by without Corey or Sereeta saying a word. Highlights, commentary, clips from old games—all NBA talk, and Corey seemed like he didn't even realize Sereeta was sitting there. She figured she would go to the bathroom and give herself one last chance at escape; this time she wouldn't come back. She would admit that she would rather watch her own television and relax.

She waited a few seconds and then stood up. She

took a step and said, "Excuse me." As she reached
the aisle, she stopped when she heard him speak.

"You must be scared of me," he said, never taking his eyes off the television.

Sereeta could feel her heartbeat speed up some.
"Nooo . . ." she said.

"Yeah, that's why you keep running away. It's
cool, though."

"I was going to the bathroom," she said.

"Mmmm-hmmm. OK," he said as he glanced
back at her real quick before looking at the television again.

Sereeta walked to the bathroom in shock. She
was trying to figure out Corey's game. Was he all of
a sudden trying to be a cool boss or something,
was he flirting, or did he really just want her to
learn more about basketball? It was hard to tell—
he was being so strange. She used the bathroom
the little she had to go and braced herself for
going back to the seats. As she washed her hands,
she looked in the mirror to assess her appearance.
Her hairstyle was on point, and her face was in
order—no boogies or crust anywhere. She had on
lip gloss, light makeup and very little eye shadow
and powder. She was thankful she had taken the
time to look a little spruced up earlier. For all she
knew, Corey didn't even notice any of that; he didn't
seem to look at her like that. That was when she realized she was probably bugging out.

Corey probably had a dozen girls he dealt with,
and most of them were probably drop-dead gorgeous or gave phenomenal brain. Either way she
most likely couldn't compete with what he was looking for. Besides, she had Mark . . . the Mark she had

been in too much of a rush to call and tell she was going away. They were far from boyfriend and girlfriend or anything, but she did like him quite a bit and was hoping to keep things moving forward.

She finally decided to exit the bathroom—thinking in the mirror had already taken a couple of extra minutes. She didn't want Corey thinking she was trying to hide out in the bathroom. She made her way down the aisle; Corey was still in his seat. She knew she would be playing herself if she sat back in her seat like she had planned. It would look suspect after he had just commented about her running away. She knew at the end of the day he was her boss, and she was getting paid to be there, so if he wanted to watch basketball with her, so be it. She remembered Debbie's creed that the job was to assist with whatever they needed assistance with.

Sereeta sat down beside him and scooted back in the chair to show she was getting comfortable and settled. "So, what did I miss?" she asked.

He seemed to sense her playful sarcasm and looked over at her with a smirk.

"Nothing much," he replied. "The game is about to come on."

"Oh, cool. I would much rather watch a game than hear the commentators talk anyway."

"The commentators are helpful because they inform you about the people's opinions and summarize league issues and stuff," Corey said.

His face was serious, like he was really appreciative of what it was the reporters had to offer.

"You really are passionate about basketball. That's impressive."

"Well, it's how I make my living, and I've been playing since I was seven. I guess I have to be passionate," he said.

"Well, that's good. I wish I was that passionate about something."

"I'm sure you are—you just don't know what it is yet."

"I know, they say think about what you would do all the time for free, and that is your passion."

"Well, that's one way of putting it. Then you can also see what makes you feel alive and free every time you do it or are around it. What makes you feel like you can conquer the world or do whatever you put your mind to."

Sereeta's eyes lifted upward as she looked at a corner of the plane. Corey could tell she was trying to think of an answer.

"Other than sex," he said.

Sereeta laughed but didn't look in his direction.

"That's how I feel about basketball. When I am on that court with the ball in my hand, I feel like magic."

"Wow," Sereeta said. "I feel sad. I can't think of anything that makes me feel magical."

"Sometimes it takes time to find out what it is. You have to think long and hard," Corey said.

Sereeta laughed. "Sounds like sex again."

She noticed two seconds too late that that had probably not been the best thing to say. If she was trying to keep things professional, references to sex probably wouldn't cut it.

"That's fine. Sex is a passion for many."

"I guess you're right. Too bad I can't get paid for doing it."

"It depends. There's always the option of getting paid *while* doing it."

Sereeta could tell from the suggestive tone of his voice that he might have an idea in mind of how she could enjoy her passion. She looked away and pretended to still be thinking, although all she could think about was what to say next and if she should end this or pursue it.

"Well, I don't know. I will try to figure out what my passion is, and I'll get back to you," she said as she looked back over at him.

"So sex doesn't work for you? You don't like sex?" he asked.

Sereeta could feel her heart racing. Her hands became clammy, and her underarms felt tingly. *What the hell? Why are you flipping out?* she asked herself. *Calm down.* "Who doesn't like sex? Of course I do," she said.

"OK, so getting paid while doing it can work for you."

She knew what he was hinting at. She got paid to work for him, so if she dabbled in some sex while she was still on the clock, it could be a nice arrangement. *Do I look like a prostitute? Don't you think I like sex, but with people I care about and who care about me?* She could feel Corey looking at her, but her mouth wasn't moving. Finally, she replied, "I guess it could work for me, but it may not."

"It depends what it is, I am sure. I'm just saying when you're looking for your passion, don't rule anything out."

Corey turned back to watch the game.

"I guess you're right," she said.

She sat there wondering if he was playing a

mental game or if she just couldn't read him whatsoever. His words were flirtatious, but his actions showed no interest at all. She didn't know, so she decided to just ignore it and go over to her seat to get her little sweater. As she got up, he reached out and touched her hand. She looked down at him.

"Where you going?" he asked.

"Just right over there to grab my sweater."

"I don't know what it is, but I really want to have sex with you right now."

Sereeta's eyes shot open. She couldn't lie—random thoughts of sex were popping in and out of her mind, too, but this was the last thing she had expected him to say. "Really?"

"Yes, and I know you work for me, so I understand if you'd rather not. I'm just telling you because I'm hard as hell right now, and it's because of you—not the NBA highlights."

Sereeta giggled, but inside she was as nervous as hookers in church.

"I'm flattered, Corey, but you said you wanted us to remain professional."

"And I do. Maybe there's just some sexual tension built up between us. We can diffuse the tension and then act like it never happened and remain professional."

"Is that even possible?"

"Sure it is. I've done it before."

That didn't make Sereeta feel any better. She was thinking about everything Debbie had said about assisting players with what they needed and being expendable. She was also remembering Debbie saying how once you were intimate with them, they took care of you. Then she was also remembering that it was a form of prostitution. She didn't know what to do. She had to admit that she was feeling him, and she also felt the sexual tension. "I don't know. . . ." she said.

Before she could get the words out of her mouth, Corey was unbuckling her pants. The instant she felt his hands on her waist, she could feel her body quiver slightly. She was standing up, and he was still sitting, so he was eye level with her waist. He opened her pants and began to run his fingers along her bikini line.

"You don't have to know anything—let's just enjoy the ride," he said.

He reached in and began to softly kiss around her navel. Sereeta could feel herself moisten. As he kissed around her belly button and bikini line, he was gently caressing and grabbing one of her butt cheeks. Sereeta's eyes scanned the plush plane as she took in every sensation her body was feeling from his touches. He began to slowly lower her pants as he rubbed and kissed in all the bare areas. She kicked off her pants once he had gotten them low enough, and then she stood there in her underwear and shirt. She was wondering if he was going to remove her panties and continue to kiss, but she wasn't sure ballplayers went that far with their "girls." He had gone under her shirt and begun to rub on her breasts. Sereeta pulled her arms out of her shirt and removed it. Her demi-cut green bra matched her yellow and green thong, and from the reflection in the window, she was looking sexy.

She felt like she was in a movie; it didn't take long before all her thoughts and fears disappeared. She was feeling Corey and enjoying the ride. By the time Corey stood up and began to unbuckle his pants, Sereeta was dripping wet and beyond anxious to feel him inside her. He bent her over the recliner chair he was sitting in and entered her. The next five minutes were filled with long, hard thrusts. Sereeta moaned and screamed as she received her first sexual penetration in over a month. She had forgotten about everything, including all the rules, as she grabbed on to the chair for dear life.

Chapter 29

Madison was looking out the window of the cab. She knew she was close to the venue but she was looking for the exact location. She looked down at her BlackBerry and read the address for Sexiness on the Rocks. She had told the cab driver the exact address. Cîroc, the latest luxury liquor, was sponsoring an industry mixer at which all the VIPs were requested to dress their sexiest. This was right up Madison's alley, so although she hadn't been out too much lately, this was an event she planned to attend. She was supposed to meet up with Tamika from Bad Boy Records, but Tamika was running behind, and Madison had told her she would meet her there.

Madison wore a black and gray fitted mini dress with black ankle boots. The dress had thick stripes of black and gray alternating side by side; the black stripes were made of a see-through material. She had wanted to wear her strappy shoes, but she hadn't been sure if the weather was warm enough. This dress was one of Madison's many one-of-a-kind, customized dresses that she loved. She'd had it made for a celebrity wedding and had never gotten to wear it again, so she figured tonight's little festivities were a good opportunity to get a repeat wear. Her hair was swept up in a slicked-back ponytail; a small bang dropped over one eye. Her drop diamond earrings, a simple diamond band on her right ring finger, and a tennis bracelet were all she wore for jewelry. She felt like a million bucks when she stepped out of the cab.

As she approached the entrance to the loft, she could see some of her colleagues standing out front. Cathy, the VP of promotions from Capital Records, was standing in the front of the line speaking with security. There were several others standing around, which usually meant they weren't "found" on the guest list, and someone was going to have to come get them, or they were going to have to go home. Madison said some quiet hellos to a few folks and made her way to the front of the line. The bouncer asked her name, and she told him. He scanned the list and removed the red rope for her to enter.

"Are you with anyone?" he asked her.

"Yes, she's my guest," Madison replied.

Madison pointed to Cathy, who was at the other end of the rope still talking to the security guard. The bodyguard called the other bodyguard and signaled to let Cathy by. Once Cathy was on the other side of the rope, Madison was waiting for her.

"Thanks," Cathy said and gave Madison a hug.

"No problem, I know how these promoters get the lists messed up. Then they expect you to stand

out there while they find someone. It's so annoy-
ing," Madison replied.

"And embarrassing, for that matter," Cathy added.

"That, too."

"Please, that never happens to you."

"You'd be surprised. There's been an error or
two. I can't say that person still has their job, but it
happened," Madison said with a laugh.

They made their way to the elevator that was to
take them to the main loft where the party was taking place. The security guard held the door as they
got on the elevator with two other people. It was a
small elevator, only enough for a few people at a
time. Once everyone was in, the elevator conduc-
tor pressed the button to close the door. Just as the
doors were closing, Madison saw a glimpse of a familiar face on the other side. A familiar face—but
not one she wanted to see tonight. She'd seen the
side of Neil's face right before the doors had
closed. He'd been standing in the lobby and more
than likely was with Polytics. In the back of her
mind, Madison was hoping there was some rare
chance that Neil was with some other executives or
another artist—anyone but Polytics.

"I have to run to the bathroom when we get inside. Meet me by the bar," Madison said to Cathy,
preparing for her escape.

When the elevator doors opened, all that was on
Madison's mind was to stand at the other end of
the room, away from the elevator. She tried to walk
along the wall where there was some space, but as
soon as she walked in, she was approached by Kelly
from Warner Music.

"Hey, babe, how are you?" Kelly said.

Kelly was a longtime colleague, one of the few in the business with whom Madison never had any issues.

"Hey, missy," Madison said.

"How long have you been here?"

They hugged, and Madison tried to walk and talk, but Kelly seemed to not want to walk along with her, so Madison had to stop so she could listen.

"Just about a half an hour, not long."

"Will you be staying a while? I have to run to the bathroom," she said as she positioned her body to head to the back.

"Sure, go ahead. I will see you."

Madison felt like she was running from the feds or something. All she could imagine was Polytics and Neil stepping off the elevator and then her being forced to have to have an awkward conversation with them. She made her way through the crowd. She just simply smiled at, waved at, or told she would be back to everyone who spoke to her.

She got to the rear and noticed a small sitting area with an empty seat. She sat and pulled out her phone. If only her BlackBerry were her KITT car, and she were Michael Knight—if only her phone could suddenly inform her of some escape route or some amazing tips on how to handle the situation. There were no incoming e-mails, missed calls, or electronic advice, so she put the phone away.

She sat there and looked around the room at all the sexy ladies dressed in their short dresses and stilettos. The men wore suits and dress pants—a few had dress shirts with the top buttons undone.

This was their way of bringing sexy back, she figured. And then there were quite a few people who had paid no damn attention at all to the sexy theme of the night. Some folks were wearing sweat suits, jeans, baseball caps, and whatever else they had worn to work that day. That was the music industry for you—no one had to comply with anything. The industry was filled with people that were "too cool" to care.

Madison felt movement beside her. When she looked over, a young man was sitting down next to her. She turned away and then looked back, realizing she knew him from somewhere. He was talking to another young lady who was standing beside him.

"Is your name Corey?" Madison asked at a lull in their conversation.

"Yes," he replied.

"Hi. Yes, Corey Cox—you play for the Knicks. You did an interview at my radio station a few months ago."

"Oh, yeah, you work at Drama Ninety-Nine, right?"

"Yes, I do. I'm the program director. I'm the person who allowed you to come up there and promote your new sneaker and athletic line," she said, laughing.

"Well, thank you very much, it's a pleasure," he said, reaching out his hand for a shake.

As Madison shook his hand, she noticed that the young lady he was standing with had looked away.

"This is my assistant, Sereeta," Corey introduced.

"Nice to meet you," Madison said as she shook her hand as well.

"Let me give you her business card in case you ever need anything from me or tickets to one of the games," he said, gesturing for Sereeta to give Madison a card.

"Sure, and I'll give her mine as well, in case you need anything."

Sereeta and Madison swapped cards.

"Great, I'll surely be in touch. You two take care," Madison said as she stood up.

She looked toward the front of the loft and didn't see Polytics or Neil anywhere. She refused to hide out in the back all night—she hadn't come to this party looking hot to trot just to have some artist keep her boxed in a corner. She began to walk through the crowd to see if she saw Cathy or Kelly. She looked over by the bar, didn't see Cathy, and figured she had gotten tired of waiting or hadn't reached the bar just yet. So she walked around a bit more to see who else had shown up. There were several executives from different record labels, some radio people from competing stations, and a bunch of people Madison had no idea who they were. She mingled with several and caught up with a few colleagues.

Eventually, Cathy walked up. "Where were you?" she asked.

"I was walking around looking for you," Madison said.

"I went looking for you in the bathroom. Thought you got kidnapped."

Madison thought to herself, *What, did you find out about stalker Polytics?*

She laughed. "No, I'm still safe."

"I saw Tamika from Bad Boy. She is looking for you, too."

"Oh, she's here. Good. I was supposed to come with her, but she wasn't ready when I was, so she told me to come ahead of her."

"Yeah, she told me. She asked me if I'd seen you when I bumped into her. She was over by the front," Cathy said.

Cathy pointed over to the second bar in the front right-hand side of the loft. Madison looked over but instead saw Neil walking in her direction. *Aw, damn.* She had almost forgotten, for a split second, that she was hiding from them. She didn't see Polytics, so she was relieved about that. Neil was walking with a girl Madison didn't recognize.

"What's up, Madison?" he said when he reached her.

"Hey, Neil."

"How are you?"

"Good, yourself?"

Madison figured Neil knew all about her situation with Polytics, and she wasn't sure how he would act or if he would say anything. She was ashamed of her actions, but Madison wasn't the type to hang her head low for anybody.

"Neil," he said as he extended his hand to Cathy.

"Cathy—nice to meet you," Cathy said.

Madison turned to look at the young lady with Neil, hinting at the need for an introduction. She was just being nosy—for some reason she was curious about this girl's relation to Neil and Polytics, if any.

"Hi, this is Naomi. She works at Intheloop. She's Tiffany's assistant."

"Oh. How nice to meet you. I love your boss," Cathy blurted.

"Thanks, nice to meet you as well," Naomi said.

"Hi, I'm Madison. Nice to meet you. I have probably spoken to you before because I speak to your boss all the time."

"Do you work for Drama Ninety-Nine?" Naomi asked.

"Yes, that's me."

"Oh, yes, I do know you. Tiffany has asked me to get you on the phone several times."

"Yeah, and my assistant, Alexis, probably speaks to you more so."

"Yes, Alexis. We're usually trying to coordinate meetings for you two or good times to call back," Naomi said with a chuckle.

"Well, nice to meet you, and I am loving your dress," Madison said.

Naomi couldn't believe that Madison Cassell had complimented her dress. Naomi was finally feeling like she fit in with her new life. The dress was a BCBG dress she had gotten on sale. It was brown and cream with an off-the-shoulder cinch top. The bottom was flowy and free, and she wore a brown knee boot with gold accessories. She wasn't showing off much aside from her shoulders, but she felt sexy.

"Naomi has only been living in New York for a few months, so I'm trying to bring her out to more events so she can get to know people and mingle."

Naomi hung her head in embarrassment that he had told them in a nice way that she was lame.

"Oh, well, call me any time you want tickets to any of the shows. We will help get you acclimated to New York life," Madison said.

"Thanks," Naomi said. She realized she should actually thank Neil for saying that—she was thankful for Madison's offer. But she still had a bad vibe from Neil—the truth was that Neil had been there the night of the Weezy party, and he had noticed—like many others—that she and Tyreek had disappeared; it seemed that tonight he was just trying to get his shot at the goods. Naomi had found it a bit odd that he had offered to take her with him to this event and had told her the theme was to dress your sexiest. She had been suspicious and thought about declining until she'd figured she would rather not just watch television all night. She hadn't heard from her boyfriend in a few days—he seemed pretty upset about his unanswered calls the night of Tyreek and her lack of explanation for not calling until the middle of the next day. Naomi felt guilty talking to him, so when he'd hung up, upset, she'd figured it was best to let him call back when he had cooled off.

A woman walked up to the group, and Neil took it as a chance to say good-bye. He and Naomi headed toward the bar in the back.

Approaching the group, Tamika smacked Madison on the hip. "There the hell you are," she said.

"I was looking for you." Madison laughed, looking to Cathy for support.

"Yeah, I told her you were looking for her," Cathy chimed in.

"Yeah, yeah. I'm about to go soon. I'm about to

be wasted with all these free drinks flowing around here."

"I know. The Cîroc and lemonade is pretty damn good, if I must say so myself," Madison said.

"Yeah, they have this Cîroc and strawberry juice drink. The waitress brought me two of those, and I downed them in, like, four gulps. I am definitely taking a cab home," Tamika said.

Tamika had used to work at Drama 99, and she and Madison were pretty cool. She had left to get a marketing position at Bad Boy, but they had remained in touch and known each other for at least seven years. The industry was like a revolving door, people coming and going year after year. To have a friend for years was always something to be cherished in the music business. It was a cutthroat field—people were all about what you could do for them. Tamika was one of Madison's colleagues who Madison felt was a good friend, for real.

"Well, if you're leaving, I'm leaving, too," Madison said. "I thought we were going by Cafeteria after this."

"We can still go, I just don't want to stay here much longer. But no rush," Tamika said.

"Did you guys notice Corey Cox?" Cathy asked out of the blue.

"Yeah, he did an interview at the station. He's a nice guy," Madison said.

"Yes, he *is* a cutie," Cathy said.

Madison and Tamika looked at her, shocked that she would say that. Cathy was an older white woman, and Corey was a younger black man. They just didn't think Corey would be her cup of tea.

"I love the Knicks, what can I say?" Cathy said when she noticed their surprised looks.

"Yeah, he's here with his assistant," Madison said. "Nice guy."

"His assistant—yeah, OK. We both know what that means," Cathy added.

"Yeah. She's assisting him, alright. Assisting him on her knees," Tamika said.

Madison and Cathy laughed at Tamika's comments. They knew it wasn't right to talk about folks, but everyone knew that was what these parties were all about. They were marketed as networking events, but very little networking was done. People usually ended up with people they already knew, and entry-level staff were too afraid to approach the business executives. As a result, the networking was minimal; people were too cool to look eager or ask someone for something. So these events usually ended up being about showing off status and getting gossip about who was with whom and who had left with whom. Industry events served very little purpose most times—that was why Madison didn't attend many. This one was cool, though, because she got to be sexy, and she enjoyed the free Cîroc.

After about three or four more generic conversations, Madison began to feel as though she had done her time. Cathy had gone to the bar to get another fruity Cîroc concoction, and Tamika was a few feet away talking to a VJ from Fuse. The room was still pretty filled; plenty of people had shown up since Madison had arrived. She could tell that the evening was nowhere near over, and the loft hadn't seen all its guests for the night just yet. Still, she was ready to call it a night—she still had to work in the morning, and she felt as though a true VIP should know to come late and leave early. She walked across the room to the other side of the floor, figuring she would finish the last few sips of her drink, place it by the bar, and then signal for Tamika to leave with her.

She leaned against the wall and fiddled with her straw. She knew it wouldn't be long before someone came over to talk with her—everyone wanted a chance to speak with a woman of her influence if they could get a moment alone. Realizing that she might get cornered by someone she really didn't want to talk to, she began to slowly roam along the wall. There were three big gentlemen standing a few steps away, so instead of walking around them, she decided to just take her last few sips there. Just as she lifted her head from her glass, she felt someone bump into her. When she turned around, it was one of the gentlemen in the group.

"Excuse me," he said.

"Excuse me," she said as she reached out her arm to gain some room between them. Just as she stepped away, she recognized one of the other gentlemen in the group. Her head leaned to the side as she tried to register his face and remember where she knew him from. By the time the memory hit her, Polytics had stepped in front of him and was walking toward her. Just as she grasped that Polytics was coming, she also realized that the three gentlemen were his bodyguards.

"What's up?" he said.

"Hey there, Poly," she said.

"Why didn't you tell me you were coming tonight?"

"Uh . . . I didn't know I had to check in with you," she said.

"Oh, you being a smart ass, I see," he replied.

"You know, I don't know where we crossed paths, but you seem to have some things twisted."

"No, I think you have some things twisted. As I told you the other day, I am no little boy," Polytics said.

His voice was raised by this time; people had turned around to look to see what was going on. As though his presence didn't draw enough attention, the sound of his raised voice and the sight of his angry face were not helping at all.

"Would you calm the hell down?" she said.

"No, I am tired of you trying to fucking play me," he said.

Madison was in shock once again. She realized she might have a bona fide psycho on her hands. Who in a million years would've thought a street dude like himself, with this shiny new music career, would act like this? Madison was hoping to avoid a scene and turned to walk away. As she took a step, she felt a large, strong hand grab her arm. She tried to yank it free, but the grip was tighter than she thought. She turned around to see the look in his eyes, and she discreetly asked for the removal of his hand from her arm.

"Yo, come with me downstairs before you make me show my ass in here," he said.

She looked at him, and he bucked his eyes back at her to send his message to her that he wasn't playing. Madison knew that if she did not comply, there was a very high possibility that he would only behave worse and embarrass the hell out of her. "I am not being escorted out of here. Let go of my arm, and I will walk with you," she said.

He let go of her arm, and she began to walk. She glanced over her shoulder, and he was a step behind. From what she could tell, the security guards were only a few steps behind him, and although the five of them exiting at the same time seemed to be attracting all the eyes in that area of the loft, she preferred that the security and others would come with them. She was also kind of hoping that Tamika was close enough to see her leaving with him and would tag along, but for some reason she reached the elevator, and neither Cathy nor Tamika came running up to her asking where she was going. She was heavily contemplating each of her moves, and she quickly decided that trying to get Cathy or Tamika would only incite Polytics to say or do something stupid. She wanted to curse him out, but she couldn't afford to do it in that room with all those people watching. It was bad enough there would be rumors surfacing from the little scene he had caused; she wasn't trying to make it worse.

The elevator held just the five of them as they went down. The elevator operator stood stuffed in the corner, trying to squeeze in with these muscular men; he had asked one of them to stay behind when they were all getting on, but they had refused. Madison stood a few feet away from Polytics, from this artist who had seemed so charismatic and respectable in his music videos and in the public eye, but, as she was realizing, was not quite mentally stable.

The elevator doors opened, and they were back on the lobby floor. This time it wasn't as crowded as when Madison had arrived. They all trickled into the lobby. A few cameras went off—seemed to be some Web-site photographers and possibly some press. Madison couldn't tell at all because her main goal was trying not to be in the shot. Polytics didn't seem to realize that leaving the party with the program director of Drama 99 FM would make for a good news story on AllHipHop.com.

Once they made it outside, Polytics's Suburban was parked right in front. As much as Madison didn't want to be with him, she was happy to get in the truck, knowing no one could see them any longer or take any more pictures. They got in, and two of the security guards went to the Suburban across the street; one got in their front seat. Madison and Polytics were in the backseat.

"You just love drawing attention to yourself, don't you?" she asked.

Pow! He suddenly smacked the shit out of her. Madison's head swung around. She instantly touched her face and looked at him, shocked. Her mouth was dropped open, and no words would come out.

"You got me twisted," he said. "I am not one of these little artists that you play puppet with. I know who you are and what you do, but at the end of the day we are both not untouchable. You are not going to disrespect me as a man," he said.

Madison sat quiet. She had never been hit by a man before, and she had no desire to be hit again. When she faced forward, the driver and security guard were faced forward as well, bopping along to the music on the stereo as they drove, or at least they were pretending to.

"So you not going to say anything?" he said.

"What do you want me to say, Clarence? I obviously don't know you very well, and to be quite honest, I don't know what to say to you."

"What does that mean?" he asked.

"It just means that I don't know what you want from me!" she said. She was hoping he couldn't hear the fear in her voice and think he should continue to intimidate her, but she was scared to death and knew it was probably obvious.

"All I want from you is your respect, Madison," he said.

Madison couldn't help but think how he must be truly crazy; she wondered if he had a real psychological problem. She couldn't imagine that she had got caught up with the one deranged rapper in New York. What kind of luck was that?

"I respect you," she said.

"When I met you, I wasn't flirting with you so you could play my record. I was really digging you," he said.

"I understand," she said.

"When we had sex in your office, I didn't want that to be the end of us. That was not all I wanted from you. I could get sex anywhere," he said.

"I understand."

"Stop saying you understand, yo! Say what you feel," he said.

She could tell he was becoming a bit flustered. "Clarence, I am going to be honest with you. I have never slept with an artist before while I was in this position at the station. You were the first. It was something I did without thinking. You were attractive, and there was something about you I was feeling. I wasn't trying to play you, but I realized that if anyone found out about you and me, it could cost me my job and my relationship," she said.

"Relationship?" he asked. "You never told me you were in a relationship."

"Clarence, we barely had a chance to talk about our personal lives. I don't know, I assumed you had a girlfriend, too."

"Well, I don't. I am single, and that's why I thought it was possible that things didn't have to end after that one night."

"My man and I have been having a lot of problems—to be honest, I haven't been that happy with him. I wasn't trying to play you. You were definitely what I wanted and needed at that time. However, as flattered as I am that you wanted to be with me, even if I were single, due to my job, it wouldn't work," she said.

"I could take care of both of us. My money is right," he said.

"That's nice of you, Clarence, but it's not that simple."

Madison had almost forgotten for a second that she had a red, throbbing cheek. Just hearing him open up and finally listen to what she was saying without going postal was alluring to her. She felt her phone vibrate through her purse. She pulled the bag open, flipped her phone over, and saw it was Tamika calling. She knew now wasn't the time to answer.

"Yeah, well. It can be worked out if you want it to be," he said.

He sounded like a ten-year-old boy. She knew he was younger than her, but she never would have thought he would be the one catching feelings. It was sweet, she had to admit, but his dose of psycho behavior dampened all his charm. Hoping to keep him calm and not feeling "disrespected as a man," Madison thought it was best to just keep the conversation at this level. She didn't want to seek an apology for his violence and invoke another outburst, and she didn't want to sound as if she weren't open to options and possibly upset him.

"I will think it through, Clarence, and we will talk about it next week, I promise. I just need some time to think about all this," she said. "For now, can you just drop me up the street on Fourteenth? I am supposed to meet a friend."

"Why can't I come? It's a guy friend?" he asked.

"No, it's a girl. I was at that party with her, but I left without her to talk to you," she said.

He looked at her and then sat up and leaned forward.

"Yo, stop at Fourteenth Street," he told the driver.

"Thanks," she said as he leaned back.

He sat back and looked out the window. "Listen, Madison, I'm sorry if I've been rough or too aggressive. I am a man who knows what he wants. I really am feeling you. You are a successful, attractive, mature young woman, and I can use you on my team," he said.

"Thank you," she said. "You want me to join your team, Clarence? I have a job."

"No, like, to have my back. Hold me down. Be my lady," he said.

"You can have any woman you want. Why do you want me?"

When she'd first felt attraction toward him, she recalled being a bit insecure and competitive with his exotic women company, but now she felt totally different and could care less if she wasn't his cup of tea.

"They come a dime a dozen. I can have truck-loads of them, but ones like you aren't as easy to find," he said.

Madison couldn't lie to herself and say she wasn't flattered. He was a younger, richer man. She had to admit that if she didn't have to worry about her job and he wasn't so unpredictable and possibly crazy, she would consider leaving Jamahl for a walk on the fun side with Polytics.

"I appreciate that, and I will definitely consider your offer. It's just that my career means a lot to me."

"If you end it with me, I am going to share our little secret, and then your career won't be all that sound anyway," he said.

She looked at him, shocked again. "Are you threatening me?" she asked.

He looked back at her with a blank stare.

"You *are* joking, right?" she asked.

"Not really. I want you, Madison. I won't do you dirty—just give me a chance."

Madison just sat there, trying to think exactly what she was supposed to say at this point. This man was really off his rocker. She wondered how he had ever gained this much power and popularity without anyone noticing. Then she realized how accommodating his team was—they probably all knew and just didn't say a word because he was feeding them all.

Fourteenth Street was the next corner, and she could feel the Suburban slowing down.

"I will call you soon—I'm just asking that you give me time to think," she said.

"I will be out of the country for the next few days. How much time?" he asked.

"A week or two, just give me that. Don't come to the office, don't stop me if you see me out. Just give me the time to think."

"OK, but in two weeks we will talk," he said.

"Yes."

The car stopped, and she got out. As soon as the black Suburban pulled off, she hailed a cab to go home.

Chapter 30

She was running late for work. Naomi had been out late the night before and had had a rough time waking up this morning. She spent the entire train ride trying to figure out her thoughts and to self-reflect. She didn't understand how things were happening so fast. All of a sudden she felt like the popular girl in school—and even when she'd been in school, she hadn't known what that felt like.

She got off at her stop and began to walk toward the staircase to exit the subway. She noticed a man walking directly in front of her. She could only see a portion of his profile from behind, but from what she could see, he looked like he was a handsome young man. The train platform was too crowded to walk closer to him to get to see more of what he looked like. She could see the tag sticking out of his hat, which was obviously there by mistake—she was close enough to read the XL imprint. She thought maybe she could use that as an

excuse to tap him and get a better look at his face
and possibly the start of a conversation, too.

She felt desperate, trying to walk as fast as possible to keep up with him in the crowd. She didn't
know why she was so intrigued by a man she didn't
even know and hadn't seen fully. Maybe it was the
curiosity that was killing her—the curiosity about
whether his profile and cool demeanor did him
justice or whether it was a false advertisement. She
could see his fair, medium-brown skin tone, his
well-fitting jeans, leather jacket, and stylish paperboy cap. Something was making her follow this
man as if she knew exactly the reason.

Finally, he made a turn past the staircase—a
turn she had no intention of making—and she realized she would be crazy to follow him. All for
what? So she continued her way up the staircase to
the upper level of the train station, all while trying
to get a few last glances at him. She felt like she was
defeated, having never actually seen his face. If
she saw him another day with another outfit, she
wouldn't even know it was him. *This sucks.*

As she walked down Broadway wondering "what
if," she realized she was overanalyzing something
that wasn't such a big deal. After all, he could have
been a married man with eight baby mamas and a
jacked-up face. Why did she even care? Being away
from her boyfriend was causing her heart and
mind to wander much further from him than she
cared to admit. She knew that working in the entertainment business had subjected her to only the
worst of options half the time, but was she that
hard up?

She didn't know why she would even be considering getting to know another man after last night anyway. The longer she thought about it, the more she forgot about the strange guy in the paperboy hat. She began to remember that she had enough on her plate for the time being. She had spent the entire night with Neil, drinking and hanging out. When they had left the Cîroc party, they had headed to some other industry party hosted by some artist and his band. She knew there was a chance he and Tyreek were cool enough to share stories, but that didn't stop her from rolling with Neil until three o'clock in the morning. She had a feeling that maybe Tyreek wasn't feeling her all that much, or at least not the way she was hoping he would.

Naomi knew there was a chance she could bump into Tyreek while hanging out with Neil, and a small piece of her wondered if Tyreek would be concerned or at least a little jealous. It seemed she couldn't say no to the attention. She told herself it was just innocent fun, but at the end of the night, it wasn't innocent anymore. When Neil dropped her off, he reached in for a kiss and began fondling her breasts. Naomi, buzzed off a few drinks and a bit afraid to say no to him, went ahead and participated. It wasn't until she felt his hand trying to go up her dress that she stopped short and pulled away slightly. She wasn't ready to have sex with yet another guy in less than a week. It surely wasn't out of respect for Tyreek—he had barely spoken to her since their night together. She just knew she could never speak to her boyfriend again if she was going to wild out like that.

As for Tyreek, she had seen him twice in the department, and both times he had been quick and short with her. They had spoken once on the phone one night after work. However, aside from that, there wasn't any talk about what had happened or any plans to hang out again. Deep down, Naomi felt a little used, but she didn't want to succumb to the emotion. Not only was she not wanting to appear weak, she knew she still had to manage to clear things up with her man back home. Yet for some reason, she had kissed Neil, only adding to her disrespectful behaviors. She wished she could confide in her boyfriend, but she was well aware that he would very likely break up with her if he knew what she had been up to. She had sent him a picture of her new look via text, the same day she had gotten the haircut. His reaction seemed concerned with her new attitude more so than her new look; he'd said he liked it but that it was just so different for her. Naomi could tell it only added to his fears of the way the city life was affecting her. Naomi was beginning to realize he had some valid concerns.

She walked into her building, past security, and pressed the elevator button, waiting patiently for it to arrive. The sound of heels clicking began to get louder in the hallway. When she looked up, Tiffany was walking up to her.

"A bit late, are we?" Tiffany asked.

"Yes, sorry."

"I heard you were out partying last night. That's no reason to get here late."

"I know. It was the trains," Naomi said, knowing damn well it wasn't the trains.

"Well, leave earlier if the trains aren't dependable."

The elevator arrived, and they both stepped in. Naomi didn't say anything, because she knew anything she said would sound like an excuse.

"Speaking of, you need to be careful who you hang out with. You are a grown woman, and I'm not telling you what to do, but you don't want to risk your career messing around with these men."

Naomi was beyond confused how her boss knew about Neil and was wondering if and what she knew about Tyreek. Then she also wondered if it was Tiffany's business who she dealt with outside the office, and she began to get upset.

"Many people have lost their jobs in this business because they couldn't keep their personal preferences under control. It's just a note to the wise—take it how you want," Tiffany said as she walked off the elevator.

Naomi trailed behind. She could feel her face fill with embarrassment—it was hot, and she knew it was red. Tiffany walked fast enough ahead of her that there was no chance to really explain herself unless she sped up after her. She was too embarrassed to do that; besides, she didn't know what to say. She didn't even know what Tiffany knew.

Naomi got to her desk and glanced into Tiffany's office to see what she was doing, but she couldn't see her from that angle. She sat down at her desk and placed her purse in the corner of her cabinet as usual. Naomi's mind was racing with thoughts; she was trying to remember where she was less than a month ago before her makeover and how she wished she could go back in time. It was as though she'd lost herself just that fast. Cheating on her boyfriend—sleeping with Tyreek and kissing Neil—all of it was just a lot for such a short period of time. Even if she tried to say it wasn't that big a deal, she was feeling the consequences now. She didn't want to get fired because she was characterized as a ho.

She opened her cabinet to get out the employee manual to see if there was anything regarding having relations with other employees. She realized that a lot of companies had those boundaries, but they were all different, and she wanted to know if what she had done was grounds for being fired. She was scanning the handbook page by page when she noticed Tiffany walking toward her.

"Can you take this file and bring it to Frank in the art department? Then bring the CD they're going to give you to the business and legal department. Tell Adam I need him to listen for samples," Tiffany said, handing her a file.

"Sure," Naomi said and jumped up.

Tiffany walked away without looking back. Naomi could feel the tension all through her own limbs. She sensed that Tiffany might be mad at her or just disappointed; either way, she didn't like it one bit. She was hoping that all she knew about was that she'd hung out last night with Neil. She was hoping that the Tyreek story hadn't spread that fast and that far.

She entered the art department on the fifth floor and walked straight up to Frank's desk.

"Hey, Frank. Tiffany told me to give this to you and to get a CD from you," she said.

"Oh, sure. I have the CD for you, but give that artwork to Susan. She's at her desk," he replied.

Naomi walked away. From the reflection in the glass ahead, she could see him glance back to look at her derriere. She put an extra sway in her walk; she figured if he was going to look, she wanted it to look right. She continued over to Susan's desk and saw she was on the phone. She walked up, waved the file in her hand, and slowly placed it down on her desk so Susan could see she was leaving it. Susan lifted her finger and mouthed *Give me one minute.* Naomi stopped and leaned against the wall behind her. Susan gestured toward the seat. Naomi was a bit confused but sat down anyway.

She hardly ever spoke to Susan, so she knew it wasn't gossip or anything personal. She figured Susan had a message she wanted her to relay back to Tiffany. She looked around the floor at the rest of the people in their cubicles and offices. Everyone seemed to be hard at work except for a few over by the coffee and water station. The art department designed all the album covers and posters and most of all the images of any sort needed by the label. Naomi thought to herself that if she had a bit of artistic skill in her, she would want to work in art. It was all creative and innovative; it could never get boring when it was something new every day, she thought to herself.

Susan hung up the phone. "Hey, Naomi, sorry for the wait."

"It's OK. Tiffany just told me to bring you that."

"Great, I needed this back today. She's always right on time."

"Yeah, I have to go bring this CD to business and legal now and then go back to my chambers."

Susan laughed. "OK. But listen, I just wanted to give you a bit of advice from an old-timer to a new-timer," Susan said as she looked Naomi right in her face to let her know she meant business.

Naomi instantly became concerned with what she was going to say and looked puzzled and afraid of what was to come next.

"We as women in this business have a thin line to walk. It's a male-dominated business, and we are making a lot of strides, but we aren't there yet. We can't do what men do and get away with it. You have to be careful how you carry yourself around here, how you dress, and who you deal with. People talk, and things can look real bad."

Naomi could feel that tension filling her body again. Her underarms were getting sweaty. *What the hell?* she asked herself. *Was there a label-wide announcement made about her?* Naomi was thinking there had to be other interoffice relationships that took place—she couldn't have been the only one. At this point she knew all this couldn't have come from the Neil situation. It had to be Tyreek.

"Thank you for the advice. I will be sure to keep it in mind," Naomi said. She didn't know what else to say. She felt she was getting a "whore intervention." She was beginning to become more offended than embarrassed. She knew that what she'd done wasn't necessarily the smartest thing, but it wasn't as if she'd murdered someone. She didn't understand how this had become such a big deal so fast. She knew she was new to the company, was young and from out of town, but she didn't know where everyone got off putting their noses in her business.

"No problem. I just like you, and I don't want to see you get taken advantage of," Susan replied.

"If you don't mind me asking, why did you figure I needed these words of advice?"

Susan looked away and began to move some papers around on her desk. It was evident that she would've chosen not to answer that question. Naomi figured if *she* had to be put on the spot, she was going to expect some information in return.

"Let's just say people talk. I am not implying you did anything, I just don't want you to be the topic of too many conversations. You are still new here; you don't want a tarnished reputation."

"Who was talking?" Naomi asked.

"I don't want to start anything, Naomi. I was just trying to give you some advice."

"Susan, with all due respect, you kind of already started something."

Susan looked at Naomi with her eyebrows raised. She seemed a little surprised that Naomi was being confrontational.

"You are not the same young woman I met when you started working here, I see," Susan said.

"No disrespect intended. I am just curious because you are not the first person to speak to me today, and I feel like the butt of some company-wide joke."

Susan looked sympathetic. She looked around to see who was near, and then she leaned in close to Naomi.

"I believe Tyreek told someone something about you and him, and that someone has a pretty big mouth. I don't think Tyreek was intending to embarrass you, but the person he told wasn't a wise choice, if you know what I mean."

Naomi knew just who that big-mouthed person was. It had to be Monique. She worked closely with Tyreek, and even being the new girl, Naomi knew about Monique's mouth.

"It was Monique, wasn't it?" Naomi asked.

Susan's eyes widened. "I didn't say that," she replied.

"But that's who it was. She told my boss, Susan, and I can get fired. Regardless of if it's true or not, it's just a rumor. She shouldn't have done that."

Susan just looked at Naomi. Her eyes said she had something else to say, but her mouth didn't open.

"It's fine. You don't have to say. Thank you so very much, though, for your advice and honesty," Naomi said as she stood up.

"I know you're upset, but learn from this. Some of the men in this business will chew you up and spit you out. Don't get caught up in it. Do your work and date outside these walls," Susan said.

"Thanks," Naomi said.

Her footsteps seemed heavy and swift as she walked down the aisle toward the elevator. She could feel her breathing patterns varying and her chest tightening up. Now was no time for any kind of anxiety attack because she had to put an end to this. She stepped onto the elevator and pressed the button. She was about to press her floor, but instead she pressed Monique's floor.

Everything was a blur. She was so pissed off she didn't stop to think about what she was going to

say or if saying anything at all was a good idea. She
knew there was a good chance a scene could be
made, but she figured she couldn't make the situation much worse than it already was. She walked by
a few desks and offices and saw people working
and talking to one another. She didn't slow down
at the sight of any familiar face; even if she weren't
focused on her target, she wouldn't feel comfortable talking to anyone not knowing who knew
what. She knew it was more than likely that the
people on the ninth floor—where Monique
worked and where everyone worked closely with
Tyreek—knew the most. *Shit, there wasn't that much
to tell.*

She could tell from a few feet away that Monique's
door was open. She couldn't see inside just yet, but
she was ready to attack. The few minutes it took
her to get to Monique's office, she rattled off in her
head all the things she wanted to say to Monique. As
soon as she approached the door, she saw the back
of a man's head. Monique's desk was facing the
door, and as soon as Naomi appeared, their eyes
locked. The guy in the chair was Tyreek, and he
turned around once he saw Monique looking past
him. Naomi was a bit shocked and wasn't expecting to confront Tyreek just yet, but she had come
all this way, so she couldn't turn back now.

"May I help you?" Monique asked.

Her smart undertone gave Naomi just the refu-
eling she needed to complete her goal to shut
Monique's mouth.

"Actually, yes, you can. I don't appreciate you walking around spreading rumors like we are in high
school. If that's what you choose to do, please just

keep my name out of your mouth," Naomi said. Her neck was bobbing so fast, and her hands were swinging so much, she barely knew what she said herself. She looked at Tyreek, rolled her eyes, and walked away. Neither of them even had a chance to say anything, and if they wanted to, they were going to have to chase after her, because she was gone.

She could see a couple people pretending not to look at her as she walked by. More than likely they had heard her when she was in Monique's doorway, and some of them probably knew exactly what she was referring to. By the time she got to the elevator, she was proud of standing up for herself and scared at the same time. She didn't know if this would bite her in the ass—she was just an assistant, and a new one at that. She had just become a bit known around the building, and just that fast she had become the most popular girl at the company—it just wasn't the type of popularity she was seeking. She wanted to be among the "in" crowd of the label. She had figured if she dressed nicer and made some more friends who had the cool jobs, she would fit in better. Now there was a nasty rumor circulating about her, and she was an enemy to the cool floor. She had no idea how she had gotten to this point so fast.

She felt like every person she passed on her way back to the elevator was pointing and laughing at her. She considered finding the staircase and taking the stairs back to her floor, assuming she would have to pass less people. When she realized she would have to go back in the direction of Monique's office to get to the stairs, she opted to stay en route. Eli from the fourth floor passed by, and when he greeted her, she thought he seemed a bit more flirtatious than usual.

"What are you all giddy about?" she asked.

"What?" he asked. He stopped dead in his tracks as though he was truly confused as to what the hell her problem was.

Does every man think they can just show me a bit of attention now and they will succeed at getting in my pants? Or am I just paranoid now? What have I done? she asked herself.

"Nothing, Eli, my bad," she said as she pushed the elevator button.

He began to walk off, but she could see that he was shaking his head and mumbling something under his breath. *Oh, boy, that's just another tale to tell about me,* she thought. She was thankful that no one was in the elevator; she didn't want to have any more hallucinations. The elevator stopped on her floor, and she got off. She swiftly walked down the hall, practically trying to drop and roll into her cubicle. She made it there without anyone stopping her for conversation or ogling her.

She sat down at her computer to begin checking her e-mails. She wanted to call Devora or someone to scream and cry, but she figured she was better off waiting a few moments in case her boss came out to question her. That was when she remembered she had never brought the CD to Adam in the business and legal department. She had been so distracted she had carried that CD in her hand the entire time, placed it down on her desk, and thought nothing of it. She grabbed it and jumped back out of her seat, hoping to leave the department without Tiffany seeing her. As soon as she stepped out of her cubicle, she saw Monique storming down the aisle.

Naomi stopped midstride, unsure of what to do. She made eye contact with Monique and could see that it was no coincidence she was on her floor moments after Naomi had left hers. Naomi began to continue on as if she didn't care what the hell Monique wanted; she was holding on to her fearless face. They were walking toward each other, but Naomi had every intention to just pass on by.

"I don't know who you think you are," Monique said when she was close enough to be heard by Naomi.

It was obvious that Naomi was in ear range, but she just kept strutting right past Monique toward the elevator banks. When she glanced over her shoulder and saw that Monique was still going in the opposite direction, she realized *Oh, shit, she is going to Tiffany.* Naomi quickly turned around and headed back to her desk. Her heart began racing, and she was filled with fear as to what Tiffany would say or think about the tantrum she had thrown in Monique's office door. *I wasn't insubordinate, because Monique is not my boss . . . but it was unprofessional,* Naomi was telling herself.

She watched Monique step inside Tiffany's office. Naomi got back to her desk only a few seconds later; she figured she wanted to be close by to try to hear what was said and defend herself, if need be. She could overhear Monique telling Tiffany how Naomi had shown up shouting in her doorway while she was in the middle of a meeting.

Meeting? Yeah, right—sharing more gossip, Naomi thought. Monique went on to say how she didn't appreciate what Naomi had done, and if she weren't a professional businesswoman, she would have told her off. She said Tiffany needed to handle her staff. The words that heightened Naomi's anger were when she heard Monique say, "This isn't a club." As soon as she realized that she had nothing much to lose, Naomi walked over to Tiffany's office.

As soon as she arrived in Tiffany's sight, Tiffany sat up and folded her hands. She probably hadn't expected Naomi to come confront her or Monique at this time, but from her body language and expression, it seemed she preferred that it be addressed.

"Tiffany, I am sorry to have this childish issue in your office because I know you have a lot of important work to tend to," Naomi started off.

Sensing the butt-kissing intro, Tiffany waved her hand in a "get on with it" motion.

"It was brought to my attention that rumors had been spreading about the building that concerned me and my reputation. I was also told that these rumors were being started by Monique here, and upon hearing these false rumors about myself, I reacted by confronting Monique and asking her to please refrain from spreading stories about me. Maybe it wasn't the correct time or place, but I felt as though it needed to be stopped immediately, and I reacted."

Tiffany turned to look at Monique as if to ask her if she had anything to say about it. From the way Tiffany turned without a response, Naomi got the impression that she agreed that Monique should've been confronted.

"Well, listen, that it came from me is a rumor as well," Monique said. "I could care less what you thought or what you heard, but if your sexual escapades can't be kept in your personal life, don't bring that to me. The next time you come to my office waving your hands and raising your voice, I won't be so nice."

Tiffany didn't stop her or assure her that Naomi would be reprimanded, and that must have pissed her off even more.

"The next time you put my name in your mouth, I won't be so nice either," Naomi said.

"Whatever," Monique said as she turned out of Tiffany's office.

Naomi looked back at Tiffany, and instantly her anger subdued some and she became nervous again that Tiffany might lash out at her.

"Where did this little fireball come from?" Tiffany asked.

"I apologize, Tiffany. I just really didn't appreciate what she was doing."

Tiffany laughed a bit and shook her head.

"You are surely not the little girl I hired from Texas, I tell you that," she said.

Naomi smiled, trying to relax for just a second. "I *am* the same girl," she said.

"I don't know about all that, but I do hope that you're just as angry with Tyreek as you are Monique because she isn't the one who told me," Tiffany said, dropping her head but raising her eyeballs.

"Hmmm," Naomi said. She was very appreciative of Tiffany's ability to treat her as an equal at this moment and not belittle or berate her. However, she didn't feel comfortable enough with her yet to admit that those rumors were true. At this point she figured she would be better off just denying anything had ever happened and let it be her word against the rumor mill.

Chapter 31

Sereeta wasn't sure what to expect when she pulled up to Corey's house. They had been back from Los Angeles for three days now, and aside from the night before when he had asked her to attend the Cîroc party with him, she had been off work. The entire time in LA, they had pretended almost as if what had happened on the plane never had happened—just like Corey had said. Her hotel room was down the hall from his, and after the long days of meetings, sneaker stores, and press, they were in their hotel rooms the entire night. On the ride back to New York, Corey didn't seem to mind that Sereeta watched MTV on her side of the plane.

He had called earlier that morning and asked her to come by his house to gather some of his belongings to have them shipped to his cousin in Detroit. There was no car sent for her or any specific time given, so she figured she would just get there as early as possible. After she spoke to him, she got dressed and headed on over. When she got there, only two of Corey's cars were in the driveway, and it looked pretty quiet as usual in the neighborhood. The houses on his block were huge and far apart from one another; it was a beautiful neighborhood.

Sereeta parked her car and went up to the house. She rang the bell once and then used her key. She walked inside the house and instantly noticed a few things were out of place. She saw a gym bag in the corner that was open and some sneakers in another corner. Sereeta locked the door and began to walk farther into the house. She saw a few bottles of Grey Goose and Hypnotic on the coffee table and glasses by the end tables.

"Corey!" she yelled, unsure where he was or if he was even still home.

"You can come up!" he shouted.

She walked past more disheveled clothes and a pink overnight bag. She realized then that this was the site of a party of sorts the night before or that morning. She walked up the stairs, and voices became louder as she got closer to the top. She reached the top and saw a brown-skinned young lady with just her panties on run down the hall and into one of the guest bedrooms. Sereeta stood where she was at the top of the stairs, afraid to walk any farther and see any other private parts. The girl closed the door behind her, and then Sereeta was standing in the long hallway alone. A few seconds later, Corey turned the corner, coming out of the master bedroom.

"What's up, Sereeta?" he said.

Inside she felt let down that he had had no thought as to whether her feelings were involved after what had happened on the plane. She was hoping he would be a little more caring than he was. No apology given for her having to see that, no explanation, no anything. She knew if she said anything she would sound like a jealous or nagging girlfriend, and she wasn't going to lose her job over this. Still, the look on her face couldn't hide how disappointed she was feeling that Corey had called her upstairs while a half-naked girl was in the hallway.

He knelt down to tie his sneakers and fix the bottom of his sweat pants.

"Nothing," she finally replied.

"Cool, I just received three shipments from And One and Nike. I wanted you to take one of everything and package it in a box and ship it to my cousin," he said.

"OK, boss," she replied.

He looked up at her and tried to make eye contact, but she turned to walk down the stairs.

"Sereeta!" he called.

"Yes?" she said.

"The boxes are in the third bedroom to the left, and I wasn't done," he said as he stood up.

"OK."

"Is there a problem?" he asked.

Sereeta figured she wasn't doing a good job hiding her attitude. "Not at all. Why?"

Corey shrugged his shoulders as though he was in no mood for any side conversations. "When you're done, go in the bottom drawer in the small closet and take out a few packs of the socks and shorts and put that in the package."

"No problem," she replied.

Corey didn't bother to acknowledge the sarcastic undertone in her voice that time.

"A'ight, and call me when you are done. I have a few more things I need you to do," he said before he headed down the stairs.

Sereeta walked down the hall to the third bedroom to the left. She heard a male and female voice coming from the second bedroom to the right but kept walking. *How many people are in the house?* The young lady she had seen had gone into a different bedroom, and the rooms didn't connect. Corey's master bedroom was closed, and she couldn't see inside to make sure he didn't have any sleeping guests. She walked straight ahead to the room she'd been sent to and tried to mind her business. She realized that just because she had grouped out and fucked Corey, she had no rights to him or any right to know any of his business.

She walked into the room and headed straight for the closet. She heard a loud noise, and she jumped. She turned and saw Corey, who seemed to be tickled by the light scream she had yelled out.

"I forgot something," he said.

"Where are you headed?" she said.

"I have to go get a haircut and handle some things," he said.

"Who is here?"

"A couple of my teammates, and they have company," he said, tossing his keys in the air as he headed toward the door.

"Oh, *they* have company, OK."

Corey stopped and looked at her.

"Oh, you're funny, huh?" he said.

Before she could reply, he was walking out of the room. She wanted to take something and just throw it at him. *Damn,* she thought. *How did you let yourself even get in this situation?* Did she really think he was going to make her his girl or something just because she'd had sex with him? For some reason, she had been hoping it had meant more to him than just that. She didn't want to admit it, but it had meant more to her.

She tried to come home from LA and talk to Mark, but her mind had been on Corey. She had even hung out with Mark, and he had spent the night with her. The last thing she had wanted to do was fall for a man she couldn't have. Mark was fun, smart, handsome, and not an unattainable NBA player. Still, even while she and Mark were fooling around, she was enjoying every second of it, but her mind would drift to when she had been with Corey. She wanted to know if Corey had thought about it for even a second after it was over or if it was just all business for him.

She pulled out a few pairs of socks and shorts from the bottom drawer in Corey's closet and brought them with her into the bedroom. She placed the socks and shorts on the bed and walked over to the six large boxes in the bedroom. She noticed one was open, and when she peeked inside, she saw a bunch of shorts with AND 1 logos on it. She began to open the flaps on the box so she could see what was inside, and she began to separate the items. She heard a noise from the hallway and stood still so she could hear better. She recognized the sound of someone vomiting. Sereeta went to the door, and she could see someone bent over the toilet bowl in the bathroom. She could see it was a male, but all she could see were his size-thirteen flip-flops and bottom end. She went back into the bedroom to continue what she was doing.

Corey needs a wife. He lets his house get treated like a hotel or something. She knew it wasn't her place, but it was way too common for the team to utilize his house as a place to get drunk and bring their groupies. Sereeta found it a bit distasteful. Although she hadn't seen him in the mix of it yet, she knew he was. It was pretty likely that they were using his house because they had girlfriends or wives at home. Sereeta reminded herself that it was best she just listen to Corey's advice and stick to trying to get to know Mark. As much as it would be dreamy to be Mrs. Cox, there was just too much hard work and baggage with that package, and she wasn't up for trying to create a miracle.

She began to pull some of the items out of the box when she heard some bumps in the hallway. She figured it was the same guy trying to make his way back to the bedroom. She placed three pairs of shorts, one of each color, on the bed and then went back over to the door, and stood still. The noise was closer, and when she looked up, there was a guy in the doorway. It was France Thomas, one of Corey's teammates.

"What the fuck are you doing here?" he asked.

"Corey asked me to take care of something for him," she said.

It was obvious he was out of it. He reached over to the top of the tall dresser closest to the door and grabbed a condom out of the box.

"I need a pair of those shorts," he said.

Sereeta picked up a black pair and tossed it to him. He caught them and looked at her as though he wasn't too pleased that she had thrown them instead of handing them to him. Sereeta began to remove another black pair from the box as if she didn't notice him still standing there. She looked over at him again to see if anything was wrong.

"I need a shirt, too," he said.

She began to sift through the box for a T-shirt. She had seen some in there a few seconds ago. As she pulled out a shirt and went to check the size, she noticed France removing his shorts. She assumed he had boxers or something underneath, but when she looked she saw a clear shot of all his business. Sereeta quickly walked toward the door in hopes of getting by him so she could exit the room while he changed.

"Here you go." She handed him the T-shirt as she tried to pass.

"Don't run," he said as he grabbed her arm.

"I'm not running, I'm just going to get something to drink," she said.

"You're just scared of my big dick, aren't you?"

"No, I'm not looking at your penis. I just want to go downstairs." She tried to wiggle her arm free, but he had a firm grip on her.

"Get your ass back to work," he said as he pushed her back in the room.

Sereeta flew back a few feet and then looked up at him in fear. Instead of challenging him, she began folding the shorts on the bed while she tried to keep him in sight. She could see through her peripheral vision that he was removing his T-shirt, which had vomit on it. He was drunk, his eyes were bloodshot, and the smell of liquor and vomit was permeating. Sereeta began to hear a female voice down the hall, and she was hoping he would leave to tend to her. Instead he stood there. Still.

Sereeta went over to the box to remove more items. She was taking deep breaths, trying her best to remain calm. She turned to place some of the shirts and wristbands on the bed. Just as she turned around to get more items and see if France had left, she noticed something directly behind her. France was standing a few inches from her.

"France!" she screamed. "What are you doing?"

He was standing there buck-ass naked with some socks on, and he had this look in his eyes, like he was a street gangster and not the familiar guy from the basketball games.

"You know you want this long dick," he said.

She looked down and noticed he was placing on his penis the condom he had just taken from Corey's dresser.

"No, really, I don't," Sereeta said.

He was directly in front of her, and his large frame blocked her view of the door or anything beyond him. However, she took a step to the left and tried to walk past. As soon as she thought she was home free, he grabbed her shoulder and tossed her back on the bed.

"What did I tell you about running? You have work to do," he said.

"Stop," she said. "I'm leaving."

"No, you aren't."

She tried to get up again, pushing him back with all her might and trying to jump off the bed, but by the time she made a little distance from the bed, he pushed her right back. She began swinging her fists against him and trying to kick him in his balls, but he moved out of the way just in time. He took one of his large hands and pinned her down by her neck. He took his other hand and lifted her skirt up over her waist. Sereeta was regretting at that very moment that she had worn a skirt this particular day, trying to be cute for Corey, only to lead to easy access for France. She was screaming, and almost nothing was coming out—his hand on her neck was blocking her vocal cords.

"Corey told me this pussy was right. I'll be the judge of that," he said.

Sereeta's body tensed up even more when those words resonated throughout her body. *Did I bring this on myself by opening my legs in the first place? Now the entire team thinks I'm a groupie?* When she felt him pull her panties to the side and begin to probe his penis around for her opening, she went numb. Her mind went blank. It was as if she passed out and became unconscious, but in reality she was right there underneath two-hundred-thirty-five-pound, six-three France. She was looking up at the ceiling, asking the angels or someone to come help her out of this situation. She saw glimpses of France's face, and she could slightly hear him groaning, but it was all like part of a blurry dream.

"Stop it! Get off her!" she heard someone yell.

It was a female voice. When Sereeta looked down, she saw the same brown-skinned girl with no bra pulling at France's arms.

"Get off her! What are you doing?" the girl screamed.

France must have realized from the shocked

look on the girl's face that he was bugging the hell out. He jumped off Sereeta and pulled her up by her arm.

"Are you OK?" the girl asked.

Sereeta placed her hand around her neck as she began to breathe heavily, trying to catch her breath.

"Are you fucking crazy?" the girl asked France. "Isn't she Corey's assistant? How the hell you go and do something like that to her?"

Sereeta could tell from the look on the girl's face that she was extremely pissed off and disgusted, but definitely not more than Sereeta was.

"Are you OK?" France asked her. He had knelt down some to look in Sereeta's face.

Sereeta took all the strength she had left in her body and slapped the shit out of him, and before he could react, she darted for the door. When she reached the end of the hall, she looked back and saw France trying to come after her.

"Wait—I'm sorry!" he yelled. He stumbled and almost fell, and by the time he gained his balance, Sereeta was running down the stairs. She grabbed her purse off the table and headed for the front door. She walked as fast as she could to her car and began trying to find her keys. Her hands were shaking, and she was trying to slow down enough to get her keys into her car. She felt the metal keys and began to pull them out of her purse when she heard footsteps walking up close behind her.

"Leave me alone!" she yelled as she turned away and pressed herself up against her car door.

It was Corey with a fresh haircut and some bags in his hand. His eyes were squinted; it was obvious he was confused and thinking. "What is wrong with you, Sereeta?" he asked.

She quickly turned back around and began trying to fit the car key in the door.

"Sereeta," he said.

She could hear the concern in his voice. She got the car door open, threw her purse in the passenger seat, and plopped down in the driver's seat. By this time, Corey was standing right next to her in front of the open driver's-side door.

"Corey, please move and get away from me," she said.

"What's wrong? Are you OK?"

"Corey, move!" she screamed.

His eyes widened in shock. "What the hell is wrong with you? You finished the package?"

"I quit," she said.

"What?" he said.

There was a sound from the balcony door opening upstairs. Corey looked back and saw France standing there in a pair of shorts and no shirt. Sereeta looked up, and when she saw him, she began to put her keys in the ignition.

"Yo, my bad, Corey. I fucked up. I wasn't thinking," France said.

"What are you talking about?" Corey said.

Sereeta was starting her car, and Corey looked back at her.

"Please move, Corey, so I can close my car door."

"What is he talking about?" he asked.

"Ask him. I'm just the help."

Corey turned around and saw that France was still standing up on the balcony watching them.

"Somebody better tell me what the fuck is going on!" Corey said.

France turned around and headed back through the balcony doors. He stumbled slightly.

"France!" Corey yelled.

France quickly turned back around.

"Yo, I said I'm sorry, Corey. Shit just led to another and . . . I don't know, man," he said.

Corey's head turned fast toward Sereeta. He scanned her face and seemed as if he could see through her to the anger she wasn't speaking about and the tears she was fighting back. "He did something to you?" Corey asked.

Sereeta remained silent, looking out the front of her car. Corey bent down on one of his knees to be eye level with her.

"Sereeta, did he do something to you?" he said.

Sereeta had her eyes locked on the tree in front of her car. "Don't pretend you care about me, Corey," she said without taking her eyes off the tree.

"Sereeta, please don't go there right now. I need to know what happened."

"France wanted to see if you were telling the truth when you told the team I had some good pussy, I guess," Sereeta said, looking Corey right in his face.

Corey shut his eyes and dropped his head. When he lifted his head back up, there were tears in her eyes. Her bottom lip was trembling; she was trying so hard not to break down, but her spirit was getting weaker and weaker each second. Corey looked back and saw France walk back inside the house.

"Sereeta, I don't know what happened, but please come and talk to me."

"You expect me to go back inside that house? You are out of your mind."

"What happened? What did he do?"

"He . . . he put . . . he . . ." Sereeta couldn't finish her sentence.

Corey could see the pain all over her face. He reached into the car and put his arms around her. As much as she wanted to hate Corey, she needed the shoulder to cry on. She needed to feel like he cared and she wasn't some expendable slut. Feeling him hold her tight felt so good, even in the midst of how horrible the situation. She buckled in his arms. She was ashamed and hurt and didn't want to face what was really happening or what had really happened. She tried to forget the thoughts of having to lose her job over this and focus on the bigger picture, but she was embarrassed that she was even considering that. She felt as if she had no self-worth, like she deserved what had just happened to her. At least, that was how she felt until she envisioned France on top of her—then she felt anger, and she knew he deserved to be punished. She was way too overwhelmed with all her thoughts. She had to get away. She needed downtime.

"I have to go," Sereeta said as she lifted herself out of Corey's grasp.

"I still don't know what happened," he said.

"What do you think happened?" she asked.

"I honestly don't know. He made a move on you?"

"A *move* on me?" she asked and gave him a puzzled look. *Was he really that clueless? Was it not obvious from what she and France had said?*

"Well, then, tell me. Listen, Sereeta. I like you. You are a cool girl—I've never kept an assistant this long. You are reliable, and you are professional. You were becoming more to me than just an assistant, and what happened between us . . . I'm sorry I told him. I wasn't bragging, though, I was just having guy talk. You are a very attractive and good type of girl; I just didn't want to mess things up. I'm sorry if you felt taken advantage of—that was far from the case. Please don't hate me because I told him that. He's drunk, and he probably was just trying to see if you would do something with him."

Sereeta looked down at her steering wheel while he talked. It was all a bit comforting, she had to admit. Aside from all her mixed emotions, it was nice to know what he was thinking, for once. Still, she wished she had known a few days or even a few hours earlier. Now it was all almost irrelevant.

"He raped me," she said.

"What?!" he snapped.

"You heard me."

Corey reached over to her ignition and removed the key.

"What are you doing?" she asked.

With the key in tow, he stormed off into the house. He banged the door open and ran through the front living room to the staircase. Sereeta followed behind, but by the time she got to the living room, he was upstairs. She could hear him yelling, and she definitely wasn't going up those stairs again.

"What the fuck, man?" Corey yelled.

"Yo, it wasn't like that," France replied.

Sereeta could hear a few more muffled shouts, but she couldn't make out what was being said.

"Get the fuck out of my house!" Corey barked.

Sereeta sat on the couch with her face buried in her hands; she couldn't believe any of this was happening. She heard footsteps and jumped up to see who it was. The brown-skinned girl who had come in the room, along with another one of Corey's teammates—Aaron—and another light-skinned young lady were coming down the stairs. The brown-skinned girl had an overnight bag with her, and the light-skinned girl had just her purse. The brown-skinned girl had this look of shame and guilt on her face, and when she saw Sereeta, she immediately turned away. Sereeta knew why the girl couldn't look her in the eyes; she wouldn't want to either. At that very moment, Sereeta didn't even want to face herself in the mirror.

The three of them walked out the front door and closed it behind them. Sereeta assumed it was just her, Corey, and France left in the house, and she didn't feel comfortable with that. She wanted to go get her keys, but she didn't want to face France. She could still hear them arguing.

"Are you bugging?" Corey asked.

"She was going along with it at first, and then she changed the game up. Then I stopped," he yelled.

"She said you raped her, France. She wouldn't make up something like that."

It felt good to hear him say that—he believed her. He could just as easily have believed what

France was saying, but Corey knew her better than that, and if there was anything positive that would come out of the whole fucked-up situation, in Sereeta's mind that was it.

"My bad, Corey," France said again.

You could hear in his voice that he was still drunk. His words were slurring, and he just seemed out of it.

"And how you going to do that shit in my house? You dragging me into this. She can press charges, and I will be caught right in the middle," Corey spewed.

Is that all he was concerned about, his name being in the paper? Is that what all his anger was about? she asked herself. She wanted to leave, and she had no idea why Corey wanted her to stay and hear all this. As if what had just happened weren't bad enough, now she had to sit here and listen to France make excuses for it and Corey worry about himself and not about how she felt. She wanted to get out of there, but she was way too far out in the boonies to walk or to try to find a bus. She started to realize that Corey probably wanted to coach her about how to handle the situation—tell her who to talk to and who not to talk to.

Sereeta felt trapped again, like she had when France was holding her arm. She sat up straight, scanning the room, looking around for a solution. She looked at the table by the wall and noticed that Corey's keys to the Range Rover were lying there. She thought for a few seconds and then jumped and grabbed them and headed toward the front door.

Chapter 32

Calling out sick for two days probably didn't help the situation at all, but Naomi wasn't up for whatever drama was brewing at the office. Her coworker had called her and told her there were a lot of folks gossiping about what was going on, and quite a few new faces passing by her desk were trying to get a peek of her or something. Her original plan was to miss just one day of work with the intent to let things subside. However, that evening her cubicle neighbor, Jared, had called her and told her how it seemed to be even worse that day. Naomi was so glad she wasn't there to be the fish in the glass bowl for all her nosy coworkers to stare at. She knew Tiffany didn't believe her when she'd said she'd eaten something bad. She was sick to her stomach, but not because of bad food—because of bad decisions.

What clinched Naomi's decision to call out another day was when Jared had told her that the stories circulating were different from what she knew. He said one of the guys from the dubbing office asked him if Jared had slept with her, and when he told him no, the guy had said to make a move because she was an easy knock-down. Jared had apologized for telling her this, but he'd thought she needed to know. What put the nail in the coffin was when he'd told her the version of the story he'd heard was that she was in that hotel room with both Neil and Tyreek, and they'd taken turns. All Naomi could do was shake her head in disbelief. She'd told Jared those stories weren't true, but he'd said before she could even finish that it was unnecessary—he hadn't believed it when he'd heard it. It felt nice to know that someone in the office knew she wasn't the slut whore Tyreek had everyone believing.

The first day she'd stayed home, she'd talked on the phone with everyone she could confide in from back home—and Devora—to let them know what had happened and to get their advice. Everyone had a different opinion, but many of them felt as though she had made herself a bed she wasn't going to enjoy having to lie in. No one seemed to encourage her, aside from Devora.

"Girl, I say you go back in that office and you let them all know you don't have anything to be ashamed about," Devora said.

"I know, but that would be way easier if I didn't."

"Half the bitches there have probably slept with someone in that building. They can't talk."

"Yeah, but the difference is the whole staff doesn't know all their business."

"Well, yeah, it does suck that Tyreek gossips like a girl, but so what? Gossip back about him."

"What do you mean? No! I am not even going to

admit that I slept with him. I would rather pretend he's just lying."

"That's if people believe that, Naomi. Sometimes the best way to save face is just to confront it head-on. Admit you did, but let it be known that he was horrible in bed or was stinking or something. Make him regret blabbing."

Naomi liked the idea, but she couldn't imagine herself walking around talking about her sexual life with just anyone. Before she hung up with Devora, she'd said she would think about it, but she wasn't quite sure if telling one or two people at work was going to have the same effect. She didn't have the advantage of being friends with Monique; if so, she could just tell her, and the word would spread like wildfire.

Naomi really tried to take the time at home to evaluate where she'd lost herself. She had even called Charles the night before, but he hadn't seemed too sympathetic. She'd told him a twisted version of the story, but he hadn't seemed to believe it or care either way. She'd told him that people had just seen her and Tyreek leave together and begun to assume and gossip about it, but she swore Tyreek was just her colleague and friend. From his response, Naomi could tell he probably believed the "gossip," too. Afterward, Devora had told her she was stupid to even mention it; she now regretted telling him anything at all. She figured because their relationship was practically dead anyway, maybe sharing this would help or make him want to console her. She realized after the fact that she'd had the wrong idea.

The television was on all day, but Naomi barely

paid it any attention. She kept drifting off into different thoughts and imagining what people were thinking about her. She still didn't see how she'd been living a dream—working in New York City at a top record label—and now here she was, less than a year later, a cast-off at work, still underpaid with no boyfriend back home anymore, and only a few steps away from losing her job. She'd had no idea that this was what would come with a taste of the life.

Chapter 33

Corey had sent someone to retrieve the Range Rover and drop off Sereeta's car that same night, but since then there had been no communication. He had called several times and left messages and texts to call him, but Sereeta hadn't responded to anything. She hadn't decided what her next move would be; she had been too emotional to think straight.

Reyna had told her to press charges, and although she wanted to, she knew that because he'd used a condom and because he was a famous millionaire, she would likely lose and look like the slutty groupie. Four days had gone by since the France fiasco, and she had finally slept off all the guilt and shame—she was ready to make him pay. She didn't know what she could do, but she thought Debbie might have some words of wisdom. Sereeta sat on her couch and dialed Debbie's number.

"Hey, girl. Where you been?" Debbie said, sounding all energized when she answered the phone.

"I've been home," Sereeta replied.

"Oh, I didn't see you at the Players' Appreciation Dinner last night, and most of their assistants were with them," she said.

"Yeah, that's why I was calling you," Sereeta said. "What's up?"

"I was at Corey's house the other day, and some of the players were there, and they had company and had been drinking . . . Long story short, France forced himself on me," she said.

"Oh, my God!" Debbie said. "Are you OK?"

"I am now. I just don't know what to do."

"What did Corey say?"

"He was mad, but I left the house with his Range. He sent his driver to get it, and I haven't seen him since. He's left messages asking me to talk to him and not react in any way. He's just begging that I call him. I think he doesn't want to say too much over my answering machine, not sure if I'm pressing charges or not."

"Well, are you?" she asked.

"I don't know. That's why I'm calling you. I am so confused."

"Well, more power to you. There is a lot of money to be made if you go that route," she said.

"It's bigger than that, Debbie. I just feel stupid."

"Well, most people settle, so that's up to you."

" 'Most people'? How many other people has this happened to?"

"This is a male-dominated field—there are sexual-harassment suits and rape charges of some sort on a regular basis. You aren't the first and won't be the last. These men are used to getting whatever they want, including pussy."

Sereeta just dropped her head in her hands. "What's the point then? In the end they will win."

"The point is to get some money at least and hit him where it hurts. I hate France anyway; he's always been an arrogant asshole."

"Do you know of anyone else who's had a problem with him?" Sereeta asked.

"He's grabbed Tamara's ass before while they were at Nate's barbecue, and one time one of the other girls who helps Tyrone during the playoffs told me he was groping her one day in the locker room, but he stopped when someone walked in," she said.

Sereeta began to get flashbacks of his heavy body pressed on top of hers and the smell of his sweat and Hennessy mixed together. She was trying to just block it all out. "Alright, thanks. I'll look into my options."

"Alright, call me if you need me."

The two of them hung up, and Sereeta sat there. She felt so alone. Mark wouldn't take her call the last time she called—turned out France was his brother. When he'd told her his brother played in the NBA, he never had said which player it was. It wasn't until Sereeta had called him crying about what had happened that he'd told her France was his brother and there was no way he would do such a thing. He coincidentally had had to get off the phone right after that, and she hadn't heard from him since.

She was tired of sitting at home crying, avoiding calls, running from what had happened, getting little advice or guidance. She saw Corey's name highlighted in her call log as a missed call, and she stared at it for a few moments before she hit the TALK button to call him back. As the phone rang, she could feel her heart begin to race.

"Hello?" he answered.

"Hi, Corey," she said.

"Sereeta! Hey! Thanks for calling me back."

"It's cool."

"Listen, I know you're upset, and I'm *so* sorry about what happened. I feel at fault for having you in my house, but I had no idea he was that twisted, Sereeta. You know I have never tried to put you in harm's way."

"I don't blame you, Corey," she said.

"I know that nothing can really fix what happened, but I'm asking that you meet with France and me so we can try. I'm really hoping we can avoid a scandal."

Sereeta remembered when he'd yelled at France for doing such a thing in his house—as if out of his house would be OK. "Is that all you care about?" she asked.

"Not at all, Sereeta. I care about you, too. You are a good person and didn't deserve that."

"And I think he is a bad person and deserves to suffer," she said.

"Yes, but something like this—not only he would suffer. I'll suffer for it, our team, the entire NBA . . . It's a bad look."

"He should've thought about that," she said.

"I agree, but he didn't. Where we are now, it's just best we handle it among us. Besides, he said he had on a condom, so it will be extremely hard to prove it even happened."

"Is that what you think, Corey? Well, thanks for having my back," Sereeta said.

He didn't get a chance to reply because she hung up. Her mind was racing, and so was her heart. *He's an asshole, too,* she thought to herself. She wanted everyone to suffer; she wanted not to be some silent victim so they could carry on with their lives and do this to whomever else.

She got up from the couch on which she had spent way too many hours the past two days and walked into the kitchen to pour herself a glass of water. She moved a pile of papers so she could put her empty glass down, and a business card fell on the floor. She knelt down to pick it up and recognized the large DRAMA 99 FM logo. She continued to pour herself a glass of water and recalled meeting the program director at her favorite station over a week ago. She was a nice lady, and Sereeta only wished she could have that much power and not have to be a prisoner to someone. They said you shouldn't compare your life to someone else's because you never knew what problems they had, and this could be a prime example.

After Sereeta was through wishing she were in the powerful music executive's shoes, she put the water back in the refrigerator and walked out of the kitchen with her glass in her hand. She sat on the couch, and as she sat there in silence, she thought that maybe seeing that card at that moment had been a sign. She placed her glass down on the coffee table in front of her and headed back into the kitchen with her cell phone in hand. She picked up the business card, looked it over front and back, and analyzed its details. *Madison*

*Cassell, Program Director. Drama 99 FM. Drama and
Hits.* Drama and hits. The station played music
and executed interesting interviews and dished
the dirt and drama of the entertainment business.
This might have been just the answer Sereeta was
looking for.

She dialed the number on the card.

"Hello, Drama Ninety-Nine FM," a young lady
said.

"Yes, can I speak to Madison, please?" Sereeta
asked.

"May I ask who's calling?"

"Can you tell her it's Sereeta, Corey Cox's assistant?"

"Hold on, please," the girl said.

DJ Citrus's voice filled the phone, as the radio
station was to keep Sereeta entertained while she
was on hold. She sat there and began to wonder if
she was losing her mind to even think about calling this strange woman, whom she hardly knew,
and involve her in such a personal issue. A song
came on—one of Sereeta's favorites by Keyshia
Cole. She also began to wonder if Madison would
be upset she had even told her this information.
Would she refuse to get involved and curse her
out? What was Sereeta thinking? Just as she was
getting ready to hang up . . .

"Hello?" a voice said.

"Hello?" Sereeta replied.

"Sereeta?"

"Madison?"

"Yes, hi. How are you?"

"I'm OK. I hope I didn't interrupt your day,"
she said.

"Not at all, you caught me at a good time."

"Do you have a minute to speak to me in private?"

"You mean now, or do you want to meet?" Madison asked.

"Now is fine."

"Yes, you have my undivided attention."

Sereeta was surprised at how open and kind Madison was. She knew she should be honored just to get her on the phone. She didn't know if it was strictly because her boss was an NBA player or because Madison was a down-to-earth chick, but either way Sereeta was thankful to have her ear.

"Well, Madison, something happened to me that I'm ashamed to talk about. However, I feel if I keep it to myself, the person who did it will get away with murder—it's not murder, of course. But . . ."

Madison must have sensed the fear in her voice. "Calm down, hon, take it easy. You can relax and just talk to me," she said.

Sereeta began to tear up. She felt like Madison was a therapist or something, allowing her to just let it all out. Reyna had listened, but Sereeta had felt like, in the back of Reyna's mind, she was judging her and thinking she should've complained about the nakedness in the locker rooms long ago or should've put her foot down. Sereeta felt enough at fault without having others ask her questions as if she were a fool. Hearing Madison just say "talk to me" were the most comforting words she could hear at that moment.

"One of Corey's teammates raped me and—" She heard Madison gasp, and she stopped midsentence.

"Oh, my goodness. Did you go to the police?"

"No, I was afraid to. He used a condom and I didn't think anyone would believe me and the case would be dismissed anyway."

"I believe you, Sereeta. Don't worry about people not believing you."

"I don't care what people think. I don't want to be his victim and just sit still and quiet and be controlled by money."

Madison realized she, too, was a victim sitting still and quiet and being controlled by money.

"Go to the cops. Press charges and get an attorney," Madison said.

"The press is going to run with it. Corey will be caught up in it. I just don't want to regret it," she said.

"I'm curious—why did you call me?"

"I was hoping maybe I could just come tell my story. Tell what France did to me, tell my side of the story."

Madison fell quiet. Madison could hear the pain in Sereeta's voice. She recognized it. Madison felt ashamed that she herself had chosen to keep secret what had been going on with her and Polytics, and yet this young woman had wanted to stand up for herself despite what others would think. "If that's what you would like to do, Sereeta, you are more than welcome. I am assuming an attorney may advise you otherwise, but you let me know what you decide."

"Thanks, Madison. I will consult with an attorney today, but something in my gut is telling me this is what I want to do. A lawyer is going to try to get money for me, but they may settle, and his name may never even be tarnished."

"I understand," Madison said.

Little did Sereeta know that Madison really did understand. She understood enough to realize that she had only a short window of time left herself before she was going to have to face her own demon. Living enslaved to a secret wasn't fun or easy. Sometimes, just by telling your story, the truth would set you free.

Sereeta and Madison hung up the phone, and Madison couldn't help but think what Sereeta was thinking and how she must feel. Madison took no more than sixty seconds before she picked up the phone, filled with motivation, and called the host of her Wednesday night news-formatted show and told her of her show assignment: "Women Prisoners in the Entertainment Business."

Chapter 34

Everyone left in the office at Drama 99 FM had their ears glued to the radio. It was Wednesday night, prime time, and Laura Lissette was hosting her show, *Source Stories*. She had been promoting all week that she would be doing a show on "Women Prisoners in the Entertainment Business," featuring some of the music business's most well-kept secrets. The phones had been ringing all week with audio-bite requests, industry executives wanting to contribute stories anonymously, and of course labels asking for Madison's mercy with what was allowed to be aired. No one knew who the guest panelists were, but the promo that was running made everyone curious.

Laura spoke into the mic; four women were in the room, aside from herself and her board operator.

"Drama Ninety-Nine FM—you are listening to *Source Stories*, and today our show topic is 'Women Prisoners in the Entertainment Business,'" Lisa began.

The audio clip of applause began and slowly quieted down.

"Today we have with us Sereeta McFarlane, assistant to NBA player Corey Cox; Kayla Frater, stylist to King Mercy; Naomi Mitchell, executive assistant to the VP of promotions at Intheloop Records; and last, but certainly not least, our very own program director here at Drama Ninety-Nine FM, Madison Cassell." The audio clip of applause began to fill the room again.

All the ladies were nervous; they looked around the room at each other, and from within each other's eyes, they found the strength to continue. They all knew that there might be consequences to pay, and they all knew the price for coming forward on the air might be higher than anyone was willing to pay. However, all of them thought about what they had to gain, for themselves and for several other women in the business, and they sat there with their heads held high.

Naomi had still been home "sick" when she'd heard the promo for the show. She knew the topic was much bigger than her, but she felt she had a story to tell, too. She'd already spoken to her father and been planning to move back home. After school, she had had a job offer on the table from a colleague of his to work the news desk at the local news station, but at the time she had thought New York had had so much more to offer. The job was still available, and it wasn't music, but it was communications, and she preferred to start all over than to try to continue down the path she had started. She was just happy that with Madison's help she was going to be able to go out with a bang.

Naomi had called the station and asked to speak with Madison. She reminded Madison that they had met at Cîroc, and then Naomi had told her story. After Naomi had also told Madison she was resigning and going back home, Madison had decided she didn't want to deny her an opportunity to share her story before she left. Naomi knew she had been no angel in the situation, but she wanted other women in the industry to learn not to be mesmerized by all the wrong things and to stay true to themselves. She only hoped that hearing about her embarrassment and ridicule would deter anyone from wanting to compromise who they were in order to fit in. It was a hard lesson, but she had learned firsthand that record-company people were shady.

As soon as the introductions were done and Laura was going through her summary of today's issues, Madison received a message on her Black-Berry. She looked down, and not really to her surprise, it was Polytics. Yo, what are you doing on the air right now? he wrote. She looked at it, and it made her even happier that she had made this decision because it was just a reminder that until her secret was out, he would forever think he could control her. I am giving the answer you wanted from me, she wrote back. Her face lit up; she loved it. She loved reclaiming herself and fixing what she had done. Yeah, she might get fired, and, yeah, Jamahl might leave her, but she would have her pride back, and she wouldn't have to be Polytics's victim. Even better, women around the world would learn from her mistake, and people would know what Polytics was really all about.

Naomi was well into her story by the time Madison had refocused on the room. Though she'd heard it before, it was no less captivating the second time. She heard Naomi telling how she'd liked this guy at her job, and he didn't pay her any attention for the longest time. She spoke of her haircut and stylish change of clothes and how instantly he was her new best friend. She admitted she was naive and flattered and fell for his game kind of easily. She said how she'd gone with him to his hotel room after a party, and less than a week later everyone at the company knew all about it, and she was being treated like a piece of meat. She made it very clear that she had regrets, but she wanted it to be known it all wasn't worth it.

And Madison burst out laughing when the thin, shy-looking Texas girl said, "It really wasn't worth it—I barely felt anything, and it lasted for less than two minutes." Although everyone else started laughing, Naomi hadn't been looking for a reaction—she was dead serious. She was being very clear that it hadn't been worth it. She ended her story with, "They spread all these rumors when there was nothing to tell. No one thought about how it would affect me. Out of the entire company, only one person cared enough about me as a person to keep it real with me, but to everyone else, it was funny."

Once Laura noticed the tears welling up in Naomi's eyes, she interjected. "Ladies and gentlemen, we are talking today about women in the entertainment business and the issues they face, the double standards they deal with, and the secrets they live with."

Laura looked at Sereeta and nodded for her to begin. Sereeta swallowed real hard before she began to speak. It was obvious that she was fighting back tears, but on the microphone she sounded strong. She told the listeners about how she'd had to deal with sexual harassment for months, and there was nobody to go to about it. It was just the way things were in the day-to-day environment of a sports assistant. Thoughts of Mark and him hating her went through her mind as she began to tell what had happened with France. They were quickly erased when she remembered that Mark hadn't even given her the benefit of the doubt to believe her when she'd confided in him. She knew that no matter what had happened after she "snitched," she would feel better that her silence for the protection of France's reputation hadn't been bought. She made a point to say that her boss, Corey, was a gentleman and had had nothing to do with what happened to her. She went into the details of the day that France had raped her, and everyone in the room seemed to be deep in thought.

The young lady Kayla had to wipe her tears away. No one in the room knew her secret just yet, but it was clear that she could relate somehow. Sereeta wiped away a tear or two herself as she finished sharing what had happened to her—how no one had seemed to care how she felt. It hit Madison right in her heart when she heard Sereeta say, "France wanted this to be kept a secret, but I didn't want to share a secret with a man I had no respect for. He abused me and then played a basketball game the very next night. So I am here today to let him see that his money couldn't buy him a secret." The applaud audio began to ring out, and Madison, Kayla, and Naomi clapped right along with it.

Laura chimed in once again. "Folks, as you hear this show about airing these dirty dudes' dirty laundry, some arrest warrants will be given, some careers will be shattered, but these women are empowered by refusing to be afraid. For those of you who don't know, entertainment is a male-dominated business and a business where money has all the power. All the dirt gets brushed under the carpet with a checkbook around here, and I am proud to have these ladies on my show who are willing to let it be known their dignity doesn't have a price tag. We will be right back on Drama Ninety-Nine FM."

A commercial break began, and Madison looked back at her BlackBerry. Polytics had written back, What the hell are you talking about? Madison typed back: Just stay tuned to Drama 99 FM.

Chapter 35

Madison had had to hold a meeting with the human resources rep a few days after the show aired, and although they didn't fire her right there on the spot, she figured it was only a matter of time. That wasn't why she had given her two-weeks' notice, though—she just didn't want to be subjected to all the backlash she would likely get. She had started a blossoming consulting company years ago, and she figured now was a better time than ever to go full force with it.

Polytics had called her and threatened her that same night after she'd told the world how psycho he was and how he acted like such a hard-core rapper but was extremely insecure about not being a real man—so much so that he had hit a woman just because he didn't think she respected him as a man. She told how his team ignored his crazy behavior and how they seemed to allow him to behave this way. The look on Laura's face—and everyone in the room—when she was sharing had been sheer disbelief that she was giving that much dirt on him and on herself, but it didn't stop Madison. She told how he was pussy whipped after just one time in bed, and how he had looked like he was going to cry when she'd told him she had a boyfriend. Madison knew it would embarrass him, but that was what she wanted. She wanted the press to tear apart his macho tough-guy image and show that he was a weak little boy who bullied women.

Sereeta pressed charges on France, and after all the hype from the radio show, he was eager to settle and settle quickly. Sereeta was fine with that because she had gotten what she wanted already. She knew if she had settled first, there would very likely have been a gag order or a clause in the agreement saying she couldn't tell what happened. Yet she had already told, so she had won twice, and she was happy with that. She had spoken to Corey a few times since the show, and he wasn't upset— he had said he understood that she had had to do what she'd had to do. He'd also told her he wished things could've been different because he would've kept her around for a long time. Although he'd tried to make amends, he'd made it very clear that she couldn't work for him any longer, even if she did decide she wanted to, because it was a conflict of interest. She didn't mind because she, Kayla, and Naomi were now hired by Madison to work on the consulting business.

Although Naomi had been homesick and finally accepted that she would be moving back home, she gladly accepted Madison's offer to work for her when she called her up after the show. Naomi was glad to stay in New York and remain in the cap-

ital of media. She was making more money and
had shed her old skin. She was still fashionable
and chic, but she was Naomi. She wore her glasses
and fit her short hair into a ponytail as much as
she could on those days she just didn't feel like
prettying up. Tyreek had gotten fired. Tiffany had
reached out and told her she was proud of her,
too. Her boyfriend had never heard the interview
way down in Texas, but she had come clean to him,
too. He admitted he wasn't interested in continu-
ing the relationship anyway long distance, but he
was surely willing to remain friends and stay in
touch. Naomi knew deep down they had outgrown
each other, and she was fine with that.

   The success of the consulting company skyrocketed after the press got ahold of the news that the
four fearless women who had shared their dark industry secrets had formed together to work at a
company. They had been in almost every television show, newspaper, and magazine there was—
everyone wanted them for an interview. They had
all made a remarkable shift in the way women in
the business were viewed; they were thanked daily
by women who said their male bosses had been
more respectful and they had been treated less
like sex objects. They never imagined they would
go from being ashamed of their stories to proud. It
was the power of drama.

Want more from Janine A. Morris?

Turn the page for a preview of
DIVA DIARIES,
SHE'S NO ANGEL,
and
PLAYTHANG

Available now wherever books are sold.

From *Diva Diaries*

"I am such a fool—I am getting too old for this crap," Dakota said to herself as she sat on the edge of her king-size bed. Her bed was covered in peach silk sheets, with two scented candles burning on both nightstands. The lights were dim all through-out her condo, and her Bose stereo in the bedroom was quietly playing Avant's latest album. Right outside her building was the busy traffic and chaos of midtown Manhattan, but on the inside of 4D was a romantic getaway.

Dakota had already spent thirty years on this earth, but there were times she felt like she hadn't learned a thing. It still amazed her how, with all the street smarts she had from her years of grow-ing up in Brooklyn, she was able to make her way through life and through corporate America, but she couldn't seem to prevent nights like these.

She had made her way from her bedroom into the living room, attempting not to focus on her rising anger. She hit PLAY on her TiVo box, and her television began playing back her recorded episode of *Judge Judy*. After about twenty minutes, she had stopped paying attention to what the evidence was from the plaintiff and her mind started to wander again. She began to analyze what was happening on yet another Friday night.

"I can't believe I am lying here alone in this expensive lingerie, freezing my butt off, and God knows where he is or who he is with," she murmured.

A dozen thoughts ran through her head as she slowly felt herself losing any bit of romantic or sexy vibes she had left in her body. The more emotional she got, the more she knew it was only minutes before she would completely lose it and leave Tony a nasty message on his answering machine. She would have told him to his face, but he was m.i.a. and wasn't answering his house or cell phone. He was supposed to be at her place at 9:00, and it was now 11:30, and not even a simple call was made to inform her of any change of plans.

Maybe he fell asleep, maybe he had a car accident, maybe something really urgent came up, maybe he is on his way and his cell battery is dead. Maybe, maybe, shmaybe. She knew he was just fine and he was just being a man. She was tired of making excuses for him, to herself, to her friends; she had to fill in his blanks constantly. It was just her way of delaying having to face the reality that he was up to no good. She couldn't give him the benefit of the doubt, because he didn't deserve it. She had done that early in the relationship, the first few times he pulled something like this, but at this point she knew from experience.

She sat there and envisioned just how the night was going to play out, how it would happen and what he would say and do. He would eventually call or show up and actually almost pretend like nothing was really wrong. He would just hope his sorry excuse would be enough, or at least his sorry attempt at apologizing and seduction. On nights when she just wanted not to waste her preparation for the night, she would just let it go, but on other nights, when her self-pride was shaking its head at her, she would make a big deal out of it.

Some nights she would call up her girls to vent, and try to get some sense talked into her head. But this relationship was becoming way too dysfunctional, and quite honestly, Dakota was not in the mood to face that. At least not tonight, not as she sat in her room in a teal-and-pink Frederick's of Hollywood negligee. Besides, she knew what they would say, or at least what they would think, even if they didn't tell her. She knew so well because she knew what she would think when she heard a story from one of her female counterparts getting played by her man. Even when the girl is in denial, it's not hard to tell when she is getting played. Dakota was a realist—she knew her man was up to no good.

Dakota didn't know if she was more frustrated with herself or with men, because before Tony, the last guy she let into her heart was her college sweetheart, Chris, who turned out to be a real barking dog. She spent years trying to work through stuff with him and forgive him for his infidelities. Once she realized he was just taking advantage of her obvious fear to let go of him and be alone, she promised herself she would never be that way with any man again. She had convinced herself no man was worth losing her self-respect, and she wasn't taking any nonsense from any of them. She had decided she would much rather greet them, freak them, fuck them, then duck them. She preferred that over getting all caught up in fairy-tale land. In a sense, she adapted to the ways of men; she wasn't looking for a serious commitment and wasn't trying to make one. So, Tony was the first one to break through some of that wall in a long time. Still, she had made all of these rules for herself about things she wouldn't accept, but once again, love and emotions found her back in the same predicament. Dealing with the same excuses, different man . . . or, better yet . . . same shit, different dog.

Tony was probably the worst man that she could have let her guard down for, too. In no time, she allowed good sex to turn into feelings she had no business having. Tony wasn't just a professional athlete who was often traveling—he had another woman in his life. Dakota heard at some point they were engaged, but he told her differently. Either way, she was aware there was a woman out there whom he kept protected. He would tell Dakota he was only with this girl for the sake of their child and that he didn't love her. Of course, he loved Dakota and wanted to be with her—at least that's what he said. Whenever Dakota would complain or catch him in a lie, he would say *I just ask that you be patient with me and understand my lifestyle.*

Dakota was naive when she was in love—that's why she tried her best not to feel that way. It wasn't worth the headache or heartache. Even as naive as she could be, she could usually see through Tony's b.s. Unfortunately, she really wanted to believe him. He was just the kind of guy that Dakota felt was a match for her. Successful, handsome, charismatic, and he had great taste. If she settled down, she wanted it to be with him, if she could only get him to do it. So she sat here on nights like this, trying to show him what she had to offer. Except he was nowhere to be found.

It was now about midnight, and Dakota broke down and called her girlfriend Chrasey. Just sitting there watching television was not making her feel any better; she was leaving room for a variety of angry thoughts to fill her head. She needed some type of human contact.

"Dakota, leave his behind alone . . . stop putting yourself through this . . . I don't even know why you wait on him . . . You know how it goes—he fooled you once, it was shame on him. But now he *keeps* fooling you—shame on you," Chrasey rambled on as soon as she heard Tony was pulling one of his disappearing acts.

See, this is exactly what I didn't need right now, Dakota thought to herself. It wasn't that she wanted to be in denial, but she wanted to try to keep from getting upset, and letting negative opinions cloud her thoughts. Besides, every female knows we love our girls until they are talking junk or telling us to leave our man. Then it's a totally different situation. It was moments like these when she understood how some women say they don't have female friends. She could see how jealousy, envy, deceit, and all those things could make females distrust one another. She could see how a female telling you your man who deep down you're hoping you can share a white picket fence with, ain't worth a darn could make a chick choose the man over the friend. Lucky for Chrasey, that was not the case for Dakota. She and Chrasey, along with their third amigo, Jordan, had been friends since college and they were almost like sisters. Of course, most close friends say that, but these three came the closest to that bond. Most friends say that until they have some really big fight, and then they can't bring themselves to put it behind them. Or better yet, that's just the case until they grow apart, or jealousy and competition or another female trait gets the best of them and they decide they are too grown up for that play-sister crap. These three, though, had been through over a decade of real sisterhood, fights included. Not the little fights, either—big fights, fights most people don't make up from—but in the midst of those fights, if one was going through something like a true sister, the others would still be there for her. So, when Chrasey or Jordan told her something, she knew it was from the heart and one of the reasons she hated listening. The truth can hurt. So she sat there and listened to Chrasey, and she knew deep down that she was right; she was breaking all of her own rules and putting up with even more than she did from Chris.

"Chrasey, it's just that when things are good,

they are so good. Then he goes and pulls some-thing like this and messes it all up."

"I know, 'Kota . . . and if it was the first or sec-ond time, I would tell you you're overreacting. But he does this way too often—you can never depend on him. And let me guess—you got all sexy and ready for him, didn't you?"

"Girl . . . my favorite teal-and-pink teddy I had been waiting to wear," Dakota responded. They both giggled.

"Look, 'Kota . . . you just need to put your foot down. Any time you guys have plans, he feels no obligation to keep them or even call you to cancel. Each time he apologizes, and you step back out there and expect him not to do it again, there is disappointment after disappointment. It's just out of hand." As if she was more upset than Dakota, Chrasey rambled on. "Showing up hours late with-out even calling—you don't even do that to a hooker, let alone someone you care about. You need to let him go or get serious and let him know that this is the last time. If he does it again, you're through. I know you two don't have a commit-ment, and deep down you know there may be some side pieces somewhere, but he has to know he can't take you for a fool."

"Yeah, you're right. When he does show up, I am going to have a long talk with him."

After about another ten minutes, Dakota got off the phone and jumped under the covers. After ten seconds on her plush peach pillow, the tears began to roll down her cheeks. She didn't want to cry. What if he showed up right now? She would look terrible, with bloodshot eyes and a runny nose, and on top of that she was messing up her silk pillow covers. She realized, though, she wasn't crying because of what Tony was probably out there doing, but because of what Chrasey had said. Just hearing that made her feel really low.

When it came to Tony, she could barely understand herself. It wasn't like Dakota wasn't well put together. Dakota was in great shape for her age. She was five-feet-five, 125 pounds, with just enough titties and ass—not too much and not too little. She had a pretty, dark-chocolate complexion, with off-black long hair reaching about a quarter of the way down her back, and brown eyes. Her high cheekbones brought character to her face, but her full lips and slanted eyes were what actually made Dakota beautiful. However, Ms. Dakota Watkins wasn't all looks—she had brains, too. She was the top publicist at her PR firm, and the youngest female on her level. She had several high-profile clients, was making over $95,000 a year, had a nicely furnished loft in a chic area of Manhattan, drove a 2004 purple BMW, and had what would be considered a great life. Despite all that she had accomplished, her love life overall was still chaotic.

Here she was, letting Tony ruin another Friday night for her. Regardless of how many times she asked herself why, the only answer she could come up with was because she allowed it. Feeling disgusted with herself, for lying in an empty bed wearing lingerie, she finally got up and threw on an oversized night shirt. She took her stereo remote control and hit PLAY. Keyshia Cole's single, "I Just Want It to Be Over," seeped from her Bose Wave speakers as she wrapped her hair and got ready for bed. She had just put her Razac Perfect for Perms hair crème away and finished tying a scarf on her head when her phone rang. She wasn't sure if it was Chrasey calling back, or Tony finally calling.

"Hello." Dakota tried to use her sexy-yet-upset voice.

"Hey, miss," a male voice responded from the other end of the phone.

"Who is this?"

"It's David—you busy?"

David was this "guy friend" of hers. They had been cool for some time; they had worked together a few years ago and never broke contact. A few years back, they'd had a few "indiscretions" between them, but they now had one of those "mature friendships."

After a few minutes of conversation, he was able to hear in her voice that she wasn't at her best and offered to come over and cheer her up. She was hesitant at first, but then he offered to come make a late-night meal. Full of emotion, anger, and lust, she accepted his offer. Fully aware that she had no clue if Tony was going to just pop up eventually or not, she left her night shirt on, combed her hair back down, put on some lip gloss, and waited to see who would arrive first.

From *She's No Angel*

"**O**h, my goodness!" Jasmine screamed into the phone as Charlene told her the news.

Jasmine was sitting on her couch curled up in her lavender cotton pajamas watching *The Office* when her phone rang. Two towns over, Charlene was still fully dressed sitting on Isaac's loveseat with her cell phone, smiling from ear to ear as she shared her breaking news story. Charlene would have died if she hadn't gotten Jasmine on the phone right away to tell her.

Jasmine was one of Charlene's closest friends; they'd known eath other since A. B. Gail Junior High School. They had been through a lot together, and they had celebrated and suffered a lot together. Jasmine was twenty-eight years old and she had been married for only a year to her high school sweetheart. Jasmine was one of Charlene's few childhood friends who had graduated from high school. Since high school Jasmine had been working at clerical jobs to make ends meet, and raising her baby girl, Serenity. Jasmine was also one of the few friends from Charlene's youth that she still kept in touch with. Jasmine, like Charlene, tried her best to live a better life than they had once had and to become a mature adult woman. They wanted to live a life for the future, and not remain stuck in their past. So, although they were at somewhat different stages in their lives, they always had that understanding and bond with one another. It was the bond of reform; they both knew where they had been and where they were trying to go— or, rather, what they were trying to leave behind.

Charlene and Jasmine had often discussed marriage in their friendship, but it was usually about Jasmine's, and about Charlene's belief that hers would never exist. So, without hesitation, Charlene had to call Jasmine to tell her that she was finally one step closer.

"I know, I know . . . It still feels like I'm dreaming," Charlene said back.

"How is the ring?" Jasmine asked.

"It's beautiful . . . looks like it's about two or three karats," Charlene said, holding out her hand to look at the rock Isaac had bestowed upon her.

"Uh-oh . . . Souky, souky now . . ." Jasmine said.

"Be quiet," Charlene replied, blushing. "The ring is designed like a flower with petals; it is the most gorgeous ring I have ever seen," Charlene said while still staring at her ring.

"Aww, that's nice. Especially since you love flowers," Jasmine added.

"Yeah, I know. I'm still kind of in shock."

"Charlene's getting married . . . go 'head, go 'head . . ." Jasmine started to sing some silly song.

They both laughed. Charlene would have loved to sit and talk about every detail of the night, but she had to rush Jasmine off the phone so she could tell her family and call one other friend to brag. It wasn't actually bragging, most of Charlene's friends were either married or engaged, but she had to let people know she was "validated" as well. Some of it was because at Charlene's age, when everyone is getting married and engaged, it messes with your self-esteem when your ring finger is still bare. However, some of it was from Charlene's own low self-esteem. She hadn't completely become comfortable and stable as the woman of worth she was trying to be. So Isaac hadn't only made her romantic dreams come true tonight, he helped make her whole. And Charlene was eager to spread the news. As soon as there was a moment of silence she told Jasmine she would call her back because she had to call her mother.

Charlene had kicked off her shoes and buried her feet into the couch in Isaac's living room. She looked over at the pewter picture frame that held an 8 x 10 picture of the two of them at Great Adventure. She looked over and smiled as she dialed her parents' house number. Most people would be surprised to find out that Charlene had any esteem issues. She was all of twenty-six years old, and full of youth and energy. She had the body of a runway model: tall and slender with long legs. She was light-skinned with a beautiful face that most people would say was made for television. High cheekbones with naturally rosy cheeks. She was gorgeous and she knew it; her looks got her by a lot in life. Yet with all her beauty, what made her feel like a true woman was sitting there on her hand, her left ring finger, to be exact. So, as she waited for one of her parents to answer, she sat there in Isaac's living room still glowing with joy.

Isaac was in the bathroom by then, but prior to that he was walking around the apartment doing his own thing. She had noticed him on the phone at one point, probably with his boy Surge, who he called Ser-Hey, telling him that he'd gone ahead and done it. But Charlene was too distracted to be nosy enough to overhear the conversation they were having. Usually Charlene paid close attention to those kinds of things; she was always concerned with what his friends and other people said about her. She knew it was a level of paranoia, always being the subject of a rumor. She was always wondering if and what Isaac would find out.

Charlene's mom, Ann Tanner, answered on like the third ring, and Charlene could tell from her mother's voice that she already knew why she was calling. Initially Mrs. Tanner tried to sound normal just in case it hadn't happened yet. Then Charlene took her out of her misery, and told her that, yes, she was officially engaged. Between a mixture of tears and pure joy, she congratulated Charlene and told her how excited she was. Charlene also found out how and when Isaac had asked her parents for her hand in marriage. Charlene was happy that her mother was still alive to share this moment with her. It made her think about how happy Isaac's father would be to still be here to share it, too.

After she spoke with her mom, dad and sister, she called her friend Tiffany, one of her cousins and another girlfriend. Charlene didn't have a lot of friends, most of them she had lost touch with over the last few years, but there were still a few people she was dying to tell. They all started asking her questions as if she had the wedding all planned out. Charlene had to explain this wasn't a save-the-date call, the proposal had only happened a couple hours ago. She realized then that most ladies don't brag so much and call everyone they know only moments after, so she decided to stop making calls.

As for the wedding, of course, like most women there were some decisions she'd already made. For instance, summer or fall wedding, short or long engagement, big or small wedding. These are things most girls think about and figure out when they play with their Barbie dolls as a little girl. Usually the color scheme is figured out as well, and some other basics, but not every detail of the wedding. Charlene answered the questions with a basic "I will let you know" response, along with whether she would be subjecting them to an ugly bridesmaid's dress.

Isaac had gone upstairs to watch television, Charlene assumed. As she held the phone in her hand she sat for a moment to reflect, digging her toes into his plush black and light gray carpet. She thought about the entire night as well as all the nights to come. She tried to imagine married life with Isaac and leaving the single life for good. She thought about moving out of her not-so-great place, and living in the beautiful and lavish condo that she was sitting in. She tried to think about it all, all the bright sides of the new life she would live. Soon her daydreaming brought her back to the present. She let out a little giggle when she thought about a question that Tiffany had just asked her: "So, are you going to invite Lacy?"

"I don't know, but I doubt it," Charlene replied.

"That's going to be an interesting situation . . . You may have to just suck it up."

"Yeah, I know, but we will have to figure it out. I just don't want any issues that day."

"Well, it all depends who is paying for it," Tiffany said, laughing.

"That's the truth," Charlene replied.

A few moments later, Charlene was hanging up the phone and laughing out loud. *That girl Tiffany, she ain't never lied,* Charlene thought to herself with a smile. Lacy was a friend of Isaac's that Charlene didn't approve of. She had no justification for her feelings other than her own jealousy, so she was kind of stuck dealing with their friendship. Although Charlene was sure it wasn't only in her head that Lacy wanted Isaac, she knew that there wasn't much to say without evidence. So for years she sat back and played a little game with Lacy, the one that females play when they communicate in a way that no one else is supposed to see. Tiffany's point made her think even more about all the drama that was bound to surface about the guest list, exes and friends that each of them would object to. Charlene wished she could expect otherwise, but she knew that jealousy and pettiness would definitely surface when it was time to work on the list. Charlene was hoping there wouldn't be too many skeletons surfacing along with it.

The longer Charlene thought about it, the more she wondered what she was thinking telling

Isaac she would marry him. For a second Charlene thought to herself that she should run now, and give the ring back before her secrets exploded in her face. That was easier said than done, because Charlene knew that more than anything she wanted to live happily ever after with Isaac. Still, Charlene knew her life's track record, and she knew that wherever there's happiness for Charlene there lurks some amount of drama. If it wasn't the guest list it was going to be something else, so she had to brace herself for the ride.

Charlene had sat for about fifteen minutes thinking about all of that. The thought of the overall blend of guests for a quick second tickled Charlene. She started to think about just how funny this wedding was going to be. Her folks were so different from Isaac's she knew they would have quite an interesting wedding. His family members were extremely reserved and, aside from Charlene's parents, quite a few in her family were a tad more on the wild side. Charlene knew there would be some that would get along just fine; but there were a few jokes that definitely wouldn't get laughed at and a few strange looks that would be made. Charlene knew her wedding planning would be a handful and that she had her work cut out for her.

By the time she got off the phone and finished daydreaming about the wedding guests and made her way into the bedroom where Isaac was, he was already in his boxers, ready for bed. When she walked in the room, he looked up at her and smiled. *Damn, is he fine,* she thought to herself. She knew why she was the luckiest woman alive. He was brains and beauty . . . and body. He was brown skinned, 6'3", with a tight medium build. He had a chiseled chest with close to six-pack abs, more like a four-pack. He had a low caesar, which he kept bald most of the time. He had one deep dimple in his right cheek when he shared his beautiful white smile. His facial hair was minimal and well trimmed, and he had these juicy lips that she just loved. Man, did she feel lucky that he was her man, she thought as she crawled in the bed next to him. At first he just looked over at her and then glanced back at the television, but then he realized that it was a special night and he didn't want her to start complaining. So he turned over toward her again and started looking into her eyes.

"Did you tell the world?" he asked.

Laughing, she replied, "No, only half . . ." and then she thought about it and added, "Did you tell anybody?"

"Yeah, I told K.D., and I had already told most of my family before I asked."

"Well, don't you need to let them know I said yes?"

"Please, they know you said yes."

"Oh, really?" she asked. "And how do they know that?"

"Because it's me . . . And because who could turn down that ring?" he asked, laughing. He had better start laughing, because it was their engagement night and she didn't want any problems.

"What happened to the time when y'all would be scared and nervous that we would say yes?"

"I don't know, I never proposed before . . . I don't remember that time."

"Oh, you're real funny tonight, aren't you?"

Aware that their sweet night was capable of going sour real soon, he started to try to fix it up. He got closer to her and placed his arm around her waist.

"I'm only joking, baby. They knew you would say yes, because they knew what we have is real, and that I love you and deserve you as my wife and that we are going to have a beautiful life with about six snotty-nosed kids," he said, starting back up.

"Yeah, OK," she replied with a slight laugh.

Charlene didn't even want to think about kids right then and there. That stress was bound to seep up on her sooner than later, but she would rather it be later.

"Well, we can get started on some of them now," he said as he slipped his hand up her shirt to cup her breast.

She smirked. Maybe not for the sake of having the six snotty-nosed babies, but she couldn't say she wasn't all for partaking in some newly engaged sex.

From *Playthang*

Chapter 1

The look on her face expressed a clear level of discomfort. It seemed Ms. Grant wasn't prepared for the question that Jordan had asked her. Jordan, on the other hand, was poised and bright-eyed, awaiting an answer.

The young lady was sitting directly across from Jordan, alongside her colleagues. Jordan sat with only her client, Aminae Carty, who was an artist professionally known as Amina.

"I'm not sure I understand what you are getting at," the young lady responded.

"What I'm getting at is there seems to be a lack of awareness on your company's part. Amina has sold over 300,000 singles in this past month alone, without the backing of a major company. Therefore, I believe it is apparent that she is not your typical breakthrough artist, which is why I asked whether you are fully aware of her potential," Jordan said, looking directly at the three people across from her.

Amina sat in the chair, trying to look as confident as possible, but it seemed that she was uncomfortable as well.

The colleagues on the other side of the table were all employed by Def Society Records. The young lady sitting directly across from Jordan was the director of business & legal affairs, Jill Turner. The other two faces belonged to Jill's assistant and her manager of business affairs.

"Well, yes, we are aware that Amina made strides with her career prior to deciding to join us. However, the support and funds that we plan to put behind her will take her career to another level, which may take her years to achieve on her own, if at all."

"Ms. Grant, my client and I are well aware of what Def Society Records is offering. If we didn't feel it would benefit her, we wouldn't be sitting here. However, we are also aware of how adding her to your roster will benefit you. Amina has done the hard work of generating her own buzz and awareness throughout the East and West coasts. She has a recognizable name, she has received radio airplay, and she is extremely talented. Adding her is a win-win for your company, and all we are asking is that you recognize that and not offer her the same deal you would offer someone who hasn't accomplished as much."

"Ms. Moore, I see your point, and at this time, this is all I'm capable of offering."

"Well, we are not capable of accepting this offer. However, we greatly appreciate your interest and time, and hopefully we can do business together in the future."

Ms. Grant looked surprised as she watched Jordan gather her folders and papers from the table.

"Ms. Moore, we would hate to lose out on the opportunity to work with Amina. Let me have a meeting with Shewayne, the president, and see if we can rework the budget to find a better figure to satisfy you and Amina."

"That is fine. I will respectfully hold off the other offers until we speak again."

"That will be appreciated."

Jordan stood from her chair. As she pushed the seat farther back, she realized Amina was still sitting there, looking a bit perplexed. Jordan gestured to her with her eyes that it was time to make their exit. Amina immediately jumped up to stand beside Jordan. Ms. Grant and her colleagues rose as well; they picked up their files from the table and began preparing to exit the conference room. Jordan and Amina both scooted their chairs back and began walking toward the door.

Everyone pretty much reached the door at the same time, and they exchanged words along the lines of "good-bye" and "I'll speak to you soon." Once the lobby was cleared, Amina and Jordan waited for the elevator. They stood there in silence for a few moments while the receptionist watched them wait. Once the elevator arrived, they both stepped in, and Jordan pressed the button for the ground floor.

"You OK?" Jordan asked Amina.

"Yeah. A little nervous."

"About what?"

"Well, what if they don't want me anymore?"

"Amina, I wouldn't have jeopardized your career. I told you on the way over that the goal of today's meeting was to get a better deal. I am certain that they will counteroffer with a much better deal. That offer she gave was not their best. I have known Shewayne for a long time now; I know he will send Ms. Grant back to us with the appropriate figures."

"OK. I trust you," Amina said with a shrug.

"Good. You should. I wouldn't steer you wrong."

Jordan and Amina walked out of the building onto Eighth Avenue and looked around.

"Which way are you headed? You need a lift somewhere?" Jordan asked.

"I'm good. I'm meeting some friends around the corner. Thanks."

"OK. I'll be in touch."

Jordan walked down the street toward her car. Almost there, she looked up and noticed a Starbucks across the street. She began to cross the street to go grab herself a mocha latte, but halfway across she changed her mind. She realized she didn't need the extra calories, and she needed to resist this constant urge of hers. So she turned back and headed toward her car. She walked a few feet and arrived at her black BMW X5. She beeped the alarm, opened the door, and sat inside. Once she settled in her seat, before she started the car, she reached into her bag and got out her BlackBerry. A look of disappointment came over her face when she realized that she hadn't received a call or e-mail from Jayon the entire day. She was tempted to call him and ask where her hello was for the day, but she decided against it. Instead, she just started her car and pulled out into the heavy traffic of Manhattan to try to make her way home. Surprisingly, she didn't mind the traffic; Jordan was in no rush to get home to her empty house.

Chapter 2

It was the third time over the course of two weeks that Jordan had been sitting on her front lawn waiting on Jayon. The two of them had gotten so busy with work these past few months that they had to make appointments to spend time with each other. However, the times they set seemed to be difficult for Jayon to keep. The last time, he had Jordan waiting on him for almost an hour, and he said he was held up with a client at the office. This time, Jordan didn't even care what his excuse was, because nothing seemed to justify him not answering his phone or calling her to let her know he'd be late.

From up the street all you could recognize was Jordan's five feet seven, 145-pound frame slouched in her patio chair. She looked out over her garden, which she had to admit was due for some tender loving care. Her rose bushes and plants were still healthy except for a few that were wilting here and there, but there were weeds popping up and some excess leaves lying around. It wasn't hard to see the look of frustration covering her medium brown complexion. Her light brown eyes were downcast due to the frown she was wearing. Her shoulder-length hair was slicked back into a bun, and she wore a multicolored, sheer minidress with a slip underneath it and some black sandals. She was dressed for a bright and happy evening, but from the way things were looking, it wasn't going to go as planned.

Jordan slowly stood up and folded her arms. She glanced down the block and noticed the little girl playing in front of her house down the street. Sitting a few feet away were the little girl's parents. They were just sitting there watching their daughter play as they conversed about who knows what. Jordan didn't know what they were speaking of, but they looked happy. She couldn't help but feel weak realizing how she no longer had that. Her family was shattered, and she missed the hell out of her son. It was enough dealing with her ex-husband's engagement, but seeing Jason with the two of them made her sick to her stomach. Watching the happy neighbors gave her the same feeling, so she finally looked away. Jordan looked down at her feet and then back up again. She looked down the street one more time, and then she dropped her arms and headed for her front door.

Once she stepped back inside her house, she plopped down on her couch and buried her face in her hands. She sat there wondering what had happened to her and the life she had worked so hard to perfect. For the life of her she couldn't figure out where she went wrong, and every time she thought of it, she got no closer to figuring it out. After a few moments of sitting there, tears began to roll down her face. Whether they were tears of sadness or tears of anger was hard to determine. All Jordan knew was she felt like she was failing. Her home life was bad, and even things at work were bad, and she didn't know if she had it in her to fight her way back to the top anymore.

Moments later, Jordan heard a noise. She lifted her head off the taupe throw pillow she was resting on, then listened harder to see if she heard it again. As she lay there completely still, listening, she saw a figure in her peripheral vision. She looked toward the doorway and screamed. Somewhere in the midst of her panic attack, she noticed that it was Jayon. He was standing there laughing at the scare he'd put into Jordan, although she was not yet laughing back. His five feet eleven, 195-pound frame filled the doorway, and he was dressed in blue jeans, Sean John sneakers, and an Akademiks rugby.

"Where have you been?" Jordan began.

"I was at my meetings late."

Jordan scanned his outfit, and obviously enough for him to notice. "You were at meetings dressed like that?"

"Jordan. I went home to change first. What's wrong with you?"

"What's wrong with me? You couldn't call, Jayon? I've been here waiting on you . . . that's what's wrong with me."

"Why didn't you call me?"

"Jayon . . . I called your cell phone like three times."

"Oh, must've been bad reception where I had my meetings, 'cause I didn't see them."

Jordan gave him a look of doubt, a look of disappointment. It was apparent that she wanted more than anything to blurt out, "Do you think I'm stupid? Do you think you can tell me anything?" and go off on a rant. However, she just communicated her thoughts through the look on her face.

"What?" Jayon asked with a smirk.

"Nothing, Jayon. You're making it a joke, and it's not funny," Jordan said as she stood up and went to grab the remote off the entertainment center.

"What's not funny?"

"Nothing, Jayon. Forget it. Play stupid. That's fine."

Jordan sat down and pushed POWER on the remote.

"What? You in here sulking like I did something to you."

Jordan was kind of upset that Jayon found her like that. She hated to look weak.

"I wasn't sulking, Jayon. Don't flatter yourself," Jordan said with conviction, knowing dang well she was just sulking.

"Whatever, J," he said as he walked upstairs.

Jordan sat there frustrated as hell. A piece of her wanted to just break, say everything that was on her mind, including the not-so-nice stuff. But she also didn't want the drama or the argument, and she knew Jayon would say she was looking for the negative because he would think he had done nothing wrong. Jordan sat on the edge of the couch, staring at the television but paying attention to nothing on the screen. Her thoughts were all over the place, beginning with the curiosity of how she ever became so accepting of her and Jayon's situation.

Jordan could hear footsteps coming back down the stairs. She pretended that the television had her attention and that she was relaxing. Jayon came into the living room dressed in a white sleeveless T-shirt and black sweat shorts; he apparently got comfortable since he assumed their plans were shot. Jordan had assumed that he was upstairs changing. She was tempted to ask him who said their plans were cancelled, but she was aware that her attitude probably said it. After Jayon walked around for a bit doing whatever he was doing, he eventually sat beside Jordan on the couch.

"Want to watch a movie?" he asked.

Jordan paused before she answered. She wanted to say "not really," but instead she calmly answered, "OK."

Jayon put his hand out for the remote, and she handed it to him. Jayon turned to the movies on demand channel and began looking for a movie to watch.

"See anything you want to see?" he asked.

"Not yet," Jordan replied.

Jayon kept channel surfing.

"I'll be right back. I'm going to change while you find something," Jordan said as she stood up from the couch.

Jayon didn't reply, he just steadily moved through the movie listings as Jordan headed up the stairs. Jordan was trying to remain calm and put aside all of her emotions. Jayon had the ability to suppress all drama even when there was a need to address it. Jordan could admit that it helped their overall relationship from being filled with drama, but Jordan also knew that a lot of things festered between them, and that wasn't healthy. She also knew it didn't make sense to bother to bring up how late he was now that she had agreed to watch a movie with him.

Jordan opened one of the drawers to her pajama dresser and pulled out her Victoria's Secret pink boxer pajama set. She started taking off her clothes and began to genuinely calm down. Usually, changing out of clothes that she had put on to go somewhere without having gone to that place would be enough to upset her. She was feeling that way too, until she realized it could have been worse. He could've come even later or not at all. She tried to look at the bright side—they were going to spend a quiet evening at home.

Jordan hung her dress back up in the closet for another night, since it didn't get its night out. As she closed the closet door, Jayon's jeans fell to the floor. Jordan bent over to pick them up, and a piece of paper fell out along with some money. Jordan started picking the items up when she noticed handwriting on the paper. The investigator in her instantly glanced over it. Written on it was "Nicole" and a phone number. Jordan looked at the paper a few seconds longer for any clues as to where it came from. It was on a torn piece of plain white paper, and there was nothing else written on it. Jordan proceeded to return the items to his pocket while she felt herself begin to boil with anger. She knew that it seemed as if Jayon had gotten some girl's number in an attempt to "get to know her better." Just the mere thought of addressing him over this number felt so high school. Besides, she knew there were a million legit excuses that Jayon could give, like it was a business colleague or an old friend. So Jordan decided to choose her battles and let this one go, or at least save it for a later date.

Jordan made her way back downstairs, the whole time telling herself repetitively to let it go. By the time she made it to the couch where Jayon was sitting, she hadn't completely erased the negative thoughts from her head, but she was still trying.

"You ready?" Jayon said as he pointed the remote at the television to unpause the movie on the screen.

"Mm-hmm," Jordan responded.

Jayon hit the PAUSE button. "This is that movie I was telling you about with the clones. It's called *The Island*," Jayon said as he scooted back to get comfortable on the couch. "Want to make some popcorn?"

"Not really," Jordan answered.

She had been silently wishing that Jayon would stop talking to her so she wouldn't have to struggle to hide her anger.

"You don't want popcorn while watching a movie? OK, that's a first," Jayon said.

Jordan didn't reply. She just kept looking at the television screen, which was showing the opening credits. She watched the boat ride across the water on the screen, and then all of a sudden the screen froze. Jordan looked over at Jayon, and he had the remote in his hand, pointing it at the television.

"What's wrong with you?" he asked.

"Nothing, Jayon. Turn it back on."

"You are acting mad funny, and you're saying nothing is wrong."

"Jayon, nothing's wrong. I am just tired."

"Tired?"

"Yes, tired."

"OK, if you want me to believe that, I'll let it go."

Something snapped in Jordan's mind. She was tired of being nice and holding her tongue, and since he insisted, she figured she'd let him know.

"Who is Nicole?" Jordan blurted out.

"What?" Jayon asked, looking totally confused.

"Who is Nicole?"

"What are you talking about?"

"You know what, Jayon, I don't even want to talk about it. Because in all honesty, I don't know if I can trust whatever you tell me anyway."

"Where is all this coming from?"

"You show up hours after you were supposed to, acting like it's nothing, having no regard for the fact that I was here dressed and waiting for you; then I go upstairs to change and a phone number falls out of your pocket. I just don't even know what to think anymore," Jordan rambled on.

"That was a client," Jayon said.

Jordan giggled. She laughed because she was expecting something like that.

"What is so funny?"

"I just thought you would say something like that, that's all."

"Well, Jordan, how can I win then? Why'd you ask?"

"I tried not to, but you insisted on asking me what was wrong."

"Well, I'm sorry for being concerned."

"I wish you were concerned with keeping me waiting for hours."

"Jordan, I said sorry. I was held up at work. What do you want me to do?"

"Call, e-mail, something. You come in late, I couldn't get a hold of you, you didn't try to contact me, and then you have numbers in your pocket. Really, Jay—what do you want me to think?"

"It's not about what I want you to think. I can only tell you what I've told you. What you choose to think is your own decision," Jayon said as he hit the PAUSE button and the movie started again.

"It's that very nonchalance that makes me think the way I do even more."

"Whatever," Jayon responded.

Now Jordan was pissed. She hated when Jayon just shut down, when he decided that he was done talking about something. She was upset that she even broke her silence, because now she was more upset than she had been from the start, and Jayon's attitude was only going to make it harder to calm down.

The opening scene of the movie started, and Jayon was sitting with his feet kicked up on the ottoman, while Jordan had one foot up on the couch and the other on the floor. They were sitting at opposite ends of the couch, both watching the movie.

Jordan was tempted to stop faking the funk and walk her black butt upstairs. She was barely paying attention to the movie anyway, because she was still trying to lower her blood pressure. When she thought about it more, she realized that it was possible that going upstairs was only going to make it a bigger deal. She told herself not to even stress it. Jayon wanted to play innocent and play little games; two could play at that.